"Karma"

Hashim Conner

Bloomington, IN Milton Keynes, UK

authorHOUSE

AuthorHouse™
1663 Liberty Drive, Suite 200
Bloomington, IN 47403
www.authorhouse.com
Phone: 1-800-839-8640

AuthorHouse™ UK Ltd.
500 Avebury Boulevard
Central Milton Keynes, MK9 2BE
www.authorhouse.co.uk
Phone: 08001974150

First published by AuthorHouse 6/20/2006

ISBN: 1-4259-3146-4 (sc)

Printed in the United States of America
Bloomington, Indiana

This book is printed on acid-free paper.

Prologue

My mother kept telling me what goes around comes around. Karma, she would always say, "You're not going to keep treating women the way you do, and not expect that one day it won't come back to haunt you." I would usually have a surprised look on my face pretending not to know what she was speaking of. The sad part was I not only heard but, I understood what she was saying but never really took the time to listen. I even believed what she said to be true, but the truth was her words just didn't pertain to me. At the time I just didn't feel that it was anything wrong with the way I was treating women. I made them feel SPECIAL! Therefore, I never took heed to the words that my mother spoke. That is until now. Now it is my turn to feel SPECIAL, as special as I thought I was making them feel. The special feelings that I have made so many women feel before were finally going to be returned onto me.

I can imagine many different terms that can describe my behavior. To be perfectly honest I've heard many of them from the women that I have dated. Or at least they felt that way after we stopped talking. The one that sticks out the most would have to be Dirt-Bag, probably because the longer I think about the things that I have done the better it fits. It doesn't help that this is the one that I hear most frequently, but in all it definitely fits. Just a quick overview, I love women, they are the single most beautiful creatures on God's green earth. In this, I believe lies the root of my entire problem. I do not enjoy, and appreciate just one woman at a time, I enjoy them all, although I do believe I have given each and every one of them many parts of me, I have yet to share the one thing that they all seemed to want. It was unfortunate that the same thing that they wanted was the one thing that I wasn't prepared to give of myself. What is it you ask? Commitment, or monogamy. In other words, the one thing they all seemed to want was all of me to themselves. It's not that they didn't deserve it, I just wasn't ready or willing to relinquish myself to them, and only them. In the end I would always be considered the bad guy, even though throughout all the different friendships or relationships that I was a part of, the women were given a choice, it was always understood what I was looking for. This worked for me for a long time, and I was happy with how everything in my life was working, that was until I met her. She came in and turned my world upside down, I might have thought I had it all figured out but I wasn't even close. In order for you to get a full understanding I have to start in the beginning. It seems like a lifetime ago, way before she walked into my LIFE.

Beautiful Summer

As I sit in this car, with the sun barely bright enough to cause a glare and the smell of morning dew in the air, with nothing more than the melodious sounds of Harlem Blues playing in the back ground, a single tear flowing down my cheek. I'm thinking and hoping, better yet wishing that what's taking place right now wasn't taking place. The love that I've allowed myself to feel and shouldn't have has now taken over. Who ever came up with the saying it's better to have loved and lost than to never have loved at all must have been a complete fool! What got me here? What have I done in my life that was so bad that my heart should be snatched out and trampled as it has been? I must admit I have done my share of wrong, and I have hurt people, but if I knew at anytime that this was the way I was making the women of my life feel it would've never went any further. What was it that I did, where did it start, how did it land me here? Allow me to introduce myself, my name is Christopher Alexander, I am soon to be an English teacher, in the City of Detroit. I grew up on the Westside of the Detroit, or the D as we so famously call it, and before you allow your mind to ask the question? Yes, I grew up right off 7 Mile. According to a lot of my mom's friends I was a pretty good kid, guess they would have to live with me to know any different. Compared to many of my peers though I could've been considered a saint. But for now lets just say I got a late start or at least I thought so, especially when it came down to the dealings in the women department. I was just so content being a kid I didn't really worry about girls a great deal. It probably didn't help that I had terrible self-esteem, it's kind of hard to think you're nice looking when

1

you have grown up features stuck in a little kids frame. My mom would always attempt to point out my good qualities such as my near perfect mahogany brown skin that fortunately missed the puberty pimple stage all together while most guys around me caught it bad. All I was able to focus on were the things that I would be teased about from time to time. My eyes, ears, and lips were all fully formed while my face and body had yet to fill out. So I spent most of my time playing basketball, and video games. Now please don't misunderstand me even then I had it bad for women, I just didn't pursue them. I did do my share of flirting, but I didn't think I could take it much further than that. To be honest, I didn't go on my first date until the end of my senior year of high school. To continue this honesty I feel like I had to grow into my looks. It was quite similar to an acquired taste, in the beginning it's different, but after you actually get used to the taste you can't get enough. Between my summer workout regimen, the growth of facial hair to accentuate my features, and the fact that my lips were no longer looked upon as something to be mocked and laughed at. Instead I was becoming something to be loved, touched, and wanted once my growth began. (I think I owe a thank you to LL Cool J). Actually growing into my looks wasn't too bad, it allowed me the chance to enhance other qualities (personality, sense of humor, attentiveness). The actual growth happened some where between the end of my junior year, and the beginning of my senior year. Still haven't been able to decipher whether it was the actual sexual experience that changed me or something else.

The actual sexual experience happened on one of our hotter summer days, right around my birthday, I was sitting back trying my best to stay cool. It had to be at least 90 degrees outside, which had to make it around 105 in our house no air conditioning. Luckily, I had the coolest room in the house. I was lounging around trying to stay cool, and enjoy a game of Coach K on my Sega Genesis. That's when I got an unexpected visit from Marquita. Her mom and my mom had been friends since we were kids, and she decided to come on the visit with her mom, because she knew my birthday was coming up. So while they were upstairs sweating in the heat, she decided to come down to try to keep me company. Let me tell it, she just came down to stay cool. I've been wrong before, and boy was I again!

"Hey birthday boy what'cha doing?"

2

"Nothing, much on this game being bored, what up wit you?"

"Nothing just came over wit moms to visit, and to give you your present."

"Oh yeah you got a gift for me, since when do I get gifts?"

"Since now, is that a problem? You could've been getting this gift."

"No, it's not a problem. Not a problem at all. As a matter of fact I think it's kinda sweet. So what I get?"

"You're looking at it."

"Quit playing, what you tryna say?"

"I'm not playin, I've been tryin to give you this for months, and you be tryna act like you don't want it. Not today though, you gone give me what I want this time."

"Is that right? And here I thought it was my birthday."

"It is now come here, and turn that game OFF!"

Caught a little of guard because it's my first experience I slowly moved closer. As if I was following orders, she slowly slid her hand into my shorts, and grabbed my friend entirely too tight showing her inexperience. All the while, licking my lips for me, which to this day turns me on. With her free hand she slowly guides my hand under her skirt to my surprise, she had come more than prepared for the event. As soon as my hand hit center stage I felt the heat, and moisture of her own personal sauna. At that time, it was the most beautiful feeling that I had felt. She hadn't worn any panties today, and was immediately prepared to straddle me, and let me explore her depths. As soon as I felt her warmth, my mind began to race. I tried to think of anything, but the pleasure in my lap. I was told that it would help you last longer, unfortunately my body had prepared for something very different. As she frantically slid herself up then down, up then down, I closed my eyes and envisioned myself in another place, which didn't work for long at all. As she breathed and moaned oh so softly into my ear, I could barely keep control of myself. She softly expressed how much she wanted this, and how long she had waited for me to take her. As her words and moans slid out of her mouth, and into my ears, I slid just as easily in and out of her until I could feel my entire body explode. I could barely catch my breath, she must have felt the same, because her body went limp, and she collapsed on my shoulder. Afterwards, she quickly sat up and pulled her skirt down, and then took a quick glance at herself in the mirror.

"That was fun, hopefully it'll be better next time. Gotta go now, bye, bye, Oh yeah, Happy Birthday again. Hope you enjoyed your present."

A Happy Birthday it was, even though the entire event didn't last more than fifteen minutes. I never really understood why, nor, how I ended up indulging my first time with her. Meaning that she was attractive, but I had definitely seen better, maybe it was the way she demanded what she wanted. I have always been attracted to women who knew what they wanted, and at this time I was what she wanted. I guess that was enough for me. Nonetheless, I spent much of the next week grinning from ear to ear, waiting to experience the enjoyment of my first time a second time. Unfortunately, I didn't receive an encore performance that summer, so it would be up to the new school year to indulge in my new favorite pastime. I'm not completely sure what happened, but after the experience I felt different. I noticed a newly formed confidence that I hadn't had before this encounter. As the summer continued I found myself talking to girls more and more. On the street, at the mall, just about anywhere, each time I noticed myself with more confidence and I also felt more comfortable. I couldn't wait for my senior school year to begin. I just couldn't wait.

SENIOR YEAR: *First Semester*

As school started, I knew that I had an agenda to keep. First and most important to graduate, followed by picking a college in a close second, third was to enjoy my senior year and have as much fun as possible, which hopefully included much more sex. This, in my opinion, was the beginning of the end. Within the first month I found that things were much different from previous years. I noticed that I was getting totally different smiles, and stares from girls. Either that or I was just too blind to see them before. I was informed early in the year that I had a couple of admirers, which was good to hear but there was one particular person that caught my interest at the time. I remember at the end of my junior year I met a friend that I was eager to see, and find out if she still had a boyfriend. The one person I knew who would know this information was Kevin or Kev as most people called him. Now Kev was a pretty cool character, but I knew where we stood, he was a friend from a distance. For the most part he was an associate more than a friend, but the key was he was friends with the apple of my eye at this time. Her name was Maria, she was about 5'8 with shoulder length brown hair, which she kept done, or pulled up into a cute little ponytail. She was in a different crowd than me, which was cool. I was pretty versatile in High School. Even though I was a bit slow with the girls I was still one of the more popular people in the school. I knew someone in every crowd, or they knew me.

Thanks to the fact that she remembered me from last year, it didn't take long to rekindle our acquaintance. I guess Kev vouched for me being a pretty good guy. As time passed we became good friends, probably didn't go any further because she still had a boyfriend. It was real cool because we would sit up all night on the phone just talking about nothing. You remember how you use to just sit and listen to each other breathe, or fall asleep then wake up and continue talking. That was us, many nights we would just be getting off the phone, and then see each other in school thirty minutes later. This went on for a couple of months. As time went on our feelings grew. Hers grew to the point where she wasn't happy with just being my friend anymore so she broke up with her boyfriend. I can still remember the exact time that I found out, it was about 9:15 am and I was in my cooking class, (long story) Kev came in and said he had been looking for me for the last hour. He said that Maria and her boyfriend had broken up, and now she wanted to talk to me. I knew that it was coming, but I didn't think she would actually want to be with me so soon after leaving her boyfriend. I sat the rest of the hour thinking about what I would be getting myself into. Am I ready for a relationship? Since this would be a first for me, can I handle everything that comes with it? I know I can handle the sex if it comes to that. We got together later on that day and she told me the news that I had already heard earlier today, but I still acted surprised. We didn't put any titles on us at that time because it was too soon, but we were inseparable. After each class we would be together either at my locker or hers. Everything seemed great for about a month, and then we decided to actually put a title on what we had. I was now her BOYFRIEND, and that's when everything started to get twisted. I can honestly say I got scared the first time I had that title. I stopped hanging around her as much and didn't talk to her in school. This went on for a month before she was fed up, and broke off our relationship because of my behavior. Well she didn't actually do the dirty work, she had her girl call me on the phone, and tell me she didn't want to be with me anymore. This was not the best way to deal with a problem, at least it wasn't from my point of view.

So that was over before it really started, but I wasn't done with her yet. I would get her back at some point, but I wasn't ready for that move yet. While spending most of my time with her I was still getting the same stares and smiles from other girls at school. Which after being dumped, the attention was more than welcome. About two weeks after the break-up, was the Homecoming party, which was great for me. I couldn't wait to see if any of the young ladies that had been looking so hard this year would actually say something. My question was quickly answered as soon as I entered the building. Tiffany and Sonya were standing at the doorway and kept their eyes glued on me as I walked down the hall to the ballroom. Now Sonya and Tiff are both cute, but their mouths are so big, and so foul I couldn't imagine myself going out with either of them.

"Sonya look whose here all by his self and acting like he too good to speak".

"I know girl, he acting like he the shit."

"I'm surprised his shadow ain't right behind him, I know she ain't let him out all alone."

"Tiff I know you den heard they ain't together no more."

"Are you serious, I ain't know that! Well, shit maybe I need to put my bid in he is cute as hell."

"You and about twenty other hoe'z you know he one of tha cuter nigga's in Tha School."

"Well them other hoe'z ain't me, watch me get his ass girl."

Now I finally actually got close enough to actually speak to both of them, me knowing how both of them act I should have spoke from all the way down the hall. They've probably called me everything under the sun, from the time I entered the doors till I walked down this long ass hallway.

What up ladies, how ya'll doing tonight?

"We alright (Tiff decided to answer for both of them). How yo fine ass doing tonight?"

Thanks for the compliment Tiff, and I'm alive about to try ta enjoy myself for a little while. How about you Sonya you good?

"Yes I'm okay, and you do look nice tonight. I'm gonna go and get something to drink."

Well thank you for the compliment as well.

"So where's yo date tonight?"

I couldn't find one Tiff.

"I don't believe that. You just didn't look in the right place."

Is that right, well who would you have suggested I ask.

"Anybody would've jump at the chance to be on yo arm. Well I know I would have."

7

Oh yeah, I'm gonna have to keep that in mind next time. So if you would've jumped at the chance why didn't you ask me?

"Didn't know you were available."

Well now ya know, I'm about to step in and see what I can see.

"I know you are gonna ask me to dance tonight, right Chris."

Truth is I can't dance, but if you catch me out on the floor just once you definitely get the very next dance.

"Yeah I'm a get that, and much more."

Confident huh, that's cute. Holla at cha Tiff.

Now from the way that Tiff was talking, and not to mention her body language, I came to the conclusion that I could have Tiff right now if I wanted but I didn't. At this point I just want to know who all is interested, then I'll go from there, try to keep my options open. As soon as I entered the ballroom I made my rounds, spoke to the people I felt that I needed to speak to. Gave a friendly nod to the ones that spoke to me. Then I found a quiet table in the corner, and did what I now know to be my GO TO. I usually just find a quiet table and just scope the room, just to see what I can see. So I sat there and enjoyed the view, a lot of people came in jeans, then a couple of us actually put clothes on. Kev silly ass was so over dressed with his Sundays' best suit on. Which I found extremely amusing.

"What up Kev."

"Shit, just looking at all the eye candy in this place."

"Now you know damn well you on lock, and ol'girl ain't having you messing around wit nobody else."

"Whateva nigga! I hear you got a couple of admirers, and you know ya girl is gone be here tonight."

"Who? Come on dawg you know Maria ain't got a leg to stand on wit me, quit playing. You know I'm good on her she made her choice. Plus she ain't even have enough heart to tell me herself, she ain't got two words to say to me."

"Well you know I'm cool wit Carmen and she said, ever since you talked to her when she was upset, she has been feeling you. She said you were sexy or some shit."

"Oh yeah, she is sexy, what is she like Spanish, or something. (Thinking to myself) Yeah she's hot."

"Yeah her people are from the Dominican Republic. You want me to say something to her."

"That's on you. But I'm old enough to talk to her myself. She here tonight?"

"Yep, as a matter of fact there she is right there."

"Damn she looking good tonight, yeah I think I will holla at her. Myself dawg, I'll talk to her myself."

"Yeah okay, we'll see."

So I decided to keep my eye on Carmen tonight, just to see who the competition was that I may or may not be dealing with. She pretty much stayed to herself most of the night, she also didn't seem to be paying too many people too much attention. As I said before she was looking great tonight. She had a glow that I had either never noticed before, or unfortunately just hadn't paid attention to. It was then that I was hit with a revelation. I wanted this young lady, wasn't sure in what capacity at this point, but I knew that part of me wanted her. Thanks to my summer's experience I was a bit more comfortable talking to young ladies, and through a lot of trial and era, I no longer made myself look like a complete idiot, just the mini me of idiots, so I would have to find a way to get her to talk to me without letting the bigger version of the idiot out. It hit me after a minute or two, there was a vendor in the hall on the way to the ballroom, so I went out to buy her a rose. As I returned, and found her still sitting in the same area, only she had a companion now. He was a very nice looking older gentleman, didn't really seem like her type. Turns out, it was here father, I had paid so little attention that I didn't realize her father was a teacher at our school. I politely excused their conversation to hand her the rose (that had turned into roses once the vendor got done talking).

Pardon me Sir, sorry to interrupt, but I would really like to give these to the beautiful young lady that you happen to be conversing with. I hope you are not bothered by my interruption. I thought that would at least catch their attention, and hopefully get him to think I'm a pretty good guy. He politely excused himself from the table, as he walked away he gave me a little nudge and a smile. As if he was approving of my approach, which actually made me feel pretty good.

"May I have a seat?"

"Of course you can if those roses are for me"

9

"Well I know they aren't for me, plus they would look so much better in your arms than mine."

"And to what do I owe this honor?"

"Well I was admiring how beautiful you were from a distance, but I was saying to myself that something was missing. So I found these roses, I thought they might make you smile. That was the one thing that was missing, so can I get one please?"

"So the flowers were a bribe?"

"Not at all, just thought they would help you smile."

"And why do you want me to smile anyway?"

"Just hate to see a beautiful person not smiling. I spend too much time not smiling, I think I have that market pretty much sewed up I really don't need any competition."

"Boy you are silly," she said with a smile on her face.

"There it is and, it's just as beautiful as the person who is wearing it. Well I really didn't want anything else, just wanted a smile. Hopefully I get a chance to see you again soon."

"Well we do go to school together."

"Not only is the mouth cute but smart too. I knew I'd like you. You enjoy the rest of your night."

As I walked away I looked back just to view her expression. In my opinion the look on her face was that of disbelief, as if I was supposed to stick around for the entire night. As I continued my exit, I noticed the look of disgust on the face of Maria who had been watching from across the room. She had entered the party, from my understanding about an hour ago, and had been observing my conversation with Carmen. I didn't even take the time to respond to the look just continued out the door.

School became very intriguing the next week, I had a new interest that had my attention whether she new it or not. I had an ex who I found was still interested, even if it was just jealousy, and I had a silly one who would make a fool of herself just to get close. I was in good shape from where I was standing. Carmen didn't waste much time. As soon as she caught up with Kev she talked him into giving her my number, which worked out fine for me. That was just one less thing that I had to take care of. As far as Maria went, she broke up with me and I guess she was feeling a bit regretful about the situation. At least that was the way Kev explained it when he called to talk about how upset she was the night of the party after I left. He said that as soon as I got out the door she found him, and ran down the twenty questions. You know the usual who, why, when, and where did I get off talking to anyone else on earth I guess. This was really none of my concern, I usually don't hold grudges but the way in which she handled dumping me had me doing just that, HOLDIN a GRUDGE.

Now Carmen was on top of her game. She catches me in the hall on my way to class, and asked if she could walk with me. Which really caught me a little off guard because it's usually the dude who does all the work. The walking to class and carrying books, but this time she was showing more interest than me and I loved it. Nonetheless I smiled, and hit her with an "Of Course".

"So do you usually buy roses to make people smile?"

"Naw that was a first, I was tryna see if it would work. You didn't see my little notepad out so I could record the reaction? Joking, it was worth it to see that smile."

"Glad you enjoyed it, my father was a little impressed. He asked me about you the next day."

That's good to hear, but I bought them for your benefit not his. So did you like them?

"I smiled didn't I?"

I guess I'll take that as a yes. Well here's my class. So am I ever gonna get yo number?

"Is that how you ask? I think you can do better."

Oh I'm sorry, do you think I'll be privileged enough to call you one day?

"Don't say you sorry, I don't deal with sorry people. And I think I will give you that privilege, so I'll call you later today."

Okay then I apologize, let me write my number down for you.

"No need I already have it"

"Is that right? I see somebody has been talking to Kev huh."

"I have my sources, I'll give you a call tonight. Bye-bye"

As she walked away I stood in the classroom door, and enjoyed the view for a second or two. After she was gone I stepped into class, with a smirk on my face, and a couple things on my mind. I spent the next hour lost in space, thinking about everything. By now, it was a fact

I'm getting an entirely different feel from the young ladies, than I was less than a year ago. A lot more looks, smiles, it seems like every time I turn around I'm getting new attention and I'm loving every second of it. I'm really content with being single I don't really want a girlfriend, but I know its right around the corner. Carmen doesn't seem like the type who is just going to let me simply be her friend. Can't forget about Tiff and Maria, if given the opportunity they would both jump at the chance to take me off the available market.

After I spent the entire hour lost thinking about my newfound fame, the rest of the day went pretty smooth, and very quick. Before I knew it, I was at home knocking out homework, and playing video games, which at this point bored me to no end. It wasn't long before my phone was ringing. Knew I was expecting a call, didn't think it would be this soon though.

"Hello."

"Hello, may I speak to Christopher?"

"This is him, who dis."

"How many people said they were calling you tonight?"

"Hey sweetie, seeing how it's not actually night yet I was a little thrown off."

"Would you like me to call you back?"

Said nothing of the sort. How was your day?

"Was pretty good, and yours?"

"I'm alive, so I guess it was pretty good."

"So what is that you see in me, why are you interested?"

"Wow, straight to the point! Well since we're not wasting time with small talk. I think you're attractive, and I think I want to get to know you a little better. Now can you answer the same question?"

"Well actually ever since you took the time to talk to me when I was sitting in that classroom crying, I've been paying attention to you. You had always been kinda cute, so for you to show that you had some kinda heart intrigued me."

"Okay, I just did what I thought was right. Better yet I was actually just being nosy."

"You silly, that's another one of your attractive qualities. You make me laugh and that's not the easiest thing to do. I don't really laugh too much."

"That's not a good thing, you gotta laugh at things sometimes or you'll go crazy."

"Yeah I know, I'm working on that."

"We will work on it together, I think I can help."

"Watch what you say I might hold you to it."

The conversation went on for hours, and hours. She was very pleasant to talk to. For the next couple of months we talked to each other everyday, as well as walking each other to class, and spending time outside of school. Before I knew what happened I had a girlfriend. It wasn't a problem just didn't know it in the beginning. It was brought to my attention by Tiff, and her attitude. She caught me in the hall one day, and felt it was necessary let me in on the fact that she didn't like my girlfriend. I started to tell her Carmen and I were just friends, but it hit me that this is exactly what she wanted so she could run with it. So instead I politely explained that she didn't have to like her I did, and I was the only person who had to. That didn't make her feel any better, but it was a lot better then hurting Carmen, by saying something stupid.

Second Semester

I didn't officially accept the title of boyfriend until we got back from Christmas vacation, and no it's not what you think, she did receive a Christmas gift. It just never came up until then. I guess she just wanted to know where we stood before we returned to school. As soon as we got back to school I could tell the difference, she was claiming me any and every time she got the chance. Which wasn't a problem it was just different, it was to the point where teachers and councilors knew we were together not just students anymore. According to most we were an odd couple, no one could imagine me being with her, and they definitely couldn't picture her with me. She was way too serious, while I was oh so carefree. Most girls that had an interest in me thought I could do better, namely them, and a lot of teachers that didn't really know me felt that she could do better, seeing that I was one of the more troublesome guys in the school. I wasn't bad, just a little unruly, and of course very silly. What most of them didn't know, because they never bothered to either ask or find out was that I held a 3.5 grade point average. I was quite capable of taking care of business, and she was very capable of laughter.

The relationship went very well in the beginning we didn't change anything from before, we still talked as much as before, and still walked each other to each class. Plus, we ignored everyone who didn't like the fact that we were together. As time went on we grew closer, my mom, as well as the rest of my family became fond of her. It had come to the point where she was more than welcome at the house whether I was there or not, which at that time wasn't a big problem for me because the only person I was spending time with was her. Months passed and we were still happy as far as she knew, but the more people began to talk the more I began to listen. It seemed like the more I wanted to be with her the more other women were voicing their interest. The craziest part was most of them, could've had my attention at one point or another throughout my high school career. It seemed the more they told me about their feelings, the more I wanted to see what they had to say, and it wasn't the same people as before. Now I was receiving attention from young ladies that I had no idea about, although the usual people were still putting their bids in. I also now had one of the Twins, Lil Kim, Torey, Keisha, and Shannon whether they all knew or not they all had at least one view in common I was with the wrong person. If I add Maria, and Tiff, I was over a Baker's dozen. This is when the problems began to mount. Carmen had to feel the heat from these other young ladies, so she probably felt like she had to do something to keep herself in front of the pack.

We had both agreed that we weren't going to rush the sexual part of our relationship, we could wait until we were both ready for it to go there. The plan was to wait until we went to the prom together which seemed like a long wait, but at the same time, it wasn't a big deal because I hadn't had sex in the last eight months and before that it had been seventeen years, what's the big deal waiting for another three months. Only problem was other people were offering to accommodate me in my sexual endeavors, the only thing that made my life easier was the fact that these chicks didn't know that I wasn't having sex with Carmen. It was assumed we were "Fucking like Jack Rabbits" we had to be, as much as we were together. Although, the truth was, we hadn't gotten much further than some strong kissing, and touching, but that was soon to change. I remember it quite vividly, I got home about an hour late just to find that I had company that wasn't expected. I went straight into my room without seeing who was home, it was quite evident that someone had been home either recently or was still there because as soon as I entered my room I was greeted by Carmen, who as far as I knew, didn't have a key to my house. She was laying on my bed, and from the looks of things she had been there for a while, she looked quite comfortable with nothing but a pink bra and panty set on as clothing. This surprised me, but didn't bother me in the least, as a matter of fact I was extremely happy to see her in this light.

"Hey, you looking as sexy as you want to. How'd you get in here?"

"Well I hope you are not upset, I got the key from your sister. I told her I wanted to surprise you."

"Why would I be upset? And even if I was, your attire would have killed that quick! So what's up with the lack of clothes?"

"What do you think? I think it's about time we take our relationship to the next level."

"And what level might that be? (as if it wasn't obvious)"

"Well we've been together for about three months, even longer if you count the time it wasn't official. I think it's about time that we take our relationship to a sexual level. Plus I need to know if you can satisfy me before I'm disappointed after the Prom."

"Hahaha, You got jokes huh? Are you sure this is what you want to do? I can wait, we don't have to rush into anything."

"I've thought about it and I haven't wanted anything more than this in my life. I want you so bad, right now. So stop talking and come on over here and give me what I want."

"Well I haven't told you no so far in our relationship, why would I start now?"

As I slowly approached the center of the room, where she lay comfortably on the bed, looking oh so beautiful with nothing more than her pink Victoria Secret's set on, I couldn't help but stop and stare for a moment. Thinking to myself this beautiful, intelligent, young lady wants me. This was so amazing to me, I could not have been convinced I would be in this situation this time last year. But here I am about to have sex with one of the sexiest girls in the school. As I slid my hands through her jet-black hair, I heard a slight moan escape as she exhaled. I gently pressed my lips to hers, and we began a strong passionate kiss. I could feel her hands grasping at my back caressing, and massaging my shoulders. As the kiss became more passionate, I could feel her hands and fingertips more and more. As I lay on top of her and the caressing continued she unleashed one of her many talents, sliding her feet up to my waist. With one leg she held me close, and with the other she maneuvered her foot inside the waistband of my oversized jogging pants, and easily pulled them down below my thighs. By now I'm not only very turned on, but surprised by her flexibility, also by the way she has taken over the situation. Now in nothing more than a pair of boxers, and her nothing at all, she begins a very slow seductive grind against me. All the while looking deep into my eyes as if she had a serious concentration going on. She leaned forward, and placed her breast directly over my mouth as her hands roamed under the pillow under my head. As I began to enjoy the breast that my tongue and lips where teasing, I also began to notice the moisture from her softness. She pulled her hands from under the pillow and quickly ripped open the package, as we both worked on getting my boxers off, she immediately grabbed me and rolled down the Magnum. Before I could say a word she quickly slid down, and let out a loud sigh, and in her sexiest Spanish accent "Aye Papi", escaped her lips. This did something totally different for me. I had never heard anything so beautiful before in my life. She moved with so much passion it was as if she could feel even the slightest move that I made. She stayed on top of me for a while to control how much of me she felt, as she continued to ride she expressed how much she was enjoying herself. I slowly took control of the situation, as she allowed me to roll her over on her side. I lifted her leg into the air, and gave myself an opportunity to get a complete stroke in as she felt the entirety of my love, she quickly grabbed the nearest pillow and covered her mouth. She let out a muffled YEEEESSSS, which turned me on even more. I believe she could tell that her speaking in Spanish really excited me, with each stroke more and more of her Dominican ancestry emerged. I could feel each time I entered her moisture she was getting tighter and tighter. She had complete control over her muscles, which intensified the experience.

She finally asked me to turn her over, so that she could see my face. She wanted to look into my eyes to see my expression while I was deep inside her. As we slowly moved into position, with her legs wrapped around my waist, and her hands massaging my back, I could feel myself getting closer and closer to my destination. She was very close to the same. She had come to the point where she couldn't stop her legs from trembling. Her next action insured my arrival. She slowly dug her nails deep into my back, and the intensity of the pleasure, and pain that I was introduced to brought me directly to my destination. The warmth of my explosion could be felt throughout both of our bodies. I could see the excitement in her eyes, as I was sure she could see the satisfaction in mine. As the hours passed we continued to explore each other's bodies until it was time for me to return to school for my last day of basketball practice.

Before, and even after we indulged ourselves into each other, I was torn between being in a relationship, and being single. Just as before I was attracting attention from many different places, and was quite interested to see whether the grass was truly greener on the other side. Maria had continued to make her interest known, and her advances were more and more intriguing to me.

Now that basketball season was over, I seemed to have more spare time. Which I used most of to chill, with Carmen who's swim season was in full swing now, so I spent most of my time in the pool area. It was cool because I knew most of the people there, probably because I was on the team in the ninth grade (It was forced upon me). The only problem that I ran into was the fact that not only was Maria there everyday, but so were her friends Aleshia, and Sabrine. Most of the time it was cool, but every now and then we would run into problems, especially when Aleshia got going on how I should be with Maria instead of Carmen, which would only happen when Carmen was still in the locker room. So to avoid the whole situation I would just come into the pool area later and later everyday. We were all still friends, which Carmen really didn't approve of. Her disapproval was now noticeable. She could tell that there was something between Maria and myself even if she wasn't completely sure of the existence of our prior relationship. The more time I spent hanging out with the group, the more I forgot about the fact that Maria broke up with me, and the way in which she did it, was pushed to the back of my mind as well.

Everything went bad on one particular day when Carmen had a doctor's appointment, and didn't come to school. Instead of taking my silly ass home I went down to the poolroom anyway. BIG MISTAKE! I went down with Kev who had laps to do before he could go home. Maria and crew were there just sitting around, when Aleshia had one of her bright ideas.

"Hey ya'll let's play truth or dare."

This should have been my cue to leave, but before I could gather myself I heard about five or six people yell out "Bet it" which pretty much meant it was a good idea, so before I knew it, I was in the middle of an intense game of DARE. I call it that because there weren't to many truth questions asked. When it got around to being my turn I thought I was slick, when giving the choice of truth or dare I immediately said TRUTH. Thinking I was in the clear I was asked a pretty easily answered question by Sabrine "Do you still like Maria?"

"Yeah of course I do. We are still friends as far as I am concerned why wouldn't I like her?"

She hadn't realized she had given me an out because she didn't specify what she meant by like even though I knew damn well what she meant. It wasn't going to be that easy getting me to admit anything. Here I was pretty sure I was in the clear, but I must have forgot that Kev was a DUCK (which we used to describe a dude who goes with whatever the crowd is doing). He was more on their team than mine so he quickly took his opportunity to suck up, and hit me with the same question in a different way.

"Truth or Dare, Chris do you still want to be with Maria."

"What? Ain't that a bitch! First off, I just answered a question. Second, I ain't answering that. Third, you a ol'suck up ass nigga."

"Naw dude you gotta answer or you gotta take a swim wit all yo shit on."

"Let's be honest, who in here is gone make me take a swim? But I'll answer the question, NO I DON'T, because I'm with someone."

"But what if you weren't?"

It ain't yo turn, and we ain't playing the what if game. Who's up next?

I came to the conclusion that it was shit on Chris day because Aleshia was the next person to ask the question Truth or Dare, I was beginning to think that Kev set me up for failure, and I fell right into the trap. Just when I was about to quit, and get the Hell out of Dodge, the questioning took a turn for what I thought was the better, but ended up being for the worst. Aleshia took the heat off me long enough to throw my ass directly into the fire. She quickly turned her attention to Maria, "Truth or Dare?" she asked.

"I'll take Dare."

"Okay I dare you take Chris in the Coach's office and have your way with him."

"Now Aleshia you know he is in a relationship (she said sarcastically), he's not going to agree to that."

"That nigga ain't married, and I know he ain't scared. At least I hope he ain't."

I couldn't believe they were speaking on me like I wasn't right in front of them. By now the blank stares had begun to occur as well as the Ooo's and Aaa's from the other participants. Thinking to myself "Peer pressure is a BITCH!" It's not like this is something that I wouldn't mind doing, but it was something I shouldn't do. But, they won't just disrespect me like that all in my face, insinuating that I'm scared, like they tough, and shit. I know what to do. I'll call their bluff, and see how tough Maria really was. So I quickly got up, dusted myself off and began to walk towards the office, before either one of them could say anything I turned and looked at Maria and asked her in my strongest voice "You coming?". With a shocked expression on her face she slowly rose, and stepped awkwardly towards my direction. Edged on by Kevin's words "Who looks scared now?" she picked up her pace.

As we entered the lamp lit, empty office, both wanting to be there, but at the same time not wanting to. We turned and looked at each other, "So this is what you want?" I asked. With so much attitude she responded, "I'm here ain't I!" That don't mean much under the circumstances, I think you here because I called your bluff, and you weren't expecting me to. Before I could finish my sentence she stepped in and stole a kiss, sliding her tongue between my lips, and then gently biting my bottom lip. I eagerly responded by grabbing the back of her hair and holding her right where she was enjoying my lips, and me enjoying hers. She pulled away after a couple of seconds and asked "Now do you still think it was just because of a Dare."

"Maybe I was wrong."

"Chris I still like you, and the only reason I broke up with you in the first place was because, you started to treat me so differently when we actually became a couple. You were ignoring me, and treating me like I was just another female friend of yours, not your woman. Then you turn around, and start kicking it with Carmen, and she ain't even yo type. She don't want you like I want you, and I know she can't do you like I can. To top it all off, you don't like her like you like me."

20

So you telling me you still want me, and I'm supposed to just say okay. As far as our relationship went, I treated you like you wanted to be treated by all your past relationships. Remember you told me that you didn't like being all affectionate in school, so everybody wouldn't be all in your business. Even after the way you ended our relationship, the way you did. You think I should just ignore the fact that you had one of yo girls call me on the damn phone and break up with me! I don't think I can do that right now! It wouldn't be fair to me, and I'm sure Carmen wouldn't like it either. You hurt me real bad, and I'm not past that yet. I hope that I can get over it one day, but that day isn't here yet.

"If I wanted to be treated like that I would've stayed with them. But I understand I was in the wrong with the way that things ended, but that won't stop me from trying every time I get the chance, and you can mark my words I am going to get you back. You are my man not hers."

We probably need to get out of here. As I opened the office door we could see everyone scrambling back to the seats, acting as if they weren't just listening at the door. Aleshia was the first to have something to say "Damn he must be a minute man." My response was simple, you know all about them, don't you! This got a laugh from everyone else, because we all knew her complaints with her boyfriend at the time. Kev had a look on his face as if he wanted to ask right then what had happened, I ignored the look, and returned to the place I was sitting. As I sat there with the newly acquired information, I found myself debating what should be done with it. Part of me said I should ignore the fact that I still had feelings for Maria because I was happy with who I was with. But as my thoughts deepened, I had to ask myself was I truly happy? Was I really in the relationship that I really wanted? The more I thought about it the more unsure I became, if I was truly happy, what had just happened wouldn't have happened. The other part of me (the quite sinister part), thought why not have my cake, and eat it too. It's a saying often heard, but rarely understood. Let me tell it, it was one the dumbest sayings I had ever heard. Who on earth would want cake if they couldn't eat it? But my thought was I could have them both. Maria was in a place where she would accept whatever I was offering as long as she had a part of me. She was also so hell bent on having me and embarrassing Carmen, that she wouldn't mind talking to me behind her back. Luckily, my more sensible side was in control, so I decided to try my best to stay away from Maria for a while. At least until I could better control myself. After sitting there for a while listening to the others play, and completing the debate within, I stood and said my good-byes.

The next couple of weeks flew by, and as more and more time passed the closer we came to Graduation, not to mention the PROM. I felt I was more than prepared for one, and not nearly as prepared for the other. I had already decided on WMU for college, and couldn't wait to get the formalities over, and done with. I had already been to visit many times because my cousin began there the previous year. So I already had a group of friends up there. I had also checked out the class sizes, and found that they were one of the best schools in the state for my major. Carmen on the other hand hadn't decided on what school would best suit here standards, which really didn't bother me. I had come to the decision that we wouldn't be together in college anyway. Especially, because she was hoping to go to school in California, she explained that she was quite tired of cold weather. The cute part was she actually wanted me to think about finding a college in California so that we could go together. Which amused me more than anything, I didn't want to go to California. I was privileged enough to have been a couple of times, it was a nice place to visit but I would not want to live there nor go to school there. I guess it wasn't my type of atmosphere. Even still, she would throw it out there from time to time; I guess she was trying to gauge my reaction. To bad she got the same laughter just about every time. As time went on she decided not to ask the question as much, instead she replaced it with, would I have a problem if she went to WMU. I really didn't think to highly of the idea, but instead of telling her that I usually, replied with "If you think you would be happy there, it's a good school." Which didn't sit to well with her, I could tell by the expression on her face.

Although it was the truth to an extent, she really should choose a school by how she will fit in with its surroundings or at least by how comfortable she is there. Even still, she seemed to replace the notion of me following her to school with one of her following me to school. It became a serious problem when I learned from our counselor that she had applied, and been accepted to WMU.

I wasn't prepared to deal with the future at this point, I was more concerned with the present. I was with someone that I wasn't sure I wanted to be with, and I had someone else who was very interested, and very persistent that would like nothing more than to be with me. Maria had begun to let her disdain for my relationship show on a regular basis. It was at a point were if Carmen wasn't sure about whether Maria didn't like us being together before it was now a FACT. This made Carmen work that much harder to keep me happy, which made me feel even worse about the whole situation, and it still wasn't enough to make me stop talking to Maria. Was I being selfish? Did I really even care? How could I keep being with her if I didn't even take a stand, and tell Maria to back off? These were the questions that I asked myself, but these were also the questions I couldn't bring myself to answer.

Maria made it no easier. Her pursuit became stronger by the day, she caught me walking up the driveway to the side door one day. I had just watched Carmen pull off on her way home, and as I walked up the drive I noticed a greenish blue Escort pull up in front of the house. They must have hit the opposite corner at the exact same time. She got out of the car, my immediate reaction was a slight smile, but I quickly changed that to something more suitable for the situation.

"What the hell are you doing here! What if my woman was sitting here?"

"I thought you didn't play the What If Game, and if I thought she was I would've kept going."

"How do you know she ain't coming right back?"

"I don't, but if she was you probably shouldn't be out here talking to me so I think you should invite me in."

"What? You must be out yo mind!"

"Nope just know what I want."

Is that right? And what is that you want so bad that you just show up at my house unannounced, you'd think I would at least get a phone call before you just stop by. Her response angered me even worse than, her being there.

"I did call. Your mom said you were downstairs, and she guessed it would be alright for me to come by."

Shirley had a bad habit of getting involved when she shouldn't. She probably wanted to meet the other person she hears me talk about all the time. But this was neither the time nor the place, for her to meet Maria, I wouldn't be able to explain this one; no way, no how. Unfortunately, that didn't stop me from inviting her in. We went straight into the room that I entertained all my guest. I wanted to talk so that I had a full understanding of what she wanted from me. She politely explained that she wanted another chance at being my woman, she felt that since we now understood where we went wrong before, it would work out beautifully this time around. We could make each other happy. She also explained that she wasn't planning on giving up until she at least got the opportunity. Once again I found myself in a room alone with her wanting to agree with everything she said, but knowing that I couldn't. I reminded her that I have a woman right now, and I don't want to hurt her feelings. This did nothing to change her mood, nor her demeanor. She had her mind set on what she wanted and didn't plan on stopping until she got it. As I sat on one end of the couch and her the other I couldn't help but notice the more time passed, the closer she got. I closed my eyes for a second to think to myself and quickly opened them when I felt her movement, she was now close enough to run her hand across my thigh. I could feel the warmth of her breath on my neck as she whispered "What's wrong with having what you want?" As I began to think about her words I allowed my eyelashes to meet once again. Enjoying the darkness as well as the touch of her lips on my neck I could hardly remember the words that should have been coming out of my mouth, instead I replaced them with muffled sounds of enjoyment. As the temperature rose in the room I gently ran my fingers through her hair and laid her back onto the couch as her kisses elevated from my neck to my lips, and my touch descended from her hair to her breast. I noticed her breathing becoming heavier, our body heat must have rose high enough to be felt throughout the house, because there was a knock on the door, about the same time that my hands had decided to explore her curves. Who is it? I said with a certain disgust in my voice.

"It's you mother, can I come in." As if it was a question that I could answer with anything else, besides YES. What up, lady? I joked as I quickly removed myself from my current position. "Nothing just thought I'd come down and introduce myself since you didn't think it was important enough to do." I had to apologize, but I honestly didn't want them to meet especially considering that this is someone who she really shouldn't know at this point, seeing that I had a girl friend and it wasn't her. Plus I knew Shirley, I knew she was going to say something. The problem was I had no idea what it would be.

"Hello I'm Mrs. Alexander, the boys' (the boy, dang she act like I'm not sitting right here.) Mother, and you are?"

"Hi Mrs. Alexander, it's very nice to meet you. My name is Maria, I think we spoke on the phone earlier."

"Really, I think I've heard Chris talk about you before, don't you guys go to school together."

"Yes we do."

"That's good, have you guys known each other long, or did you just meet?"

"We've known each other since around this time last year, so about a year."

"That's good, so you know his girl friend Carmen too then right?"

"Ma chill out."

"What? I was just wondering if she knew you had a girl friend, and if so, I was wondering why she was allowing you to use her? Men always want their cake, and eat it too. She just doesn't seem like the type of young lady who would allow a young man to use her in that manner. You just make sure you make him choose between the two of you. Don't settle for being the woman on the side."

"Well Mrs. Alexander Chris and I are just friends, and I do know Carmen, and I respect their relationship."

"Okay well I was just wondering, because you guys were down here alone with the doors closed, I just thought I'd come down and introduce myself. You guys enjoy yourselves. It was nice meeting you sweetie."

"It was nice meeting you too, have a nice day Mrs. Alexander."

Thanks for introducing yourself mom, I said sarcastically, see ya later. As she left I was forced to wonder whose side she was on mine or theirs. It really didn't matter whether she left now or stayed downstairs and sat next to us the entire time. Her job was done, Maria's entire demeanor had changed. She was now portraying the perfect Angel that she had become for my mothers benefit, instead of the Devil she was before the introduction. The act did seem somewhat genuine, even though I knew better. It was the act that we have all put on in front of parents that we wanted to impress so that they would like us. The same

25

act that they had performed for their parents before them. Maria was noticeably uncomfortable now, the words of my Mother had pierced her in both places it needed to hit, her brain and her heart. She would not allow me to use her in the way she had planned to allow me to earlier in her visit.

"Your Mom is right I shouldn't allow you to have your cake and eat it too. You should have to choose between us, so I hope you make the right decision, because I would love to go to the Prom with you. I have to go, but you should really think about us."

Stunned by her comments more so, than the fact that she was leaving. My mom has a way with words, she'll make you think even when you really don't want to. So her leaving wasn't surprising at all, but her comments about Prom, and then about US. That was wild, crazy, surprising, even confusing all at the same time. I had a woman, but I kept letting her in. What made her think I would stand my girl up for the prom and go with her? I would be the biggest Dirt-bag on earth, I knew that wasn't an option especially since we (well she) had already decided on our colors and her dress was already in the process of being made. There was nothing to think about, I had this situation under control from this day forward. I'm with Carmen and that was that.

After the experience at my house everything between Maria and me died down. It was as if she knew I had made my decision even without me explaining it to her. This worked out perfect for me. I concentrated all my energy to making Carmen happy. With less than a week until the big day I couldn't help but be anxious, partly because you only have one prom experience that is truly your own. The other part of me just wanted to get the whole thing over with. Having to withstand only a small barrage from Aleshia telling me how I should forget Carmen, and take her girl to the prom I easily ignored that request and reminded her who my woman was.

Now with it being the day of, I was fully prepared, everything was set. My entire family had come over to witness the occasion. I thought they could have waited until I at least got dressed, but not my family, they had started arriving as early as noon. It wasn't like I was the girl. I didn't have hair and makeup to do, all I had to do was put on my tuxedo, a little cologne and I was good to go. I guess they all just wanted to support me, and that was cool. My aunt and my grandmother were snapping pictures left and right, even though I still wasn't fully dressed. Now for someone like me, it's almost impossible to catch me dressed. I only do it when I most certainly have to. This whole tuxedo thing was an event, it wasn't the first time dressing up but it had been a while. After my transformation was complete. I must say I Do Clean up Well. I had on a cream tux with a Cranberry vest and tie with some Cranberry Gators (Alligator shoes) last, but definitely not least, you could smell the aroma of Issy, (before everybody and their momma started wearing it) following my every move. I was now ready for a night on the town. My parents had rented an all black Cadillac limousine. They also rented a Cranberry Mustang, which was already parked in the parking lot for after the prom. It was so amusing when my supposed friend Erika, who had graduated two years ago, had came by to see me before I left. She had caught me just before I was getting into the limo, and gave me a hug. It was really nice to see her especially because she was one of the sexiest women I had seen up to that point. She got in the limo for a second, gave me a kiss, and told me that after the prom I should drop my date off, and come pick her up. I told her to quit playing. She politely explained that she wasn't joking and she would page me later on tonight, and then removed herself from the car.

As I arrived at Carmen's house I noticed that her driveway was even more packed than mine was. As I exited the car, corsage in hand, I was greeted by so many different people. Some I knew, some I didn't even better, some I understood, some I didn't. I had met her mother and father previously, and also a couple of her cousins. But now I had to contend with aunts, uncles and her grandmother, not an easy task when most of them were speaking Spanish. Some of the men were giving me the look. You know, that you're the one trying to touch my daughter or niece look. I just smiled, and nodded most of the time, with a couple of thank you's mixed in here and there for those who complimented me on how nice I looked tonight. It seemed that some of them were stressing tonight, as if to say every other night I was a Monster. After about an hour of poking and prodding, my date finally made her entrance as she strolled down the winding staircase in her Cranberry Strapless dress that hugged every curve of her body. She had a certain glow, a confidence so to speak, that jumped out at you, and let you know I am

27

the most beautiful woman you will see tonight. Instead of wearing her hair up, as was tradition from my understanding, she took a different approach. She wore her long dark hair down, which made her look that much sexier. I immediately approached the bottom of the staircase with one hand out, and the cranberry and cream Orchid in the other. As she finally ended her descent she took my hand with a smile that lit the entire room. "You look beautiful," I said. She responded "I'm glad you approve, you look quite handsome yourself". As we stood there hand in hand I could see flashes out of the corner of my eye, "Let me get a picture of you putting the corsage on" her mother said. I slowly removed the delicate flower from its storage area, and gently placed it on her wrist. All the while you could hear nothing but pictures snapping, and people chattering complimenting how good we looked together, and how we were perfectly coordinated. I couldn't help but smile the entire time, it was so funny to me how everyone made such a big deal about a simple date, although it was extremely enjoyable. As we exited the house and approached the car the driver greeted us with an opened door, as she entered the car he complimented her beauty and gave me the way to go wink as I got in. The bar in the limo had but one thing to offer, a nicely chilled bottle of Moet and two glasses. As the driver pulled off I popped the cork on the bottle and poured us both a drink. "Oh yeah, you went all out huh?"

Not really, I tried to get a helicopter, but my parents weren't having it I said jokingly, but with a serious connotation. (Truth be told, I did want a helicopter to drop us off in the parking lot, but that would have been a little extravagant.)

As we drank and cruised the city we enjoyed just talking, and starring into each other's eyes. There wasn't too much kissing because we didn't want to ruin her make up before my family saw it or before we got to the event. The plan was to run back over to my house so that my family could see her as well, then we would head down to the prom. Everything worked out perfectly, the bubbles from the champagne had us feeling a little tipsy so stopping by my house wasn't a problem. We spent most of the time giggling at every little thing that happened. We were there for all of fifteen minutes when we decided it was time to make our way to the party. As we pulled up to the Masonic Temple it was already eleven o'clock, as I thought to myself I'm glad I didn't get the helicopter, no one would have been out here to see us step out of it. As the driver opened the door and we stepped out onto the red carpet, we saw a couple scattered faces we recognized that had pulled up with us. There was Kev, and his date getting out of a silver Jag. Then right behind us was DeAngelo, who came with Tiff, probably after she figured that I wasn't going to ask her she just went with him, they were best friends anyway. They were getting out of a Smoke Grey Rolls Royce, it was pretty much putting the Caddy I was in to shame, but I didn't mind one bit. Because while I was impressed by his car he was impressed by my date. We all spoke to each other, and entered the building at once. Although we had to separate for our announcements, as each couple entered they were announced by one of the faculty. Kev and his date went first, and were greeted by mild applause. Then it was DeAngelo and Tiffs turn, and it seemed as if everyone in the place cheered. That would be hard to follow, but who better to do it besides me. I mean us, as we entered, we got the same exact love that the couple before us got. It seemed that you could here the Oooo's and Aaaah's throughout the building. You even heard a couple fellas yell out DAMN!!! As we walked pass Kiesha, and a couple of her girls, I heard her ask "I wonder what room he'll be in tonight." To which Carmen responded "MINE!" as if this wasn't the night for anybody to be testing her. After a small bit of mingling we found our seats, and just enjoyed the music and scenery for a while. The theme was a King's Court so everything was Cream and Gold, from the table linen to decorations lining the walls, they even went as far as too have a gigantic thrown in the middle of two treasure chests filled with fake gold at one end of the room. It was beautiful, and everyone looked fabulous, I was definitely enjoying myself. Carmen got up to walk around the room one more time just to do a bit more mingling. There were people just arriving, that she felt she had to greet. I sat back and continued to enjoy the scenery. That was until I spotted Aleshia, and Maria headed my way. As they approached I got up from my seat thinking I could disappear before they actually got to me, but I was too late.

"Hey Chris, you're looking quite nice."

"Thanks, Aleshia so do you. What up Maria you're looking lovely tonight."

"If I'm looking so lovely why are you here with her? Just kidding you not looking so bad ya'self."

"Thank you, I guess."

"You know I'm playing you look damn good. What up a girl can't get a hug?"

"Yeah of course, you know we better than that."

As I lean over to hug Maria, she whispered in my ear, 'you know you should have been here with me don't you?" And as she let the words slip from her mouth her embrace got warmer and tighter. She continued, we would've had such a good time all night. As I removed myself from her grip, she looked at me with wanting eyes and asked "can a girl get a dance?" To put her back in her place, and hopefully in the right mindset I explained I haven't danced with my woman yet. With a stunned look on her face she couldn't come up with a response quick enough. It must have slipped my mind that this was a two against one stand off, because Aleshia jumped right in "She ain't ask about yo chick." Which was easily countered by "I don't think I was talking to you." And then immediately I began walking towards my date's direction. The looks on their faces where priceless, even though I didn't want to hurt, Maria's feelings. I did enjoy shutting Aleshia's big mouth if only for a moment.

Now that everyone was in the right mindset, we can attempt to enjoy the rest of our night. After mingling for an hour or two, we actually took the time to enjoy each other for a while. We had a great time we laughed, danced, and just talked. As time passed, the last dance came up and it was beautiful. The DJ played There's Nothing Greater than Love by Luther Vandross and Gregory Hines, we met on the dance floor for the last time of the night. As our bodies intertwined slowly moving across the dance floor, we connected. She gently bit my ear, and then whispered "I am so happy we are here together, and I can't wait to be with you tonight." As she finished her statement, her body heat seemed to intensify, or maybe it was just me. But her whole demeanor changed she seemed ready to leave immediately. She didn't waste anymore time, "Are you ready to go?" I responded, "Yeah we can get out of here." We didn't have far to go, my aunt had gotten me, well us a suite at the Atheneum, which wasn't far from where we were. We made our way to the car outside while everyone else seemed to be standing around trying to decide where they were going to eat. I explained to her we could just order room service, which she responded "I'm not concerned with that right now." I couldn't help but wonder why she was in such a rush tonight. "Sweetie, we have all night. We can take our time, there won't be anyone to disturb us, we don't have to rush."

"The truth is you are only partly right, no one will disturb us but we don't have all night I have to be home before five a.m."

"Oh my fault, I didn't know you had a curfew tonight."

"Well I do, so let's make the most of the time that we have."

"Sounds good to me."

As we arrived at the hotel I pulled around to valet parking, "You're really trying to make this the best night of my life huh?" "Well most people only attend one prom in their life, and I was just thinking that I want my date to be able to look back, and say that she enjoyed hers. Plus I'm really enjoying it as well. But if you're talking about the valet I'm just lazy," I said with a smile. As we entered our dimly lit suite, you could hear the heels of our feet touching the marble floors. We toured the suite, and found an extremely large entertainment cabinet with a forty-six inch television inside with a stereo system built in, sitting across from a tan Italian leather couch, and chair set with décor to match. The most tantalizing part was the fact that instead of a table between the couch and the entertainment center, there was a Jacuzzi built in the center of the floor. That wasn't even the sexiest part of the entire suite, once you entered the bedroom all you could see was the California King that covered half the room with the four red oak pillars that looked big enough to hold the ceiling up in case of a collapse. The actual mattress was so plush it came up past my waist, and once you climbed in you could see yourself sink in. I rested my tuxedo jacket on the bed, and sat at the edge as Carmen squeezed between my legs. This was a prelude to an incredible night of passion, or so I thought. We were interrupted by my pager, which went off, around 3:30am. To which I was politely asked, "Who in the Hell is calling you this late?" A question that I could neither answer, nor did I want the opportunity to answer. Needless to say this didn't go over to well with my date. I knew the page was nothing more than trouble. My parents wouldn't call unless there was an emergency. I guess I could hope for an emergency, but I knew better. I tried to look without Carmen seeing me, but she had her

Eagle eyes working overtime after the page, constantly asking me if I was going to return the page. As I looked at the number immediately recognizing it, and the 69 code that followed several times. It was Erika's cell number obviously wanting me to return the call.

"So who is it?"

Now how on Earth do I explain this? Is it the truth: It's my supposed best friend and she wants to know if I can drop you off, and swing by and pick her up for a good time. Or is it a lie: It's a wrong number, or a family member calling to check on everything. Which will it be?

"Are you gonna return the call?"

I could now hear the disapproval in her voice, which was also mixed with her anger. The anger was easily detectable because her usually Golden skin tone was invaded by a hint of red. This didn't help my decision at all, so I did as most guys would do in a similar situation. "I DON'T KNOW WHO IT WAS!" What a way to end a close to perfect night instead of an incredible sexual experience, we are about to have an argument about something that was uncontrollable.

"So you're telling me you don't have a clue who that is on your pager."

"What I'm saying is I don't recognize the number. Can we please just let it go I really don't want to argue tonight?"

"I don't think I can just drop it not until you return the call."

"Is it really that serious, is that necessary?"

"You have a choice either you can call the number back, or you can take me home right now."

Now if I have one pet peeve, it would have to be being given an ultimatum. It's like your backing me into a corner, and I hate being boxed in. So even though I could be deemed wrong, or the whole situation could be considered a misunderstanding my response was to get up, and take her home. Yes, I could've made the call or even a fake call to resolve the issue and there is a strong possibility I would've done that, if it wasn't for the ultimatum. This has been a horrible end to a beautiful night. After dropping my more than upset date off at home, I had to debate whether to return the page or not. I quickly decided that wouldn't be in my best interest, and returned to the suite to soak in the Jacuzzi alone.

The next morning I awoke to the sound of the pager that had ruined my night, fortunately it was Carmen, so I quickly returned the page as if to give her some form of security that I was alone. With a raspy morning voice I said "Good Morning, feeling better?" She responded, "Are you still picking me up today so we can hangout or are you busy." (more sarcasm, just what I need this morning)

"I'll be there just give me a minute to get up."

"What, you need to drop her off, before you pick me up?"

"What are you talking about? I'm here alone."

"Yeah whatever, if you were planning on being alone you wouldn't have been so quick to drop me off."

"Um, I swore you said you had a curfew. Should I come or are you going to be acting like this all day?"

"Maybe you shouldn't, maybe you should just forget about us all together."

"Oh yeah, all this because my pager went off."

"No it's because I wasn't important enough for you to explain yourself. I was supposed to just get over it, and that's not fair to me. You should have much more respect for me than that. Then you act like I'm wrong for having an attitude, you ruined a perfect night. My perfect night!"

"That wasn't my intention, it's not like my plan was to mess everything up so you would get upset and go home early. What would you suggest I do to make up for it?"

"That is something you will have to figure out for yourself, and I would appreciate it if you would refrain from calling me until you do."

"Are you serious? So is this how this conversation is going to end? You with an attitude about nothing."

"Funny how you're the only one who thinks it's nothing, and until you feel it's something that is exactly what we are to each other. NOTHING!"

After the short conversation laced with lies, and deception I rolled over and ran my index finger down the spine of Erica's back, and kissed her shoulder and whispered good morning in her ear. To which she responded with a slight smile. Erica showed me just how shameless chicks could be, and at the same time she helped me to see them as such. The reality of it all was that chicks are chicks NO MATTER WHAT!

The next couple of days just flew by, most of my time was spent with the fellas chill'n and getting ready for graduation. I couldn't wait to be done with school for good. Even though college was less than two months away, I already had it in my head that it would be so much different from High school. The mere fact that I would be pretty much on my own was enough for me to be looking forward to the experience. The more time that passed the less I thought about Carmen, or our forgotten relationship. Before I knew it Graduation was here, and I could think of nothing more that crossing that stage. Shaking the hands of teachers and faculty, some of which I loved and was loved by, some of them I could care less about. All so that I could collect my empty paper rolled with a ribbon around it, (The faculty thought that by given us just a blank sheet of paper, would keep us from acting a complete Monkey on stage and ruining the entire graduation. They said if you did act up they would keep your Diploma. Ha-ha... what a bunch of Bull). The most I had planned to do was not shake a couple hands, knowing that my Grandma was in the audience kept me from cutting a fool. Everything went extremely well as far as graduation was concerned, I walked across the stage, shook some, hands missed others, grabbed my piece of paper, turned to the crowd and waved to everyone. I was done, finished, if I really wanted to, I could go and tell a couple of those so called educators what I really thought of them, but it didn't matter anymore I didn't have to see them they would never have to see me again. After graduation my family took me out to Benihana's for dinner. We had a great time. They let me know how proud of me they were. I guess with all the young black men that don't graduate, it was a bigger deal than I made it myself. I just sat back and enjoyed the moment, it couldn't get much better than this. Well maybe it could, there was still a graduation party tonight that was supposed to start the summer off the right way.

I had to get home to get ready the party. It starts at ten, and I still have to swing by and pick up Kev. Which is a task in itself, especially if his old dude ain't trying to let him out tonight. Only guy I know who has to be home before the streetlights come on. Better call and find out if he can get out tonight or if I should I plan to go solo.

"What up Kev, you coming out tonight or you stuck?"

"Tryna, find out right now. You know how pops be trippin."

"You tell him who you going with, you know he be cool when you tell'em you wit me."

"I know, I told him, that's the only reason he's thinking about it anyway, yo ass got him fooled like all the other parents you meet."

That ain't it. I'm just your more sensible friend, unlike the rest of the cats you be hanging wit.

"Look why don't you just come on through, and if he on that tip then just go with out me."

Bet it, now don't think I'm gone just sit there with yo ass all night if you can't go. I'm out soon as he say the word. I'll be there in a minute.

"Yeah okay, whatever!"

When I pulled up, Mr. Moore was in the backyard shooting that sweet ass jumper that he never transferred to his son. Mr. Moore was an ex-athlete, which he badly wanted at least one of his sons to be as well. Unfortunately for him, Kev never really excelled in that department. So by default I ended up with all the backyard time shooting, and playing one on one. On my way up the driveway I yelled out "BROKE". After he sunk the shot nothing but net, he politely asked "How's my biggest fan doing today?" To which I responded, "You wish!" We both laughed, and said our hellos.

"So what brings you this way tonight? I know you didn't come to get embarrassed during your finest hour."

If I'm not mistaken I think I lead the series a billion to one.

"If I was ten years younger, I would show you a thing or two."

As long as I still win, I'm always in the mood to learn. But I was stopping by to see if Kev could hang out for a while.

"I guess so, where are you guys going?"

It's supposed to be a party or something for graduation.

"Oh really, a party huh? You think I should throw some clothes on, and come on out with you boys?"

If you think you can sneak past Mrs. Moore, I said with a smirk on my face.

"You boys have fun."

As I walked in the side door and headed for the basement, before I could turn and hit the steps. Kev was on his way up with the biggest grin on earth. "I don't know why my old dude likes you so much, if he only knew you were the Devil." What? I'm the good one, you ain't heard. Take it you're ready to go already? "You know it." We pulled up at the party, which was at Lee Bell's house (one of our classmates) about thirty minutes later after we rode around bull shittin for a little while. You could see it was gonna be a long night as soon as we pulled up. There were chicks outside with next to nothing on, just waiting for a little attention. We entered the house and voices rung over the "One More Chance" remix by Biggie. Most of the people there were from our school that either graduated today, or last year. We scanned the house for a while, before running into some faces we've seen all too much. Maria and company had showed up after all. Kev tried to warn me that they would be here tonight. I guess I just don't hear well. Though I had to admit she was looking good tonight, and from my understanding I was as single as they come.

"Congratulations Mr. Alexander on your graduation today, it was nice seeing you cross that stage."

"Thank you, it was nice walking across that stage. I was happy to see you cross as well. It's just as good to see you tonight."

"Is that right? I'd never imagine you'd be happy to see me here."

"Why wouldn't I be happy? It's not like we hate each other. That is as far as I know. Is there something I should know before I make that statement?"

"Now you know better than that. You know I don't hate you, and if I did we wouldn't be having this conversation."

"That's good to hear, you had me nervous for a minute."

We spent the next couple of hours laughing, and just talking about our individual plans for the future. It turned out to be a very entertaining night and nothing wild even happened, just a lot of laughing and good times. After the party we decided to go to breakfast, so I gave my keys to Kev so that I could ride with Maria. Aleshia, and Sabrine jumped in the car with Kev and we all set out for IHOP. On the way to eat, the conversation some how ended up on my relationship with Carmen, and I politely explained that we weren't seeing each other right now and I wasn't sure if we ever were again. She asked what had happened, which I answered that we had a disagreement.

"So she won't be following us to breakfast waiting in the bushes will she? You know she had that stalker look in her eyes all the time."

I sure hope not (I said sarcastically).

"You silly, you are gone have me worried out here tryna go eat. I'm a leave ya ass out here."

That's not me you went there not me, I just agreed with your assessment of the situation.

"SMART ASS!"

As we sat eating breakfast we came to the conclusion that spending this time together tonight was fun, and that we should do it again before I left for school, and that we did for the next two weeks we were almost inseparable. We saw each other everyday up until it was time for me to leave. It was understood that we were about to attend separate schools, and didn't want to put any pressure on the friendship that we had established in the past couple of weeks, so we just kept it as friends. On the day before I left for school Maria came by to spend the day with me, and to say our good-byes. As we sat just staring at each other most of the time, I couldn't help but wonder what could've been if I had treated her right in the first place. Would we be trying to go to the same college now? Would we be even deeper into each other than we are now? Who knows, I wish I didn't have to leave right now. She told me that she had a gift for me when she first arrived that day, but I couldn't have it until later. I couldn't help but remember my last gift received in this particular room, but didn't want to jump to conclusions. I guess later on had finally arrived, because she went out to the car and returned just as quickly as she had left. When she returned into my bedroom she had a small gift bag, with a purple teddy bear sticking out and an envelope behind it. She handed me the bag with a smile, as she spoke "I hope you like it, it's from my heart to yours." I pulled the bear out of the bag, it was my first stuffed animal from a young lady. It was even kind of cute. After looking and smiling with approval I moved on to the card that was still hanging out of the bag. As I removed the card from its envelope, I couldn't help but notice her blushing just a bit. I could tell that she must have put a lot of thought into making this particular card with the new card maker at CVS. It allows you to put your own words, or in this case the words of India Arie. As I began to read, it became more and more evident that she felt that these words described me to a tee.

"Cause he is the truth, yes he is so real
and I love the way that he make me feel
And if I am a reflection of him then I must be fly
Because his light it shines so bright.
I remember the very first day that I saw him
I found myself immediately intrigued by him
It's almost like I knew this man from another life
Like maybe back when I was his husband, maybe he
    was my wife
And even the things that I don't like about him are fine
    with me
Cause it's not hard for me to understand him cause he
    is so much like me
It is truly my pleasure to share his company
And I know its GODS gift to breathe the air he breathes.
Cause he is the truth, yes he is so real
And I love the way that he makes me feel
And if I am a reflection of him then I must be fly
Because his light it shines so bright.
How could the same man that makes me so mad
Turn right around, and kiss me so soft
If he ever left me I wouldn't even be sad
Cause there a blessing in every lesson
And I'm glad that I know him at all.
Cause he is the truth, yes he is so real
And I love the way that he makes me feel
And if I am a reflection of him then I must be fly
Because his light it shines so bright.
I love the way he speaks, I love the way he thinks
I love the way that he treats his momma
I love that gap in between his teeth
I love him in every way that a woman can love a man
From personal, to universal, but most of all its
    unconditional."

I was speechless. It was almost impossible for me to put how I was feeling at that exact moment into words. All that I knew was I had never felt that way before. I stood there for a moment, before I was able to utter one of the biggest understatements I had ever made "That was beautiful". We stood, and stared deep into one another's eyes for the next ten minutes. Finally I stepped closer to her, extending my hand to her neck gently pulling her close to me. I leaned in and pressed my lips to hers, caressing the back of her slightly tilted head. Quickly separating her lips with my tongue, I could immediately feel the warmth of her mouth, and the softness of her tongue that had eagerly meet mine. With each second that passed the kiss became more and more passionate, until our bodies became just as intertwined as our tongues were. As we continued, and our temperature continued to rise it became a must for our bodies to escape the constraints of our clothing. Our bodies yearned to be free. Free to explore the newfound lands that were us, and explore we did. Neither of us could be considered virgins, we were both experienced by now. Although this time was so much different than any other. It didn't feel like just sex, it wasn't wild. We just took our time, and enjoyed our exploration. I didn't want her to feel like just another girl that I had been with. I wanted her to feel comfortable, I wanted to be gentle, I wanted her to feel my soul and I wanted to feel her body yearning for more of mine. We continued to indulge ourselves in the pleasure that was us until we could barely move. Afterwards, we laid there without movement for hours before it was finally time to say our good-byes. As we walked to her car, we promised to keep in touch. We did however decide not to start something serious that would be long distance, a relationship that neither of us would be ready for. We spent the next couple of hours on the phone until I fell asleep, she insisted that I call her before I leave in the morning. I spent the entire drive to school wishing that I didn't have to go so soon. The new experience that just a couple weeks ago I couldn't wait to start, was the one that I wish could wait now.

FRESHMAN YEAR: *Summer School*

I arrived on campus that afternoon, after the long and exhausting drive with my parents. The summer program was for students that wanted to get a jump on their college experience. Basically it was going to better prepare us for our college years. When I arrived, I found that college life was going to be very enjoyable. It had a beautiful view and I wasn't talking about the landscape. It was understood what we were there for and I knew what my parents expected of me, but who said I wasn't supposed to enjoy myself? There were new people to meet, and I was in the mood for introductions. We had people from many different places, most areas clicked up at first if you were from the D you pretty much hung around people from the D, people from Chi-town stayed in their own circle, and so on and so forth. This presented a small problem because, the Chi- town circle had a few more attractions than Detroit. The other problem was that the dudes from Chicago didn't really like the dudes from Detroit. It was mainly this little dude with what I call the Napoleon Complex. He has to prove to the world he's tough because he's shorter than everyone else. Lil dude's name was Lee and he was especially funny to me because here it was nearly two decades had passed, and he was still rocking the shit out of a Kid-N-Play high top fade. Besides the complex I had a hard time understanding what the problem was until I met Tamekia. From my understanding, or at least the explanation that Tamekia gave me was dudes from the D tend to floss too much. We were always talking bout what we got what kind of clothes we wear, the cars we drive, even down to the chicks we've touched. I never really noticed it myself, but maybe I was biased, seeing that I was from the D and all. Talking to Tamekia was different at first, she had a certain innocence that was rather intriguing. Another thing that I found attractive was the Southern slur that came out on certain phrases and certain words when she spoke. Being that she was from the Southside of Chicago, you could hear it more in her speech than the young ladies from other parts of Chi-Town. Now Tamekia didn't just have innocence and a twang in her voice to attract the opposite sex, she was a beautiful Chocolate brown with shoulder length Jet-black hair. Around 5'6 and 140 pounds, she was thick in all the right places. She was also blessed with a great personality once you got to know her. First you had to get pass the fact that she was a bit high on herself (a defense mechanism if you ask me).

We had arrival day to enjoy each other and mingle, then it was straight to business, classes started the very next day at eight in the morning. I was in for a rude awaking, here I was thinking college is finally when I get to pick my own schedule and not have to wake up at the crack of dawn. First class on my agenda was something that I really wasn't looking forward to. Reintroduction to Trig, which I wanted no part of, too bad so sad. At least I had someone to keep me awake, Tamekia sat next to me in our first class much to the disgust of my new Nemesis (Lee) or at least he thought he was important enough to be my nemesis. He was much more of a pest than anything else. We sat together during most of our classes, spending most of the time talking, and cracking jokes. By the time the first week was over I felt like I knew everything there was to know about her, we had talked so much. The following week was a lot like the first, we just seemed to have a lot more free time to ourselves and mine seemed to be spent chillin with her. That was if we weren't interrupted by little fella, who always seemed to be around like a Leprechaun, and we were his pot a gold. By now I had my free time pretty much planned. I would spend some with her having fun, and the rest was for working out. I still had the basketball bug real bad. I would go down to the court and shoot two hundred shots everyday I got a chance. Some days I would double up just in case I might miss a day. After the first couple of days, I collected a small fan club that would sit on the grass in the shade, and watch me kill myself in the heat. This eventually brought Lil Hater (Lee) down to the court wondering what the young ladies were paying attention to.

I guess the extra attention was just one more reason for him not to like me. By the time I got around to working out the next day, there were enough people to get a full court run which I hadn't had since I left the D. Most of the dudes were from Chicago, but there were a couple from the D. I didn't join the crowd immediately, I thought I would get my workout done first, or at least that was the plan. Wasn't even a quarter of the way through my workout, before someone felt it was their duty to question me.

"So what, you think you so much better than us that you can't hoop wit us?"

I turned around to see whose voice it was, as if I didn't already know. There he was in all his glory, high-top fade and all. Standing four foot nothing with the most intense look on his face I had ever seen. I responded "Naw, that's not it at all." Then I returned to my usual regimen, which didn't last too long before he was at it again.

"So are you afraid of the competition?"

Now for the most part I'm not suckered into many things, I think I'm bright enough to keep myself from falling for the set-ups, but I don't appreciate anybody telling me I'm scared. Don't get me wrong, there are some things that I am afraid of for instance (dying, being set on fire, maybe even a couple scary movies), but to play basketball against anybody will never be something that sends chills down my spine.

"I ain't scared of shit, get it right little fella!"

"Prove it, let's see if all that practicing you do pays off."

I just smiled with a sinisterly looking crooked smile and said "Sounds good." We played about six or seven games. I spent most of my time passing the ball in the first two games. I always like to feel out the competition before I start playing hard, this too ended in time. Lil Hater just wouldn't allow me to enjoy myself. We easily won the first three games with me just passing so I didn't think it was necessary for me to shoot the ball too much but this also wasn't to his liking.

"All yo ass do is pass, you must be a practice player I ain't seen you shoot once since I been guarding you."

What's your point? We winning every game and you ain't scoring on me I'm happy.

"Yeah ya'll winning. No thanks to you though."

Look, I'm chillin right now just having fun. You don't want me to play seriously, I'M BETTER THAN YOU! So just let a sleeping dawg lie.

For the next couple of games I thought I'd wake up and bite the little fella so he would shut up. A little embarrassment should make him shut up. Since there wasn't anyone waiting to play each game went to twelve. The crowd had grown from the usual couple of young ladies to just about the whole program. Some staff even joined the festivities. I was told that one of the staff members had an inside track with the Head Coach, so I looked at this as an opportunity to kill two birds with one stone. I could get noticed by the coaches friend, and at the same time shut Lee the hell up. So for the next three games I easily scored ten in each game, and politely told him about the way I was giving him the business. In the last game, I explained that he should know who he is talking to before he runs off at the mouth. "Now that the dog has eaten I can go back to sleep." After I made the last statement, I went back to passing every time down the court to show that I wasn't a selfish ball-hog, for those who didn't get to witness the first couple of games. After the last game, I received a couple praises from the crowd, and the silence that I so wanted from Lee. This embarrassment kept him quiet for a while but let me tell, it wasn't long enough. The one thing that I wasn't really expecting was the extra attention that I received after playing, it was like no one really thought of me as being athletic in anyway. I was told as slow as I move off the court, and as laid back as I am, they couldn't imagine me running up and down a basketball court. I had to admit the statement had some merit to it, but I had never thought of it that way. I guess that is my other side, my competitive side and it takes over when it's time to play. I almost turn into another person all together. Once it was explained that the other side is a very sexy side, I was a little surprised. Although it was pretty much a consensus, Tamekia confirmed it all when she told me that she saw me in a totally different light after the game. I asked if it was a bad thing, to my understanding it wasn't. This was definitely good to know, but seeing that we only had one more week left before it was back to the D, it didn't leave us with much time to get anything going. We spent the next week together with nothing but sexual tension between us and unfortunately we did nothing about it. We said our good-byes on the last day, exchanged numbers, and promised to keep in touch. Which really wasn't going to be a problem seeing that school was starting in about three more weeks, so it wouldn't be long before we could chill again.

With summer school over, my summer vacation was on again. I couldn't wait to see the D one more time before school really started. As soon as I stepped foot in the door it was like I never left. Mom hit me with her go to line, "You need to take the garbage out." This was followed by, "You need to tell these little heffa's to stop calling my house all hours of the night." "Hey mom how are you today, really nice to see you. I missed you too!" (I replied playfully trying to give her a hug.) "Whatever boy, get out my face." "How were your classes, or were you to busy chasing girls?" "Classes were great I should be receiving my grades in about a week, and no I wasn't too busy chasing girls." "I slowed down and let them catch me." (I said under my breath so that I wasn't heard clearly.) I turned, and walked out before she could retain my last statement. "I'm gonna knock the garbage out, be back in a minute." It didn't take long at all, before the news of me being back hit. I guess some people must've had it on their calendars. No sooner than I stepped out the side door there was Cuz pulling up in his Regal, sounds loud enough to wake the neighbors a mile away. Or should I say, trunk rattling enough to wake the neighbors. "What up boy, heard you just got back."

Yeah, just got in not even ten minutes ago.

"Oh yea, that's cool so how was it? Was it some chicks up there this year or what?"

It was cool, met a couple chicks. You'll definitely have something new to look at when we go back. (Cuz really named Eric, but E-man is what everyone else called him. I just stuck with Cuz to be different, but he had been through the program just the year prior to my attending.)

"That's cool, I stopped through to see if you wanted to hit this party with me tonight."

Sounds good, what time?

"Leaving soon as you throw on some clothes. It's a barbeque first and then turns into an all nighter."

Cool let me let mom know, and jump in the shower.

"Bet, I'm a run to the store, be ready when I get back."

I went back in the house, to get ready. First I stopped in my mom's room to let her know my plans. Which to my surprise went along painlessly. Maybe I was growing up and she didn't worry as much. What really struck me as odd was the fact that I had just gotten home less than an hour ago and she still wasn't tripping. Here I was ready to debate for the next thirty minutes, and it was over in less than thirty seconds. I shot out of the room before she could return to her senses. Slid into my room and grabbed some hoop shorts and a T-shirt to put on. Then headed straight for the shower, this was more a pick me up than a clean me up. After a quick shower, and a little lotion I was just about ready. No outfit is complete without Flip-Flops and a pair of black ankle socks, at least not for me in the summertime. By the time I was on the stairs Cuz was at the side door. Right on time. I was on my way out there. So where we going. "Not too far, but you'll see when we get there. Hop in." It was so funny to me, Cuz grew up his entire life in Detroit, but his Father's side of the family was from Memphis, Tenn., and he went down to visit just about every summer, but for the last two summers last year and this year when he came back he had a slight Southern twang in his voice when he returned. This year was even worse because he came back with music to go with the twang. All the way to the party I was forced to listen to 8 ball and MJG, which wouldn't have been so bad if I wasn't the biggest Biggie fan on the planet at the time. Plus he was trying to irritate me by comparing 8 ball with Biggie I guess because they were both fat as hell. At least that was all I could compare at the time. After about twenty minutes of bull shittin around I noticed that we were going towards my Grandmothers house. "Who you know stay over this way?" His smart-ass answer was this older chick. As soon as we hit the corner I realized why my mom didn't complain at all, the backyard was filled with tents, balloons, and people. And this big ass banner that said Congratulations on your Accomplishments, I was so surprised, I just couldn't stop smiling. My mother had invited the entire family, and I guess she had Cuz and Kev invite all the friends cause everybody was there.

As I entered the party, immediately I saw Maria standing near my Aunt probably because they had hit it off so well last time they met. Her smile was just as big as mine when she finally acknowledged the fact that I was starring directly at her. I started to make my way through the crowd of family over to her, being stopped at every turn by proud family and friends. I finally made it to her just to hear her first smart comment.

"Hey, how are you? You're Chris right? It's nice to meet you, my name is Maria."

Oh yeah, is this what we're gonna go through. You could be a little happy to see me.

"Why should I? I haven't heard from you since you left. You could've called, wrote, you could've done anything to get in touch with me but you didn't. So as far as being happy to see you I am, but if you think I'm not mad at you then you didn't learn shit at that damn school!"

What could I say? She had a legitimate point, why would I expect her to run and jump back into my arms? Why wouldn't I expect her reaction to be that of a scorned lover? We had been through so much in such a short time that I owed her nothing less than to keep in touch, to let her know that I cared. She had shared with me the most precious part she had to offer. Not only did she share her heart, but she also went out on a limb and made love to me to truly express the way she felt. My reaction to all of this was that of a fool with no emotions. A selfish fool who didn't even pick up the phone to show that what she had done meant something to him, to at least remind her that she was as special to him, as he was to her. I had work to do. I had made the mistake of making someone that I cared about feel small, and unimportant to me when it was truly the opposite. For the most part it was evident that I still had a chance, because she was there. She had made the first move, and I had planned to make sure the next move was made by me, although that move wouldn't be made today, it would be made.

"You're absolutely right I messed up, and I don't deserve your forgiveness. But I am so happy that you came today, even if you only showed up to show me what I'm missing out on. Thank you for coming, and I hope you enjoy the party. But before I walk away, sick about the foolish way I behaved, can I ask one question."

"What Christopher?"

Ouch, the full name huh? You know I only hear that when you're pissed. My question is would you mind if I called you? Today, tomorrow, anytime soon.

"I don't know, do you even remember the number?"

Without another word she turned and walked away, leaving me standing there with my mouth wide open awaiting a profound statement to utter from my lips, but it never happened, I just let her walk away. The rest of the party was a blur, I just couldn't get her out of my mind. It didn't help that she stayed around and mingled so well with my family, plus the fact that all of them took to her like a moth to a flame. She stayed to the very end of the party, it was as if she was taunting me. A continuous reminder that I fucked up, and it wasn't gonna be easily made up. My grandmother asked me to take a couple chairs in the house, and by the time I returned she was already gone. No good-bye just gone. I quickly ran to the front of the house to see if I could catch her getting into her car, but I was too late. By the time I made it to the front she was turning the corner. The night was over, and I still seemed to be so far in the tunnel, I couldn't see the light at the end.

The next day started the correction of my mistake, I didn't let any of the day get away. I awoke at ten thirty, and got directly on the phone. With a little grogginess in my voice I asked to speak to Maria, which she replied "This is she."

"Did I wake you?"

"Nope it was time for me to get up anyway I have to get a lot done, today's my last day in town."

"Last day? I know you not leaving for school already are you?"

"Yep we're driving down in the morning I think we are leaving around 4:30 a.m."

"You think you gonna have a little time today for me to see you?"

"Not sure, I have a lot to do. But I guess I could stop by your house when I get out and about."

"That would be great, just call me and let me know when you're on your way."

"Okay it'll probably be about an hour from now, I can't stay long either just a quick visit."

"I'll see you then."

In about an hour, that doesn't leave much time at all, I need to get up and get dressed, and see if I can find her a going away present. Maybe a card or stuffed animal, probably both, and make sure I'm back before she calls. Hoop shorts, T-shirt, flip flops-n-socks and I'm out the door straight to the mall and back that's the plan that was set into motion. As soon as I got to the mall I went straight for the toy store to find something that would remind her of me. When I walked in I saw the biggest bear I had ever seen in my life. It just wasn't me plus she probably had limited space for the trip down to school so I had to keep looking. As I traveled deeper into the store I saw a decent sized puppy with the saddest eyes that I had ever seen, besides when I look in the mirror. If this didn't remind her of me, nothing would, so that was a wrap. On the way out I stopped in Hallmark to grab a card, this would be the time-taking-hard-part. Do they have a card that would present our situation in the best way? As I flowed through the card shop, I finally found the perfect card, it was a Between Me and You card that expressed my exact feelings toward her. After the purchase I only had about twenty minutes to get home or so I thought, so out the door I rushed. My pager went off with the message: I'm on my way, while I was on the way to the car, so I seemed to be in even more of a rush than I was in the first place. I made it home just in time to see her hitting the corner, she pulled up in front of the house as I was retrieving her gifts out of the car. "Hey, how are you?"

"I'm fine, what about you, how are you today? I thought you would still be asleep after your long night. What'cha got there?"

"I'm a little surprised myself. How bout your night was just as long as mine even though you left without saying good-bye to the person who's party it was. And this right here is just something for you to remember me by, and to express how sorry I am and how much I really want a chance to make it up. I hope we can keep in touch, I know you might be upset right now, I just want you to know that you mean so much to me and I don't want to lose you or that part that you bring to me."

"I don't have a problem with keeping in touch, I just wanted you to understand how much you hurt my feelings, and that I didn't appreciate that shit in the least bit. I can't stay mad at you, and I can't imagine my life without you in it. So you don't have a choice, but to keep in touch. If not you're gonna have me right back up here lookin fa yo ass!"

"Well if that's all I gotta do to have you back up here looking for me then maybe I will ignore you a lil bit."

"Try me if you want to, it won't be pretty."

She playfully snatched her puppy, and expressed how cute it was, and how pretty the eyes were. She refused to open the card until she was alone, she said crying over me was not an option. We sat and talked on the porch for the next half hour before she had to leave. After saying our good-byes we embraced and then kissed. As our lips touched I felt something that I couldn't explain, something I had never felt before. It felt so RIGHT. It was more than a tingle, more than a twitch. It was as if my entire body had received a jolt, and my senses were awake for the first time. The wind felt heavier, it blew harder, the heat from the sun felt hotter, the aroma of the rose bush smelt sweeter, and our embrace, as well as our bond, felt stronger. She got in the car, and as I closed the door I could see the tears forming rapidly, she quickly said good-bye and slid in an I LOVE YOU. Which I thought had caught me completely off guard until I opened my mouth and said I LOVE YOU TOO. Which seemed to astound me more than it did her. I wish I could've stepped outside my body for just a split second to see the look on my face as I said it.

"You didn't have to say it back, I didn't tell you just so you'd say it back to me."

"I know, it's the truth."

"Good-bye, Chris"

The truth was I did mean it. I did love her. Maybe I wasn't in love with her but I did love her. That's why it came out so easily, without thought, without me even realizing it. As I watched her drive away, part of me just broke down, I wasn't the same anymore. I could feel the tears building in my eyes, tears that I could never allow to appear on my face.

Fall Semester:

By the time my semi-meltdown was over it was time to return to the creature that is known as school. Although this was a chance for a new beginning, it somehow felt the same. There was going to be an adjustment period. I mean there's the fact that I'm going to be in a new environment, with new people, and new experiences. Even with all the new things going on in and around my life, some how it all still felt the same. No sooner than arriving back on campus did the festivities begin. I was in the middle of setting up my room the way I wanted it when Cuz strolled in with a proper room warming gift, a (Fifth of Hennessy). It definitely had to be hidden away until all the remnants were properly disposed of, seeing that I was under the legal drinking age. That didn't stop us from pouring a couple before I put it away.

"So what up Cuz, when ya classes start?"

"Dawg, don't start on that class shit, we got a whole week of partying to do before we have to worry about that shit."

"Oh yeah? Bet, that's cool as hell. So what up for tonight?"

"Don't know about you but I got a hot one coming through. I can see if she got a girl or something."

"Naw, I'm good, I got a couple people I know up here, I'll work something out."

"Alright Chris I'm bout to head back to the room. I'll holla at you later."

Even though I told Cuz that I would work something out, the truth was emotionally I knew I wasn't ready. I was still hell bent on missing Maria, even though she was states away, doing lord knows what. I hadn't spoke to her in a couple of days, and had yet to receive the letter that was supposed to be in the mail when she arrived. In the mess that I called my mind I realized that she didn't have my new address, and the letter would have to reach my mother's house, and then be sent to me from there. Between the long ride up, a stiff drink, and finally fixing my room the way I wanted it there would be nothing better than a little rest, better yet a quick nap. Two hours passed before I awoke to find that more of the crew had arrived and had already started to celebrate being back together. The first person seen was Phil, who had been Cuz's best friend since Elementary school so he was always around, therefore he and Cuz were roommates. Then there was Mal, who I knew from playing basketball, he was the only party that didn't attend high school with us. Dell, who was Mal's roommate, I knew him from high school, he had a striking resemblance to David Robinson (San Antonio Spurs) and he even played like him a little bit. All these rooms were right after the other, and then further down the hall you had Snoop and Marcus who were on the other side of the hall. That was it, at least for the fellas that lived in our dorm. You still had Bee, SD and Too Kool who had all decided after their freshman years to get apartments off campus. Everyone was in the hall talking about what they did last summer. The crazy part is most of the events happened when we were all together. After a couple hours of video games, and talking about the summer, we decided to take over as the welcoming committee. Dorm life was great especially because we had co-ed dorms and no real curfews for our rooms. Most people just left their doors open. My guess was, it gave them an opportunity to meet new people, and the new people they were going to meet were us. Little did we know, it would be us, that would meet someone new. Her name was Rita, she was in her junior year and could be considered an older woman, at least she was older than me and for that matter everyone else in our circle. She was about 5'10, light skin with straight hair that came down to her waist. Dell was the first one to pass her room, well not really pass he just pretty much stopped dead in the middle of the doorway. That intrigued the rest of us, and made us stop at the door as well.

"Ya'll just gone stand at the door or ya'll coming in?"

We all entered her room greeted by a beautiful smile and a hello, "It would be nice if there were introductions of the men that are sitting in my room." So as time went on, everyone introduced themselves around the room, and as each introduction was made her eyes followed each individual as they spoke, finally the introduction got around to me. Before I could say a word our eyes met, and I noticed a difference in the way she looked at me. It wasn't the look that the others received, she looked me completely up and down stopping for a split second somewhere between my waist and feet. I could've been mistaken, but it was almost as if she could see directly through my shorts as if she had Superman's X-ray vision. Just then I noticed her smile turn from angelic, to devilish just that quick. We all sat for a minute exchanging pleasantries before leaving. On the way out I smiled devilishly and waved good-bye.

It was time for me to get back in my room before trouble found me. On my way back I just so happen to run into Tamekia.

"Oh, hey Trouble, I mean Tamekia. How are you?"

"I'm surprised you remember my name, but other than that I'm fine."

"That's good, happy to hear your doing well. How's your boyfriend doing?"

"He's fine, glad you asked, and how about your woman? Oh yeah you don't have one do you?"

"No, but I do have someone that I care about."

"That'll be good to know for future references, I might need help with a thing or two one day."

"Is that right?"

"That wouldn't be a problem would it?"

"Maybe, maybe not, depending on what you may need help with. Now excuse me I have to get to my room. I'm expecting a call."

"Really and here I don't even have your number to make that call. Don't you think we should do something about that?"

Of course we should. Here, it's 4758, call me when you get a chance. I would enjoy catching up, was my response as I hurried past her in the hall on my way to the elevator. As she stood there in the hallway I decided that the elevator was going to take entirely too long so the stairs would have to do. Here I am safely confined back in my room, attempting to stay away from the College Life that is eventually going to take over. I can't hide from it forever. Eventually it will catch up, and eventually it did.

Around two weeks had past and classes were in full swing. I had papers due, tests coming up, and overzealous professors to deal with. To make matters worse I still hadn't heard a word from Maria, not a phone call, nor a letter to confirm that she was thinking of me the way that I was thinking of her. On top of that there was the occasional clowning from the fellas on how I stayed in my room as if I was quarantined. Finally one day after checking the mail, to no avail, I thought that I would walk to the student center building, and treat myself to some real food or at least the only real food you can get when you live in the dorms. I decided to grab some McDonalds. I would've been better off quarantined in my room because I ran into Tamekia on the way back to my dorm. This struck me as odd because this had to be about the fifth or sixth time I'd seen her in two weeks, and she didn't reside there. In fact she stayed in the valley, which was more than a hike to get to. I knew, because that is where all students of the summer program were supposed to stay freshman year. I had been excused because of a great job pleading my case with my advisor. My guess was she was seeing someone in the dorms, which wasn't a problem. Most freshman girls were considered fresh meat on campus. The truth was she had a female friend that lived in the same dorm as me, and she was on her way home before it got too dark to walk alone. She had already missed that opportunity by the time I saw her, so I explained that if she gave me a chance to eat my food I would be happy to walk her home. Which worked out perfectly for her, because that would give her a chance to visit with me for a while and catch up. As we enjoyed each other's company it was almost like we hadn't missed a beat since we were together last. She still laughed at all my jokes, and I was still the good listener that I had been complimented on prior. Between the jokes, and the catching up, there was still a sexual attraction that could be felt. It was apparent that being alone in either of our rooms wasn't a good idea. So before that idea was brought up I asked Cuz if he felt like accompanying us to walk her home. Luckily he wasn't too engrossed in his video game, and wanted a little fresh air anyway. Dodging this bullet wasn't the easiest thing to do. She was looking great, in all her naturalness, no make-up, her hair pulled back in a ponytail, and sweat-suit, but still had the ability to draw attention from all the fellas. As we walked Cuz took the time to take a full inspection, and as if that wasn't enough, took the time to grade the product on the low. When he first walked in the waiting area of our building he took a long look at her face and as we left the dorm he gave me a quick nudge and whispered "She has good skin, she gets a 7.0 in the face, still working on the rest." Introductions were made and began our journey to the valley. Before we even got across the street he was at it again, "She's not even dressed up and she's still attractive. That means it probably won't be a problem waking up next to her in the morning that moves her to about a 7.5." Half way to our destination he began to trail behind us just a little bit, unable to fathom exactly what he was doing at first we continued at our pace, then it hit me, "ASS CHECK!" By then it was too late, he was already done with his evaluation, and was in the processes of hitting me with a Mike Utley like thumbs up. By the time we made it to her resident hall Cuz already had her up to a 9, and was busy telling me how stupid I was. After making sure that she made it in safely we turned back for home. Preparing for the onslaught of questions that followed my pace quickened, but it was too late.

"Why the hell did you ask me to walk with ya'll? She probably would've asked you to come in and chill."

"Yeah pretty sure she would have, that's exactly why you're here."

"You serious? If it was me I couldn't wait to touch that one."

"I know, but I'm good. That's not what I'm tryna do right now."

"What yo cake ass looking for, love?"

"Not at all, just not looking for trouble and going into her room I would've found it quite easily."

By the time the "twenty-question" portion of the walk was over we had already made it back home. My eyes were low, and the bed was calling so there was no better plan than bed. Upon entree the light from the phone was blinking bright red, easy to spot when walking into a dark room. There were two messages on the voicemail. The first was from Tamekia letting me know that she was happy to get a chance to catch up, and that she wasn't tired at all. I should've stayed awhile. Hopefully she would see me soon, and our friendship could continue to grow. The second message forced me into the computer chair. It started off so great, the voice was so clear and wanted, it immediately put an ear-to-ear smile on my face. In her innocent voice she said: "Hey Boo, sorry I'm just getting a chance to call even though I had to go through alternate means of getting your number. If you're wondering I called Crystal and had her look you up in the directory so that I could talk to you. I guess you haven't got my letter yet since I haven't got a response or a phone call yet. So I'll give you a quick overview. I miss you so much, lately I've been wishing that I came there instead of coming here. But on the brighter side, schools been fun so far, and I already knew a couple of people when I got here. Plus you already know that Kevin's irritating ass is here bugging me at every turn (with a slight snicker she continued), but even that's cool for the most part. We have a whole group of girls from Detroit here and we pretty much hangout together. My roommate's from Florida, and she's country as hell, but she's real cool I'll probably go home with her a couple of times this year. Well I'm not gonna stay on this phone all night talking to your machine so here's my number at school (615) 996-4253, call me tomorrow if you get the chance Love you bye-bye." That's when the crushing blow came. She had failed to hang up the phone completely before the other voice, the male's voice was easily heard "Come on and get dressed so I can take you back home." It was so devastating that I had to listen to the entire message again just to hear the end of the message, and I wasn't mistaken, it was there plain as day "Get dressed so I can take you home." And here I am trying to stay out of trouble, and she's having a blast. Instead of giving her a chance I immediately called the number back, to no avail her roommate with her best southern accent said "She's not in right now, may I ask whose calling?" To which I responded in a whisper, "You can tell her Chris called. Thank you and I apologize if I woke you, goodnight." Before sleep really hit me, I was forced to think about the whole situation. How can I truly be upset? There was no known commitment there. So how and why should I be upset? This just gives me an opportunity to actually enjoy my college experience, and enjoy it is what I planned to do.

FALL SEMESTER: *Time For Fun*

The next day was the beginning of a new me, even though I was a tad bit hurt, it wasn't going to stop me. After my workout and class was over I realized how much spare time was on the agenda for today. There wasn't anything better to do, than taking a quick visit to the Valley to see who was around. It was crazy, everybody from the summer program lived in the same area and to be honest, the only people that didn't have to live down here were me and I believe, two other students from the program. It was almost like a family atmosphere, everyone knew each other already so they all just hung out around the dorm. I sat around for a little while and enjoyed conversation with a couple associates. As the conversations began to bore me, I decided to sneak away and go visit a friend. Before I knew it, I was in front of Tamekia's door debating on whether I was going to knock or walk away. As I stood there in an all out mind debate, I realized that I was being watched so I quickly turned to find Tamekia standing in the hallway, she quickly said "Were you planning on knocking or just standing there until I came out?" My response was quick, "Wasn't sure if I should go back to the lobby and call first, you might have had company."

"That was a pretty good response. I can almost appreciate that one."

"Well you did say that I'm quick on my feet. Are you expecting company or can I come in?"

"Of course you can come in. You should've been over to visit a long time ago."

She was absolutely right, I should have come over weeks ago to spend time with my friend, but unfortunately I didn't and for that I had missed out on a lot. Conversation didn't last long before it turned to the topic of sex, I really didn't mind but I was a little hesitant seeing that I was in her domain. She didn't waste any time with her line of questioning either. It may have taken all of three questions before she had all the information that she felt she needed. The first had to be how long had it been since I last had an encounter, which to my calculations was too damn long, and at the same time it was the best answer I could conjure at the moment. The next question was along the lines of how often do I have to have sex? This too was an easily answered question, as much as possible. Last but certainly not least, she hit me with a statement more, than a question. "So you're about due then! Huh?" To which I could do nothing less than answer, "Yep, as a matter of fact I'm over due." She hadn't come all that way in the conversation to stop there, or had she? Of course not, she had to have more to say, but the truth was it wasn't anything left to say. Her next action was better than any word she could've thought of. She came in close, and leaned in for a slight taste of my lips. This did nothing more than add to my already growing excitement, I softly caressed the nape of her neck with my fingertips. "After the line of questioning that I just answered it would be in your best interest not to start anything that you don't plan on finishing." She laughed and quickly grabbed the rim of my shorts pulling and tugging at them as to quickly get them off. I slowly intervened and just pulled the draw string and they automatically fell to the floor not far behind them were the Calvin Klein boxers that were underneath, before I could get my shirt completely over my head and onto the floor she had already pushed me to the bed and mounted me as if she was preparing to ride a untamed mustang for the very first time. Either she had been on a sexual hiatus, or she just really wanted to see what I had to offer. She had her lemon yellow sun dress hiked up around her waist with one hand, and me in the other preparing for entry. I attempted to slide my hands down to help, but was quickly turned away. She grabbed both my hands and slid them back above my head. Then she began to slowly grind in a circler motion, by this time she had my body at full attention, not to mention a very naughty smirk across her face. This was unacceptable, getting the better of me was not an option, at least not the first time. My pride wouldn't allow it, so by slowly pressing my ass into the soft mattress to gain as much leverage as possible, I quickly drove myself back up into the air, as well as into her to wipe the smirk from her face. It was replaced with a look of ecstasy, as her eyes rolled up into her head she released an incredible moan. The waves of her ocean went from calm to dangerously wild in a matter of seconds, as her eyes began their descent from the heavens they laid upon mine and our stare became intense. She could barely mumble words, but I was able to read her lips as she now ran her fingers through her hair "Oh my Gooooddddd!" was the phrase that she mouthed repeatedly. With my hands free to roam from her thighs, to her waist, and then up to her breast, yet still allowing her the pleasure of being on top and seemingly in control, I proceeded to help. By grabbing her hips and pulling her down into each of my upward thrusts, I helped her climax that much quicker. This was our first encounter but from the looks and feel of things there were many more to come. She continued to ride until I could feel her moisture on my thighs, by then she had enough she slowly rolled over onto the bed with a deep sigh. As we lay there silently it seemed to be understood by both parties what this was. It was a sexual relationship, she still had a man, and I was not on the market for a woman. I already had enough unsolved issues to sort out than to worry about an on campus woman. We could get together from time to time and enjoy each other's company, and more importantly enjoy each other. At least until one of us gets tired of the arrangement.

For the next couple of weeks it was like an every other day event, we would laugh, and talk then have a sexual escapade. To ensure that I didn't catch feelings I would still talk to other people including Maria even though she was states away, I had almost forgot about her message with the guy in the background. All the while Tamekia still had her boyfriend in the picture so that gave her limited leeway to get too attached to me. A month had passed with our arrangement working without a hitch, no snags, or mishaps. Usually when something is too good to be true that's exactly right, it was too good to be true. Somehow, the seal was broken and even though she was so in love with her boyfriend she some how caught feelings for me as well. She now had problems if I was seen with other people around campus, and there were actually arguments replacing our fun time. This was an event that had me perplexed. Was she expecting me to only spend time with her? Could she really and truly expect me to share her with her man, but she gets to have me all to herself? This can't be serious, she can't really believe that this is an agreeable arrangement. In my attempt to explain that the entire purpose for attempting a friendship of this magnitude, was to avoid arguments, guilt, and especially answering to someone. The words really must have struck a nerve, because her next statement was obstinate laced, every other word was shit, damn, motha fucka. I just knew I was listening to D'Angelo's cd, or she had been possessed by a dead sailor. Either way this was something that I didn't have to deal with, once again, this is what I was attempting to avoid. There had to be some underlying motive for her to pick an argument out of the blue. My mind couldn't fathom that she just really had grown to like me more than she should, it had to be something additional bothering her. That's when it hit me. Her boyfriend's birthday was coming up, maybe she was feeling a bit guilty and just needed some time away to gather herself. Hopefully that was the case, and if so, she can definitely have any amount of time she needed. Friday evening came and part of my conclusion had proven to be right, she and her man were spotted in the student center building ordering a pizza to take back to her room. This was great I thought, I had the entire problem solved, but as usual I was wrong again. My concerns were easily swayed from that particular problem. I had bigger fish to fry, tonight was supposed to be the party of all parties before Home Coming, which was about three weeks away. It was an opportunity to meet some new chicks, and I couldn't wait. I was an eligible bachelor, no "understood" relationship even though the way Maria's' slick ass was on the phone each night talking, it seemed as if I might be in one, from her stand point. From the looks of it I didn't even have a Cut Buddy (an understood sexual partner) anymore, though this problem could easily be resolved tonight. Well not so easily. She was my college experience so far, not to mention a pretty damn good experience. She was more than a Cut Buddy, and a friend, which was rare in itself, but even more than, that she was a walking, talking ego boost. She was the first woman to tell me that I WAS THE BEST she'd ever had. It's not so much that I believed her than it was the fact that she said it, and it sounded damn good when it came out. This was neither here nor there, her man was here now and she was unavailable. Or so I thought!

I would've expected it being his birthday and all, for them to be trapped in her room for the weekend, as we had been for many nights out of this semester we were enjoying. They decided to come out for air and stopped by the party ""Bad move!" I had been at the party for about an hour, it was decent as parties went. I guess I had something a little different in mind, maybe I was expecting a different setting than the recreation gym with a tarp over the floor. I had spent enough days in this area playing basketball. Wasn't expecting to party here too, but that's what I get for not going to a Black University like my mom suggested. The party was thrown by the Alpha's and they had produced a great crowd, with a great mixture and limited problems. I just wasn't as impressed with the music, but nothing's perfect so I was going to enjoy myself no matter what it took. Luckily, it didn't take much between the buzz that I had from the cup I had been sipping on throughout the night, and the attention that I was getting from the opposite sex. I was quite content. That's when it happened, I was standing by the entrance talking to a candidate in the quiet area. I was facing the entrance and she had her back to it, when they walked in, hand in hand it was so cute. I was truly happy for her, as well as him. They deserved to be happy if in fact they were. The look that she had on her face when she saw me was not that of a woman excited to be out with her man. She seemed uneasy or nervous as if she was in between a rock and a hard place. Her face seemed to scream out at me "Please don't trip!" as if I was going to act up or something. I spoke to her and then introduced myself to her man, gave some lame ass line about "Its good to finally meet you, she talks about you all the time, and we have class together." Then I moved on, to me it was simply better, yet it was the only thing to do. I knew our situation, she already had a man and luckily it wasn't me. There was no reason to make a fool of myself, nor get her in trouble, and no need to get him riled up for nothing. So instead, enjoying the rest of my night was my plan, every now and again throughout the night I would see her dancing with him but staring at me, this did nothing more than make my night that much better. I could almost hear what she was thinking through her stares. Just to be sure though, I would find out on the next slow song. The D.J played 112's Can I Touch You, and I thought to myself, "Perfect". I grabbed the sexiest chick in the area, and led her to the dance floor. Slow dancing can be so SINtual when done right, as the music played we'd slowly glide across the floor all the time our bodies rhythmically moving together, all the while my body grinding against hers. The beautiful young lady was in a trance, I was softly singing the words in her ear as we danced (Keep in mind I can't sing a lick, but at the right time on the right line you can't tell.) Anyway, I could feel her embrace get tighter, obviously I hit the right line at the right time. She whispered in my ear "Do you have plans after the party!" Just as I was about to answer I noticed Tamekia right next to us dancing with her man. Staring as if she could read my mind and already knew my answer, to the question she had just read off old girl's lips. The next song came on, and I politely asked Tamekia's man if we could switch, I told him that he would be doing me a big favor cause the chick was trying to attack me. He laughed for a second but didn't need much convincing, mostly because his new dance partner was sexy as hell. He just wanted to make sure it was okay with his woman if he danced with someone else, which of course she didn't have a problem with it at all. Mostly because she had a couple of words of endearment that she wanted to relay to me anyway, and as soon as we switched it started.

"So you going home with her tonight! I see how she's all up on you!"

"Is that right? I hadn't noticed, but I have noticed you staring half the night. What up wit that?" (I said with a killer smirk)

"Ain't nobody been paying yo ass no attention!"

"If that's the case how you know she was all over me, I couldn't tell? That was the first time I've danced wit her all night."

"Well that ain't how it looked just now!"

"This is cute. You actually sound jealous, and you're here with yo man. That doesn't seem a little sick to you? That can't be good."

"Chris answer my question!"

"You don't want me to answer that."

"So you are going home wit her."

"No, I'll be in my room alone"

"Whateva"

"See I told you, you didn't want me to answer your question."

"No, that's not it at all. I just expected the truth!"

"And that's exactly what you got. If you like you can stop by and check, oh yeah my fault yo man is here. So you can't!!!"

"You think you're funny, huh?"

"End of the song. You best get back to your boo." (with a smirk)

Seeing as that was the last song of the night and all, I probably should go find the fellas and get back home or wherever it is I'm going. After the party and a little flirting in the parking lot, I finally made it back to my room around 3:30am, a little tipsy, and a lot sleepy. I took my shower and got ready to lie down around 4:45am. I received a knock on my door "Who the hell is it?" "Open the door and find out!" thinking to myself "Quit playin I know that voice." What the hell was she doing here? The perplexed look on my face had to give away what I was thinking, so she was polite enough to answer the question that was racing through my brain. "You said I could stop by and check in on you. Are you alone?" My response was quite simple I already explained what I was doing tonight at the party. Must we go through that again. I was all but sure he had to be gone back to where ever it was that he went to school, so when my next question came out it was more than sarcastic. "So what you just up and left in the middle of the night?" her response was not only shocking but it also appalled me in such a way that I was almost disgusted "I had my girl Angie come get me, she had a female emergency and needed my help." This may very well have been the sickest shit I had heard thus far in my life. After explaining that she needed to get back to her man as soon as possible, she continued her assault to my "supposed" innocents, by saying that her man was drunk and asleep so she had time to get back. Not even attempting to stop there she went on to let me know how tasty I appeared earlier that night. The only response that I could conjure was "Is that so?" to which she replied "Yes it is, do you have any idea what I wanted to do to you, better yet what I wanted you to do to me."

"No I was distracted by you're boo."

"Well let me see if I can get you focused on the right thing."

She came over to the bed and laid on top of me, and began to kiss my neck. Needless to say, I easily forgot about the man she left asleep in her room, as she ran her hands from my chest down to my thighs. As I ran my fingers through her hair I aggressively pulled back so that I might attack her neck, and return the pleasure that she had so generously given to me. She let out a soft moan, inspiring me to continue slowly sliding my lips across her soft curves allowing her to enjoy every second, every minute of my touch. As we caressed each other, all the while becoming more and more excited, I could feel the heat from her personal inferno calling, yearning, wanting me deep inside her. As I entered I felt her warmth embrace me, once again she released a deep moan and whispered in my ear "You feel so good inside of me, that's why I'm here instead of there." in the same sexy voice she continued "I'm here because, YOU'RE THE BEST." With that said, I guess a switch was thrown because my pace increased, and her moans intensified. Before she could speak another word her walls collapsed, and flooded with moisture drowning me in her bliss. With her pleasure fulfilled, and my ego more than satisfied by her compliments, I let her know she should be getting back to her man, he could be getting worried. This must have brought her back down to earth because she gave an evil scowl threw her clothes back on, and proceeded to the door. "Goodnight Chris!" "Don't you mean good morning Tamekia?" She slammed the door and the room was dark again.

From then on everything started to change, Tamekia began wanting things I couldn't provide. I was more than capable, but that wasn't what I was looking for. Yes of course I enjoyed her company, and liked spending time with her and of course the sex was intriguing, but that's all it was just sex. Little did I know, our friendship had to end sooner than later. She had become clingy and wanted to be out for all eyes to see. In any other circumstance this wouldn't be a problem. She could possibly be a good woman for someone other than me. Not to mention the fact that I'm not in the market for a woman, and she can't be in the market for a man because she already has one. Plus, Homecoming was around the corner and who knew what was in store for that upcoming event. Giving up the sex was not high on my list of things to do, but all the extra stress was something I could do without. The new plan was to distance myself from her, I still wanted to keep her as a friend, but that was it. Finding someone to replace her as a Cut

Buddy wasn't going to be too hard, after all this was a college campus. Two weeks had past and the plan was going pretty good to my knowledge. She didn't spend as much time looking for me, and our sexual partnership had almost disappeared all together. Instead of hanging out in her room I now found myself in the gym that much more. Unfortunately that meant more time seeing Little Hater who seemed to be in college merely for the membership to the gym. Ever sense I started spending so much time with Tamekia, I spent less and less time in the basketball area of the gym.

Since my absence from the scene I guess he and his little crew had built up a name for themselves on the court. So as soon as I entered the court area it started. "Look who's here to get his ass whooped." This was easily ignored, because as soon as my foot hits the wood my arrogance kicks in, so I knew there was no way on earth that he was referring to me. "He so scared he don't even want to respond." Once again no response, there wasn't a need to respond to his ignorance, he didn't know any better. My mother always told me not to argue with an idiot, because from a distance you can't tell who is who. Since he couldn't get the responses he was aiming for he took it to the next level by coming over and actually talking face to face. Actually it was more face to chest, I could clearly see over his high top fade. "You shouldn't even waste your time getting on our court." By now my patience for his ignorance was running thin, talking shit was one thing, but disrespecting me was totally different and it garnered a response. In the calmest voice I could muster "Didn't you learn anything this summer? I embraced you then and after these lewd statements you've made just now, it's going to be even worse today. My suggestion is that you go and enjoy the last game you'll be playing today, because I'm on next." At the end of my statement I immediately turned and walked to the other end of the court to warm up, without another word being said. Little Hater was unlucky enough to win his next game, and actually had to face me on the court. He couldn't have possibly wanted this, maybe in another life where he would be taller he'd actually have a chance, but in this life he was in Hell. I wasn't in the mood to take it light on him at all. It was okay in the summer, everyone knew already who the better of the two was. But since I was rarely in the gym this semester the crowd probably had a slight misconception. First offensive possession I started off punishing him, one quick move and I scored. The next play down, I pulled up on the left side of the court for a long two, over his outstretched arm. The score was already three to nothing, when Lee turned the ball over. I came down on the right side and hit another two pointer over him. After that shot I explained that shooting over him was equal to shooting over a chair. That statement had to hurt especially when part of the crowd had begun to snicker. It wasn't over for him yet I had already scored five points and the game only went to nine. Two more shots and it could be over. His team had begun to smarten up. They sent another guy over to help him guard me, but his pride stepped in "I got him don't help me!" This was funny to me but hilarious to the crowd. One of his teammates reminded him that I already had five, as if he didn't know. I attempted to get my team more involved so I passed the ball to Mal who quickly gave it right back and told me to finish him off. Lee's intensity level increased, he guarded me more aggressively, which if he were anyone else probably would have been a good thing, but for him it was just the opposite. After a quick shot fake, I slid right past him for an easy lay-up. Six to four was the score and I had six his team had four, according to them they still had a chance to win. They had no idea how wrong they were. After playing the passing lane, Mal stole an errand pass, and threw it my way. I had a clear path to the basket, but slowed myself so that Lee could catch up. After waiting for him to get in front of me I pulled up for the shot directly in his face, and drilled it. All the time laughing at him, telling him next time you should keep your mouth shut little man. This couldn't have sat well with him, because he pushed through me as if he was upset. On the other end of the court he decided to throw his body around as if I was the little guy. Mistake on top of mistake is what I thought to myself. He finally scored a bucket. You could immediately tell that he wasn't use to scoring whether it was on the court or off of it. He jumped up and down as if he had just won the game, and became comfortable talking crazy again. I decided to take what manhood he had left in this gym. It was time to take him where every bigger player takes a player smaller than him on the court, THE BOX. I went down low and called for the ball. He had his forearm in my back as if to give himself leverage, this is known as the bridge in basketball terminology. To me it was just another way to get him terminated, as I received the ball he pushed trying to get me further away from the basket. He was too little and way too late. I positioned my left foot behind his left foot, and as I turned elbows out, my elbowed landed square in the middle of his back. As he plummeted to the floor, I soared up for the game winning point. After scoring and allowing everyone the opportunity to laugh uncontrollably I added to his misery by pointing at him on the floor, shaking my head and yelling out NEXT! Afterwards Little Hater came up with an excuse to grab his clothes and leave the court, as if the embarrassment wasn't enough reason to leave I added to it "Oh you're leaving already?"

In most cases after a game of basketball it would've dropped there. That would've been it but Little Hater really didn't care for me. It was a lot more than the fact that I was from the D, it had to be the fact that he use to have a gigantic crush on Tamekia. According to her it was never more than that a crush that didn't go any further, but this kid had it out for me and from what I had noticed it wasn't letting up anytime soon. To add to my misery he had made friends with an unlikely candidate. Little Hater and Aleshia had become friends in some manner of the word, but they were close enough that Aleshia told him about Maria coming to visit for Homecoming weekend. Information that I had run across simply by mistake, I called her two nights before her flight was supposed to leave out. Her roommate made the mistake of assuming that I already knew about the trip she had obviously planned with the help of Aleshia. After obtaining this new information I planned to put it to good use. Unfortunately so did Little Hater with me unaware of his intentions. He wasted no time running and informing Tamekia, as if she had any say in the matter. I had to give it to him, he had a way with words. Easily explaining that she couldn't mean anything to me because my real woman was coming in town. That mixed with the fact that our friendship was taking a drastic change, only added to her emotional distress. All the while I'm thinking I'm at an advantage, but was truly only privy to limited information.

FRESHMEN YEAR: *Homecoming*

Maria and Kev arrived together and the first place they went was straight to Aleshia's. After their quick pit stop in the Valley they made their way up to my dormitory. Thinking that she was slick, Aleshia came to my door alone as if to surprise me, or maybe she was just making sure I didn't have company, either way I was more than prepared. I answered the door and we exchanged pleasantries. She acted as if it was a regular thing to come and visit me. I got straight to the point, "So what's up?" "Nothing I just stopped by" was her response. "Aleshia you haven't stopped by all year, what's so different now?" to which she responded, "Nothing just wanted to check up on you." At that moment there, was a knock at the door, as I opened the door I noticed Maria standing there suit case in hand and a gigantic smile on her face. The excitement rushed through my body, even though I knew she was coming, the fact that she was standing in front of me still warranted a surprised reaction. I snatched her in the door and into my arms easily expressing how much I had missed her.

"When did you get here?"

"Well Kev and I arrived about forty minutes ago."

"Oh yeah, Kev is here too?" Now that I didn't know about, would've thought he would've been the one to warn me that they were coming but once again he had already proven that he was more her friend than mine.

"Yeah he came to surprise Sabrine, we left him over there before we came this way. He'll probably be over here a little later."

"That's cool, not really worried about him though, more so happy as hell to see you."

It didn't take long before she gave Aleshia the signal that it was time for her to be on her way. I asked what made her jump on a plane and come all this way to see me. The best answer she could come with was she had grown tired of just talking on the phone, and wanted to see me in person. I was wondering how long she was going to be able to stay. I knew it couldn't be much longer than the weekend, not that I was eager to get rid of her, just wanted to know how long I had to enjoy her company.

Aleshia hadn't been gone longer than ten minutes before the night started, not another second was wasted. We started off kissing passionately, as I lead her to the bedroom, touching and teasing her all the way, tenderly caressing her body, and barely making it to the bed before my jeans were unbuttoned and around my ankles. With her shirt and bra already disposed of, and hands exploring and fondling her newly released breast, I bent down and gently allowed my tongue to race over her nipples repeatedly. As I felt her heavily breathing on the back of my neck, I couldn't help but inhale the scent of the pear lotion and body spray that she had applied evenly earlier in the day. At the same time I can feel her hand run down the middle of my back. Finally reaching the small of my back, she then dug her nails in and began her ascent back up to my shoulders. Enjoying the pleasure as well as the pain of it all, I let out a slight moan. She then grabbed my neck escorting me back up to a meeting with her lips. We began the deepest, most sensual kiss that either of us had ever experienced together. It was unspoken, but at the same time understood how much each of our bodies missed the others touch. As we intertwined and our bodies became one, we could hear Faith Evans explaining how as soon as she got home she was going to make it up, and do what she had to do. The song fit the situation perfectly because she was doing what she needed to do to make me feel better. As each stroke traveled deeper into her depths, and her breathing became more and more irregular, the sense that she was at the height of her enjoyment over took me as well. I then kissed and caressed her right leg until it slid directly over my shoulder, all the while staring seductively into her eyes. Not allowing her to look away, while I reintroduced her to me in my entirety. By the look of pure pleasure on her face I could tell she was enjoying herself, as for me I couldn't imagine being anywhere else on earth. Hours passed with us still enjoying the exploration that was our love, as day became night we were finally interrupted, by the phone. My plan was to not even waste my time answering the phone, but that was eliminated by the next sound out of her mouth "You not gonna answer the phone?" thinking to myself well there goes that moment. I answered the phone.

"I'm listening" in a very distinct female voice I was asked "Where my girl at? Tell her I'm on my way upstairs so grab her stuff and get ready to go."

"Stop playing Aleshia, she ain't going nowhere yet."

"The hell if she ain't. She not just here to see yo ass. We're going to the Homecoming party tonight, so I'll see ya'll when I get upstairs."

Without another word she hung up the phone. My guess is I was the only one left out of the loop because Maria was already getting up and throwing on her clothes, before I could explain the situation. "That was Aleshia? I didn't know she would be here so soon." So it was true she was leaving. Not a big problem, I was planning on going to the party as well, but not this early, it was only eight o'clock, but I guess they had a lot more to do than I did. By the time Aleshia got up to my door Maria was just about ready to go. I opened the door "What up girl?" She entered barely even speaking.

"Oh yeah you just rush in and don't even speak, and on top of that you stealing her away."

"I don't know why you trippin, you know where she'll be after the party anyway."

"Whateva Aleshia."

Acknowledging the fact that she was right with a smile I then turned my attention back to Maria and asked her if she really planned to leave me now. Without giving her a chance to respond I pretended to be hurt by her decision, then I laughed and told her to go have fun and I would see her later tonight. We gave a quick hug, and a kiss then left it at that. On their way out Aleshia thought it would be wise to add in the fact that since they would be getting dressed in her room they would be sending Kevin to my room so that Girls night could begin. Wasn't a problem for me I could deal with him for a couple of hours. As they exited my room I began to think to myself, I hope everything goes well tonight, don't need anyone acting a fool on me this weekend.

I decided to just throw on a Polo jogging suit for tonight. It was already understood that I was okay in the clothes department, I didn't feel that I needed to impress anyone by getting dressed, plus it was just another party at the Rec. On top of that, I didn't need any extra attention. This was my first year in college, but not my first college Homecoming. I had come up last year around this time so I already knew it wasn't as big as everyone made it seem. Between the fellas and the people that I met in summer school I was kind of popular so I was introducing Kev to people every time I turned around. He fit in quite nicely, especially because of the new things he picked up a school. He had already been a drinker in high school, but he had now picked up smoking weed as a new past time. Wasn't that big of a deal because with the exception of myself, everyone else I hung out with did as well. He had no problem with acceptance especially once he pulled out his sack from the south. The party started at nine, and it was now eleven o'clock so we needed to get going. Even though I'm already taken for the night, it still doesn't hurt to be seen, or does it? When we stepped in it was packed from wall to wall, and unlike the last party there wasn't a quiet area. There were women everywhere, it was probably some dudes there too, but my eyes had trouble focusing on them especially with the abundance of legs that were out tonight. So let me see who's here, and if there is anyone that I need to avoid. Before I could give the room a good once over I instantly see Maria, we make eye contact so I smile. It's too early to be cuffed up with her plus she's with her girls right now. On top of that it's some lame ass dude in her face trying to get her number. From the look on her face he's not doing to well. Hmmm, that's too bad for him is what I stood and thought to myself, as I look at the sheer disappointment in his face. Every now and again I have caught myself being the jealous type, but it's really not my style. It only happens when I'm feeling down and someone else seems to have things going on. This however was not one of those rare cases, plus it was evident that she had the situation under control, so I could comfortably move on. As I moved on I didn't realize I was walking straight into the line of fire, because out of nowhere trouble appeared.

"What up Tamekia?" (I said politely)

"Whateva nigga, I already know yo little chick is here for the weekend!"

"Wow, news travels fast I just found out today." I said as if I was astonished by her findings.

"Oh I won't be acting like shit anymore, I'm tired of being yo chick on the side. Either you gone choose or I'm done."

"Come on now sweetie, you knew the rules before this game even began, plus there's not a choice to be made here. Honestly, do we have to go there? I'm just tryna have a good time with no drama if possible. Can we make that possible? I'd really appreciate that. Thank you in advance."

"You think this is over, it ain't over until I say it's over, you are going to make a choice."

"Well in that case can you please say it's over so I can get back to enjoying myself? I already told you there is no choice to be made. Furthermore this is neither the time nor the place for this conversation."

"That's where you're wrong. This is the time, and the place, so you need to choose Chris. Or I am going to make a scene in this party, I'm sure she's in here."

"Sweetie your making a scene right now, and when I tell you we won't be kicking it anymore, it's going to get worse. I'd really rather save you the embarrassment."

"So that's your answer, I was willing to leave my man for you and you won't leave that bitch."

"Look Tamekia, I'm going to take a couple steps away from you before you say something I won't be able to ignore. I understand that you're upset right now and I don't want to have to tell you about yourself."

"Fuck you Chris, I don't want yo ass anyway, I was doing yo ugly ass a favor by letting you touch this right here. And you couldn't even do that right."

"Wow, and all this time I thought I was Pretty Damn Cute. I take it you're done now. You've already hurt my feelings by saying that I was ugly, then topped it off with the fact that I'm sexually unimpressive. And with all that said the thing that sticks out most is the fact that you were just demanding that I choose between you and her." (My guess was that my sarcasm wasn't appreciated at that particular point.)

I decided that it was time for me to walk away from this situation, and get back in the party mood. Just hope it wasn't as big of a scene as

I thought it was. Was pretty sure she saw the entire episode, and if she didn't one of her spies. I mean her friends did. So I might as well get ready for the line of questioning that was more than likely going to be asked later tonight. Where the fellas go that quick I thought to myself? As I walked around the party searching for them and attempting to avoid everyone else, I finally I found them posted up by the wall as usual. "Ya'll to blowed to holla at these chicks or what Cuz?" He turns and gives me the look as if to say I should know better than to ask him a question, like that.

"You seen Kev?"

"I think he's over there wit his girl."

The party scene was beginning to bore me already, plus I wasn't going to be able to show this man a good time if he was going to be cuffed up with his girl all night. I already knew I wouldn't be talking to any women tonight, and there would be no flirting because that would cause too many questions to be asked. I might as well head to the house, and call it a night. "Ay, I'll catch ya'll at the crib." As I maneuvered through the crowd it hit me, I probably should let Maria know that I'm leaving. Suddenly I got an uneasy feeling that I was being watched, so I slowed up for a second and thought to myself. What if Tamekia in her angry state of mind sees me talking to her? She might take it upon herself to talk to her once I've left the building. Maybe I shouldn't leave just yet, but if I stay there might be even more trouble brewing. Then it hit me, I'll have Cuz tell her that I'm leaving, but if she saw the discussion with Tamekia earlier she's already on a mission to find out what it was all about. I may already be in harms way, and just don't know it. Maybe I should stay here for a while longer. Plus I still have this uneasy feeling that I'm being watched. As I made my way around the crowded room I saw the chick from the last party, it seemed as if she was in a daze but her dazed looked seemed to be in my direction. As I moved so did her eyes, so I decided to wave, and keep it moving. I had been drinking half the night so I was about due for a bathroom break. On top of that I needed some time to think about everything that had transpired. As I stood in the men's room trying to decipher whether or not I am over analyzing the situation. In time I decided that I was putting way too much thought into the problem, if it could even be thought of as a problem. This is usually when in the cartoons on one shoulder a small angel appears on the characters shoulder and on the other one there's a small devil. Only problem was that my devil was speaking so much louder than my angel. What really happened? I had a disagreement with a chick, that wasn't a crime. I moved on to the next question, what if Tamekia actually told her about the type of friendship we had? Answer: it was okay because I wasn't in a relationship anyway. Damn that little Devil made sense, at least he did to me.

As I exited the restroom, I noticed that the same chick that had just been seemingly staring at me was standing there as if she was waiting on someone. "I'm beginning to think you're following me." She wasted no time with her response "And what if I am?" that wasn't the answer I was expecting so I was a little thrown off. "Well if that was the case my next question would probably be, should I be worried? If I had no reason to be alarmed then I would ask you what the problem was." Her response was once again shocking. She told me that she remembered me from her room the time we all stopped in and introduced ourselves, but more recently she remembered me from the last party when we slow danced near the end, and then I pushed her off on some guy so that I could dance with his girl. Wow, I was astounded by her in-depth and detailed memory. Not only did she remember the last party, but she remembered my name from when we stopped by her room, that was wild to me. She continued "I thought we started something at the last party, and I hate to leave things unfinished, unless you are more interested with the young lady who is noticeably upset with you tonight." I politely explained Tamekia was just a friend, but I did have someone that I cared about at the party tonight who had a higher stature than the chick that was upset.

"Is that right, well in one sense I'm happy to hear that you have friends and at the same time I'm sorry to hear that someone that is not me has such a high stature in your life."

She then told me that she was going to allow me to get away this time, but the very next time that she caught me anywhere she wasn't accepting no for an answer. She told me that she would see me around campus, and then we would continue this conversation. I told her that she seemed full of confidence and it was kinda cute. Her response was that she knew I would like it, and she would see me soon. As soon as I began to walk away I could feel her eyes giving me one last once over, honestly that in itself was a turn on.

When I returned to the party I was quickly spotted by Maria. By this time it was around 1:45 am, and she was asking where I had been hiding all night. I let her know that I was just chillin and letting her have her space to enjoy her time with her girls. She decided to make me feel good by saying she wasn't there for them, she was there for me, and that we should go enjoy each other fully right now. This sounded like a plan to me, by the time we let everyone know that we were leaving it was around 2:15 am, neither of us was really ready to go in because we hadn't even had an opportunity to talk. It was a beautiful fall night, so we decided to go for a walk around campus so I could show her where all my classes were. As we walked, we talked about everything under the sun. We laughed and joked for hours, and finally when we returned to my room our time turned to a serious note near the end. She wanted to know where we stood as far as a relationship was concerned. This was a question that I didn't feel I was able to answer on my own. This is something that we seriously had to think about considering the distance between us. Were we really prepared to be monogamous, and be with only each other? She made the whole situation seem so easy, so fun, and easily accomplishable, but the truth was, this would take an enormous amount of hard work, trust and dedication, and unless we had all three we wouldn't make it. I should've said NO, this is something that I am not ready for. That would've been the truth, but between the incredible night we shared and the beautiful way she made everything so simple, I found myself just saying yes to everything, not fully realizing the consequences of what I had just agreed to. After that first day, the weekend just seemed to fly by, I barely saw Kev again until it was time for them to ride back to the airport. Maria and I spent every waking minute together, as I showed her around campus, and introduced her to anyone who wanted to meet her. On their final day they packed into Mal's car to go back to the airport. As we said our good-bye's I noticed a tear forming in Maria's eye, I asked what was wrong and she said that it was just the fact that she was going to miss being here with me.

After Maria returned to school it was now fully understood that I was in a relationship. I attempted to stay out of troublesome situations. It actually worked for a short period of time. I kept myself busy whether it was in class, in the gym, or even in the library after I found out were it was (never was the biggest on studying). This helped me stay out of places like the student center, and especially the Valley. I was doing great if I did say so myself. That was until I ran into Rita on my way from class, better yet when Rita almost ran me down, on my way to meet Cuz for lunch in the café. When she mistook me for a part of the particular street I was crossing, she pretended she didn't see me at the crossing. I could have thought of much safer and less scary ways to get my attention, although it did work. Once I crossed safely, I stopped and turned around to see who convinced themselves that they were Mario Andretti. As she rolled down her window with a huge smile on her face, she told me to get in. My first instinct told me that this wasn't a good idea, but before I had the chance to turn down the opportunity, she quickly reminded me that NO was not an option. So against my better judgment I walked around to the passenger side, and got in the car. As we pulled off she asked if I had any more classes today to which I responded "No I don't". The devilish smile on her face widened, as she told, not asked me "Good so I can take you to lunch." As I sat there in awe of the way she handled the situation so easily, I wondered if NO was still not an option that was afforded to me. At the same time I was intrigued by the way that I seemingly didn't have a choice in the matter. This actually made me want to go, and take the opportunity get to know her better. Although in the back of my mind I knew she wanted a little more than to get to know me.

At lunch we discussed many different facets of our lives, from our plans for the future all the way up to how I almost got cursed out at the first party for three reasons. First was because I grabbed her and danced, just to make some other chick jealous. Second because I didn't even remember being in her room earlier in the year. Last but not least, because I switched dance partners after she asked me what I was doing later that night. She told me I could've at least picked someone cuter if I just had to switch partners. As we enjoyed our lunch we laughed and joked, then the conversation turned for the worst. She asked me who the lucky person was at the last party, who was so special to me. I informed her that it was my newly acquired girl friend. Hoping that this new fact wouldn't interfere with the fact that she was treating me to lunch, because I walked out without any money on me this morning.

Shockingly she was impressed with the fact that I was honest enough to tell her up front about my relationship. It was explained to me that most men don't give women the option of saying yes. I'm willing to deal with this situation, they just lie and say that they're single in fear that the woman isn't going to deal with them if they know the truth. She went on to explain that women get urges just as much as men do, and if men were sensible they would be honest up front, there's no telling how far they can get. From her tone, and the passion behind what she was saying, it was obvious she was speaking from experience. After lunch we headed back to campus, when we arrived I thanked her for my meal and the great conversation. We said our good-byes and went our separate ways. Before I got too far away she told me I should stop by sometime, her door is always open. I told her that I would take her up on her offer, and then I continued on my way to grab my shorts to play ball in.

Now I was intrigued, was even more turned on by the fact that a woman in my eyes, not a girl, was interested in me, yet I wasn't completely overwhelmed by this fact. Age had never really been a factor before, mainly because up until this point if someone had been older it wasn't by much. Carmen was less than six months older, and Maria was only two months older, but Rita had a complete six years on me. I still had to keep myself under control, I had a girl friend now and I intended to respect my relationship. So just like the last person that showed any interest, I attempted to stay away from my temptation. This proved to be difficult, because of proximity. The fact that we lived in the same building hindered my attempts to stay away. This was intensified by the fact that her door stayed open. Each time that I walked pass, I was invited to come and join her in watching television. After numerous invitations, I was finally overly enticed by pizza and my favorite movie (King of New York). Once again I was caught by my appetite, but this time we had even more in common. She was a huge fan of the movie. As we watched, taking turns reciting different parts of the movie, and enjoying slice after slice, I noticed her getting closer. By the time the movie was over she had gone from sitting up on the couch to lying in my lap. Once the movie was over I excused myself, explaining that I still had studying to do and it was getting late. She expressed her enjoyment of our time together, and that she would love to do it again sometime.

This wasn't a problem for me, as long as I kept myself under control, everything would be fine. I arrived in my room just in time to hear the phone ringing, it was already an hour past midnight, and I had lost track of time. It was time for my regularly scheduled talk to Maria, since her return to school we decided (she decided) that she would call every day at this time to say good night. Myself, I thought it was just her way of making sure that I was in my room at night. We talked for about thirty minutes, before sleep overtook our thoughts and said our good nights. She sounded very happy to hear from me, this was no different than any other night that we spoke. After getting off the phone I decided a shower was definitely in order, quickly gathering my clothes I headed for the bathroom. Before truly getting engrossed in the steam and the heat of the shower the phone rang, my first instinct was to let it ring and let them catch the voice mail. Then I realized that it was probably Maria, and I didn't want her to think I was out so, jumping out of the shower as quickly as possible and rushing to the phone was my only option. Got there just into time; "Hello" I didn't recognize the voice right off, then the statement let me know who it was. "I hope I didn't make you feel uncomfortable tonight, and if I did I truly apologize, but I really did enjoy myself, just called to tell you that. Goodnight." I was slow with my response "Um uh, no not at all. I just had to study", before I could get my complete sentence out she was already gone. As I went back to enjoy my shower I couldn't help, but think of the trouble I could be in right now if I had stayed in her room. Maybe my shower needed to change from hot and steamy, to extremely cold.

The next couple of weeks flew by, and even though my mind was strong, my body was not. I had urges that were not being satisfied, it was only so much a movie and my palm could handle. I was ready to hear the moan of a woman. I wanted to feel the touch, smell the aroma, and see the pure look of ecstasy on her face as I fill her loneliness with my excitement. In some instances I cursed the fact that I agreed to be in this relationship, but at the same time I knew how happy I was with Maria when we were together. It was time to make a decision and stick with it. Either I would continue to respect the relationship that I was in, or I would make sure that she was number one with different numbers to follow. My decision was that the latter would be more beneficial to my cause. "What she didn't know wouldn't hurt her." This was my new

77

found philosophy, and in my mind it was perfect. I had enough of being good, it was time to have fun, and I had just the person to start with. I went down to Rita's room, acting as if I was just passing by, knowing that she would ask me to come in. It was Saturday night and she was looking sad, as if she had just received bad news. I inquired what the problem was, she hesitated to tell me at first and then it all came out. She had broken up with her man earlier this year, and now with her birthday being tomorrow she had no one to celebrate with. I informed her that there was nothing to worry about, I would happily celebrate her day with her. She gave me a devilish look, and asked me if I was sure that I wanted to celebrate with her. My response was "It's your day, we can do whatever you like." She excused herself from the couch and closed her door she then ventured into another room returning with a bottle of Hennessey, and then grabbed the Coke from the fridge.

"If we're going to celebrate, then we are going to do it right."

With that, she mixed two drinks for us, at the same time when she returned to her seat. I moved in closer. She gave me a clear warning.

"You might want to be careful where you sit. You might end up in a world of trouble!"

"I think I can handle myself, and any trouble that I might get into."

She quickly downed the rest of her drink acting as if the liquor had taken control just that quickly. She then laid back on the couch. I thought that this would be a good time to lean in for a small kiss, so I pecked her on the cheek. That went over without a hitch so I moved on to the next spot. I then kissed her on the neck slowly moving up to her lips. At the same time I pulled her to me. She willingly gave in and moved in close as I caressed her back, and kissed her passionately. She attempted to lean me back and take control of the situation. Control.... control was something that I wasn't ready to give up at this time, so I slid off the couch, and positioned myself on top of her, slowly unbuttoning her shirt and then her jeans. As I slid her shirt from her shoulders, making sure my lips touched every part of her body as I did so, I could feel her body tense, as if it had been touched for the very first time. As I traveled from her breast further south I could feel the heat from her dessert, which would soon be my oasis. I slowly slid apart her thighs so that I could get a better glimpse of her pleasure point. As my tongue entered the forbidden area of her body I watched her gasp, and reach for imaginary objects on the couch. Her dazed look amazed me, and at the same time made me want more, I wanted to pleasure her as she had never been pleasured before. As I gently attacked the little man in the boat, I could feel the waves of her ocean crashing, enticing me to continue my attack, and increase the pleasure. Her hands moved from clutching the pillows of the couch to clutching the back of my head. Pushing my tongue and lips into deeper depths of her warmth, I could hear her call out for God, but it was me that was in an ear shot of her moans and with each one, my power grew stronger, and made me want to do more. When I finally removed myself, and lifted my face I could feel the moisture of her wetness escaping my lips. We then traveled from the couch into her bedroom. She was a woman after my own heart. The fact was, college dorms were equipped with twin beds, which are very irritating to enjoy yourself in, but if pushed together and equipped with a bigger mattress can actually be quite comfortable. I had finally taken the time to enjoy the body of beauty that was in front of me, and beautiful it was. Her hair flowed down to the middle of her back and was a thick jet-black grade. Sliding down just a bit further and you ran into the smallest waist you could imagine followed by hips and thighs that were perfectly toned. You could tell she stayed fit and I had the pleasure of pleasing all of her tonight. I moved in close after my admiration had gotten the better of me. Smiling with a crooked smile, I gently pushed her onto the bed following her down and sliding deep into her awaiting walls of pleasure. Upon entry, I could feel her wetness engulf me in my entirety. She released an intense moan, as if she had just been breached for the first time in a long time. Her hands immediately began to race across my back, as I pushed up my torso and locked my arms in upward push-up position, so that I could enjoy her facial expressions. I kept my waist and below moving in a deep and intense motion. With each thrust I could feel more of my giant enriched by her juices. As she locked her legs around my thighs I felt something that I had yet to experience with any of my previous encounters, her inner thighs began to shake uncontrollably, and with every thrust the vibration grew. The look of astonishment overtook her face, as if I had succeeded to take her where no man had taken her before, as she whispered in my ear "I'm cummin" my beliefs were acknowledged, she had reached her climax. As she whispered I responded "Happy Birthday" and then let her know that the night had just begun.

As night became day I wasn't looking forward to the part of myself that was going to feel guilty for my acts of the prior night. Luckily, that side of me never took over. Was I really lucky? Was this a gift or a curse? I rolled over to see the person that I had spent my entire night with, the night in which I missed phone calls on top of phone calls from my woman. She looked amazing as she slept and I was happy to be there. I quietly crept out of the bed and began to gather my clothes, thinking that she wouldn't awake. I didn't want to be stuck in an awkward position, in case she had regrets about the night before. Before I could make it to the door she asked if I was leaving her already, I responded that I had to go and take a shower as if I couldn't in her room. She explained (as if she had read my mind) that she didn't have any regrets about tonight, and hoped that I didn't either, then she went on to say that she hoped it happen again very soon. I smiled, and explained that her request could be worked out. After leaving her room I couldn't help but enjoy the rest of my day, smiling about the new secret that I was keeping to myself. As I returned to my room I ran into Cuz as he was coming out of his room on his way to the activity center to workout.

"Oh yeah, so were you coming from?"

"What you talking about I'm just coming from at down the café."

"You expect me to believe that, you would've come and got one of us. Plus I've already been to your room and yo "roommate" told me you weren't home all night. You really should tell that nigga to stop divulging so much info." (For some reason Cuz didn't like my roommate, though he hadn't done anything to me or Cuz, but he did seem like a Duck.)

"I just kicked it wit a friend, why don't you give me about ten minutes to get dressed and I'll hit the rec wit you."

"That's cool I can do that, it'll give me a chance to find out where you really were."

"Whateva Cuz, I'll be ready in a second."

Knowing Cuz I wasn't going to hear the end of this until he found out exactly where I was all night, so this was going to be a long day. After throwing my clothes on, we headed for the gym. The questions never ended. It took about two hours of constant badgering before I finally broke. "I was with Rita. We chilled and I fell asleep over there, then I woke up and came home. You happy now?" Cuz was thrown off for a minute or two, my guess is he couldn't understand why I just didn't come out and tell him that one. To be honest after I said it I wondered the same thing, it wasn't like I was bragging on what happened. I just told him that we fell asleep, and that was it. We worked out for about another twenty minutes, and then headed back to the dorms.

I went back into my room just to find that I had missed Maria's call again, and that she had been calling all night. Immediately heading for the phone I knew I had all types of trouble to get out of. As my fingers dialed the numbers my mind was racing, should I tell her what happened last night? Does she deserve to be hurt this way, or should I just keep it all to myself? Before I could finish my thought she was on the phone with questions, starting with are you okay, followed by if so, where were you at all night? The last statement ended with the fact that she was so worried about me that she couldn't sleep. To ease her mind I explained that I had fallen asleep in Cuz's room after having too much to drink. It really wasn't an explanation. It was a flat out lie, and I knew it but it came out so quickly I almost believed it myself. After calming her down and putting her mind at ease, or at least it seemed to be at ease, because we then caught up on the current events. We expressed how much we missed each other, and how happy we were that Christmas break was only two weeks away. We had plans to be together for the entire time that we were home, totally disregarding the fact that our parents hadn't seen us since we left for school. I'm sure that they had plans already made for us, and they probably didn't have anything to do with us sitting up under each other everyday. We kept the conversation going for the next hour before she said it was time for her to go, and she would call me later. I retreated to my bed to rest and actually enjoy some sleep. Something that I hadn't been able to do a lot of since I'd been at school.

Awaking to the sounds of shouting isn't unusual at all in a dorm especially on the weekend, but what was unusual was waking up to perfect silence. There wasn't anyone being loud or any music playing. I rolled over and glanced at the clock it was only six o'clock. Why was it so quiet? I headed for the door to see where everyone had gone, or at least to find out why it was so damn quiet. I knocked on Cuz' door and then Mal's with no answer. I went down to Snoop's room to find out where everyone had gone. Usually even if everyone else had left Snoop was still there and as usual he was sitting in his room watching Japanese animation. He told me that everyone had went to the movies and they had stopped by to see if I wanted to go but no one answered my door. It really didn't matter, I was just wondering why it was so quiet. I left his room and ventured back to mine. I threw on a T-shirt and headed downstairs to visit Rita. She must have been waiting for company, because her door was closed. I knocked anyway just in case the company she was waiting for was me. When she opened the door her eyes lit up, not as if she was upset but just the opposite she seemed extremely happy to see me.

"Hey, I wasn't expecting you, but I'm glad you came. Come on in."

"I didn't mean to just pop up, but I still don't have your number."

As I entered the room I noticed her attire, or lack there of. She had a towel wrapped around her body and another around her hair. Politely I asked if I caught her at a bad time, which she replied, not at all. She asked if I would mind applying the lotion to her legs, and I couldn't resist. Before starting I forewarned that this could lead to other things if she wasn't careful, and that's when the seductive smile appeared over her face. She came closer to the bed and allowed the towel to drop to the floor. As the sun barely crept through the window it cascaded off her bronzed skin, and gave her an astonishing glow. She slowly unwrapped the towel around her head, and allowed the still dripping wet hair to fall below her shoulders. It was a beautiful sight, as she laid the towel across her pillow she then positioned herself across the bed face down.

"If you don't mind can you massage the lotion on my body, while I'm still a little wet. That way I stay moisturized."

"Not a problem, but once again I might not be able to control myself."

"Honestly I hope that you can't."

As I separated her hair and moved it away from her back I slowly rubbed in the Pear lotion from Victoria Secret that she wanted applied, increasing the pressure on her lower back. The particular type of lotion she used showed me that she wasn't too much different from any of the other chicks that I had been with, she fell victim to the fruit craze that had swept the nation. As she exhaled I could feel the air travel through her body, as my hands traveled further south she arched her back. Feeling her body moving beneath me as I straddled her thighs rubbing her lower back, my left hand slid lower, as I intensely grabbed a hand full of her fleshy backside, she groaned and raised herself to meet my movements. I slowly moved my right hand down to her inner thigh to which I could feel the heat pulsating. As she slid her legs apart I could barely control myself between the sweet smell of pear, and the insatiable aroma of her that was in the air. I no longer wanted to stay in control. The room evolved to another dimension of heat, it was not only hot, but it was sultry as well. Between the heat of our bodies, the window above the bed had begun to steam, and a thick frost covered it. She raised herself to her knees and allowed my fingers to roam freely, after my hand had explored her I removed it and placed it on my lips to taste her nectar. The windowpane was directly above the bed, as I continued to taste her fruits she attempted to climb away, by this time she had both hands positioned on the window. As cold as the window may have been it didn't bother her in the least, she demanded that I take her now. She wanted to feel me deep inside her. As I positioned myself behind her and then spreading her as wide as possible I planted myself deep inside. As I entered, not only were her hands on the glass, but by now so was her chest. Being that we were only on the third floor of the building, if any passer by would have been walking or riding by, she would've been easily seen. I began to thrust deep inside her walls until I heard the sounds that I had been waiting for. The quiet breathing had been overtaken by intense moaning, and slight panting. I loosened my grip on her lower cheeks, then slowly slid my left hand up the small of her back barely touching her with my fingertips. As I reached the top of her back I grabbed her hair and gave it a slight tug, increasing her pleasure with a hint of pain. Her moans intensified as she let herself go, she insisted that I pull harder, my grip became tighter as the slight tug became a pleasurable pull. I could feel her walls tighten around me, pulling and stroking her all at the same time, I kept this motion up until she collapsed, exhausted from the fluids she had recently lost all over me. I laid there with her in my arms feeling quite comfortable, too comfortable. This was a beautiful young woman, who knew that I had a girlfriend and could care less, she just wanted whatever time I had to offer. It finally hit me as I laid there that I do have a girlfriend and I was cheating on her, and it didn't bother me in the least. After allowing her to fall into a deep sleep I got up and went back to my room.

Semester Break:

My bed felt more comfortable than it had in the past, or I was just happy to be in it. The phone was right next to my bed just in case I had a call I had been waiting for. Unfortunately for me I didn't get that call, and my body was tired so I was better sleep than attempting to make the call. Didn't want to make any mistakes while tired. (Coach always told me that when you're tired the first thing to go is your mind.) So sleep was my best option. I awoke to the first day of finals week. I had two tests this morning, which wasn't a problem because I felt so rested. It may have helped if I opened a book and studied over the weekend, but no reason to start doing things that I haven't done in the past. We only had two days left before the end of the semester and Christmas break. Christmas was a huge deal in my family. The entire family would gather over my grandmother's house for dinner and to open presents. I couldn't wait to get a piece of my Grandmother's Sweet Potato Pie, and to see Maria of course. I hadn't decided if I was going back with Cuz or not. He wasn't leaving until Friday, and Rita had offered to take me because she was leaving Wednesday and wanted someone to ride with her. That would work out perfect seeing as riding back with Cuz was a hazard to my health, because of the smoke inhalation. I decided to take her up on her offer, plus it would get me home a couple of days early. I could spend time with my family and actually get some shopping done. The next two days flew by and before I knew it we were pulling up off the Freeway and onto the ever so familiar streets of Detroit. As we weaved through traffic the streets were packed. It was 5:30 in the afternoon and everyone seemed like they had all stock piled on Seven

Mile, just to prolong my arrival home. I tried to tell her she didn't want to go this way, but to know avail. When we finally arrived in my drive-way I asked if she would like to come in and meet my family to which she quickly responded not this time, because she really had to get home and take her sister shopping. After thanking her for the ride and giving her a quick peck on the cheek, I got out and waved good-bye. Before I could get up the walkway, my mom had the door open, as well as her arms awaiting her hug. The smile that she greeted me with warmed my heart. I was home, even if it was only for a semester break. Enjoying the usual lecture on whether I am taking care of my business or playing around up at school and then cracking a joke or two I ventured down to my room that was in the process of being changed into the Entertainment room. My bed had been replaced with a couch with a fold out bed in it and sixty-four inch television. It was fine with me, I was just happy to be home. With Christmas coming up, and me being in a situation that I had never been in before, having a woman that is, I was lost what should I get her. This would be the first gift that I had ever bought her or at least gift for a holiday. Should I go big, or small, should it be expensive or is it truly the thought that counts? I knew it was wrong of me to think this way, but I didn't want to be out done. I would've hated for her to go all out, and I just get something small, or vice versa. I was probably going to have to get some ideas from her, but did I really want to go that route? She would be getting home tomorrow, and I was getting more excited as each hour passed. Maybe then I can get some insight of what to do for this Christmas thing. I had a little over a week before the day would be here.

On the darker side of things seeing Maria wasn't the only thing I had to worry about around this time. I also had a huge decision to make about life as much as I loved attending school away from home, I was still missing a big part of my life. I missed competing and playing on a team, a part of my life that I wanted back so desperately, and the opportunity never presented itself at WMU. I did however have that opportunity at WSU, and this would also give me a chance to take some of the strain off my parents. WSU was offering a full scholarship to attend college on top of financial aid, and it was something that I definitely needed to think about. I had a meeting with Coach Taylor before the team was to go to a Christmas tournament in New Orleans.

I couldn't wait for the meeting, at least to see if he was just another one of those coaches looking for the next athlete to help him keep his job, or get a raise. I'm not really looking to be used or exploited in that manner, I don't have to play I want to play, I would be sure to explain that to the coach as well as the Athletic Director, I was a student first, but a chance to play college basketball was extremely exciting to me nonetheless. As I entered the gymnasium I was greeted by MB, he was the team's Captain and leading scorer from the previous year. The coach was running a little late and wanted to make sure that I had someone to show me around campus. After fully inspecting the gymnasium, we ventured onto the yard. He showed me were the basketball players could usually be found, and where the Black students usually were. The campus was located near the Downtown area of Detroit, which was entirely too close to the water. This made the wind that much colder, as the brisk winter air hit my face I could feel the chill throughout my body. MB was cool. We instantly hit it off especially because we had played at different gyms around the city together. We didn't know each other but, at the same time it seemed like we did. Finally as the tour came to a close we ended up back in Coach Taylor's office with him sitting there with a hug smile on his face.

"So what do you think of our school Mr. Alexander?"

"Well honestly coach it's pretty cold down here, but other than that it's great."

"Does that mean I can count on you being here next semester, and playing for me next year?"

"I would love to tell you yes right now coach, but this is something that I still have to think about and discuss with my parents. I have to worry about my education first, and then basketball."

"That is exactly what I wanted to hear, because you are a student first. This is why at WSU we approach our players as STUDENT athletes, not athletes that happen to be students. If you would like, I can talk to your parents with you."

"That would be great, I would really appreciate it if you could talk to all of us together so that we can get a better understanding of what WSU has to offer me on the educational side of school. This way you can also get a better idea of what I can bring to WSU on and off the court."

"I'll be happy to. We will be returning from the trip on the 28th of December, I can schedule a meeting the following day if that would be alright with you and you parents."

"I'm sure that will be perfect. Thanks Coach! Fair warning, my mom is a hand full, she's not the easiest person to convince."

"Then I'll have my work cut out for me, I'll give you a call while on the trip and fill you in on how the tournament is going and let you know what time I'll be available when we return."

"Okay I'll talk to you then, hope you guys have a good trip."

"So do I!"

As I strolled through the student center on my way to the parking lot I noticed one of the sexiest women I had ever seen, she had a certain sway in her hips as she walked as well as a certain sophistication in the manner that she carried herself, as if I could tell just by the way she walked. She was completely over dressed for just attending class, there had to be a little more than school on her agenda for this particular day. As she walked through the student area in her black pin-stripped pants, and suspenders over the shoulder of her white blouse topped of by a black Dobbs (hat) as if she was the female Mack. To end the ensemble, her feet were outfitted with a pair of stiletto-heeled boots, which at that moment I realized were my absolute weakness. This was the first time I had seen her, but it definitely wasn't going to be the last. As I finally made it to the car, I pulled off slowly admiring the site of the school that could very well be where I'd end up next.

I pulled up to Maria's house with the biggest smile on my face, excited about the opportunity to see my Boo. She had to feel the same way because before I could even get the car in park she was running out the door and up to the car. She was overly excited, but then again so was I. I think part of it was she really wanted to sell her parents on the fact that we hadn't seen each other since the summer. (Seeing that they didn't know about her trip to visit me at school.) We stood in the middle of the street hugging for about ten minutes, maybe it wasn't as big of a front as I had thought. We finally started walking towards the house, her mother and father were sitting in the living room watching the sixty-four inch television and discussing the plan for Christmas dinner. As we entered the door it immediately got quiet so that we all could greet each other. I walked up and shook her father's hand and explained that it was good to see him again. Then I went directly over to her mother and gave her a big hug, and said "Hey Mrs. Fuller" to which she responded with a bewildered look on her face.

"Since when is it Mrs. Fuller? You've went to school and came back and you can't call me Ma anymore?"

"I'm sorry Ma, I thought you might have wanted me to stop calling you that now that I'm a college student." (With a slight smirk on my face.)

"Okay you can act up if you want to, but I wouldn't recommend it. Now before you get comfortable, how was school this semester? These grades better be worth me seeing."

"Well I don't know about all that. It was my first year and most students do mess up a little bit that first year, I can only hope I did good. (While giving my best innocent look, as if to get some kind of sympathy from her.)

"That isn't an excuse I'll be accepting from either of you, and you know that. So I'll be expecting to see these grades before this vacation is over."

"Not a problem Ma, I'll make sure you see them."

The last thing that I heard from her as we moved on to the entertainment room was "Oh I know you will!" as if it wasn't a request, but a demand. She treated me as if I was her child as well. It made me feel really good to know that someone else's mother would care that much about me to take the time to make sure that everything is on the up and up. Maria and I ended up in the entertainment room sitting on the couch catching up on everything that had happened with school since the last time that we saw each other. Most of my discussion stayed on the school aspect because anything else I did was with Rita for the most part, and I was pretty sure she didn't want to hear about that part of my life. I also left out the part where I was deciding whether to transfer to WSU or not. I didn't really want to discuss it at this time, partially because I hadn't decided what I was going to do and didn't want anyone else to sway my decision. So most of my side of the conversation was on how much I missed her. The rest of the time was spent listening to her tell me about all the different parties she had been to, and how much studying that she hadn't done. We sat and talked for hours on end, before she moved closer to me on the couch.

"Did you really miss me?"

"Come on now you know damn well I did. What would make you ask me something silly like that?"

"You haven't even attempted to touch me since you've been here. What's up with that?"

"What do you think is up with that? Your parents are sitting in the other room wide awake."

"So! They ain't coming in here, and I want to feel you."

"You must be out yo damn mind, we not going there. Control ya'self girl."

"I don't want to! Come here and let me show you something."

"Listen this ain't gone happen, you need to calm yo'self down before you get in trouble."

"Actually I'm looking for a little trouble tonight, and you don't have a choice but to help me out. Plus you really don't want to miss out on this special offer."

Before I could fix my mouth to make a statement, she extended her hand to my thigh, barley missing the rapidly growing member of the party who was dying to break out of confinement. In my mind I was thinking move, and move quick, but the signals from my brain to my body were completely confused. The next move was hers and she made it work for both of us. Her hand unzipped my oversized jeans, and then her head dropped as she leaned over my lap. Feeling nothing but the heat from her mouth and the moisture of her tongue, the kid that was trapped in the jeans had instantly become a full-grown man. Her head moved slowly up and then down again, and again her tongue moved from the top to bottom of the shaft repeatedly. My mind had changed within seconds. I was no longer worried about the parents that were only two rooms away, or controlling ourselves, but now I was more concerned with how long would these motions would continue before I erupted. (My only other concern was who had she been practicing her new found talents on.) My answer wasn't far away at all. She continued her motions until I couldn't help but lean back and close my eyes at least for a second. (I had to remember where we were, I had to be on watch.) This was my first experience of this sort, but it seemed as if she knew exactly what she was doing, I couldn't really be a good judge at this time, it was way too much going on for me. Before she got me exactly where she wanted me, the footsteps started. She quickly removed her head from my lap and her hand from my jeans allowing me to pull them back to their proper place. She positioned herself on the couch leaning on my shoulder as her mother walked into the room, and explained that it was one o'clock in the morning. That was my hint, so I gave her a kiss on the cheek and told her that I would see her tomorrow. Luckily my jeans were as big as they were, or we may have had some explaining to do, I said goodnight to her parents and was on my way, still excited as I walked to the car.

Christmas was finally here, and I felt I had done a great job picking out her gift, and couldn't wait for the praise that was going to come along with my decision or at least I hoped so, though it would be a long morning before I could finally see her expression, Christmas was a huge holiday for both our families. My younger siblings were up and at it around seven in the morning. New toys, games, and clothes wouldn't allow them to sleep in this morning. So in turn that meant that I wouldn't be sleeping in either, I believe my little brother was the first to wake the house with his new fire engine. I wouldn't have been surprised if the box it came in read "Real Fire Engine Siren!". This is a gift my parents would soon wish they had left in the store. Not to be out done in anyway, my youngest sister had a talking Barbie with the most irritating voice you will ever hear, and it echoed throughout the halls of the house as I was making my way to the living room in my groggy state. My middle sister was going through package after package finding gifts that I would've loved with her name on them. Everything from a new stereo for her room, to enough clothes to cover half the homeless people in Detroit. If she didn't have a good Christmas then I don't know who did, because on top of all the gifts she still got a hundred dollars to do with what she wanted to. (I can say she deserved it, seeing that she had an immaculate report card again.) Now my oldest sister and I just got money, she was a senior in High School this year and I was a Freshman in college. We had both long gotten over our parents shopping for us. So money was the gift that we chose, the only knock with that is the fact that none of it was wrapped up, it was just handed to us. So there wasn't much for us to do besides watch everyone else have fun. It didn't matter to me much, I was used to it. As a matter of fact I kind of enjoyed watching them open gifts and playing with their toys. Plus it was Christmas and I wasn't going to let anything bother me, especially because I was going to be giving Maria her gift today. The hours of the day went by pretty fast, and before I knew it I was on my way with her gift in hand. When I arrived at her house I pulled the huge box out of the passenger seat. I could see her peeking out of the window on my way up the walk-way. As she opened the door I greeted her with a joyful "Merry Christmas". She had this astonished look on her face.

"Christopher Alexander, what in the world have you done?"

"What?" (I said with an innocent look across my face as if I had no idea what she was talking about.)

"You've gone too far, what's in this big ass box?"

"It's your Christmas gift, you can open it whenever your ready, I hope you like it."

"I hope you didn't spend too much."

"I hope I didn't either."

As she ripped the wrapping paper off, she could see that the box underneath was just a plain packing box, I guess the weight of the box never came into question, because it was light as a feather. She opened the box and fumbled around in it for a second or two just to find buried in all the wrapping tissue a medium sized teddy bear, with a smaller box in his hands. She looked up at me and laughed, as she pulled the light brown teddy bear out with his Santa Suit on. "He's so cute!" So I told her to open the other part of the gift. She grabbed the smaller box and unwrapped it to find 14k gold bracelet. Her eyes lit up, and she smiled so bright it seemed like I could see every tooth in her mouth. She seemed happy, which in turn made me ecstatic. I felt great being able to make her feel this good and seeing that my taste was in line with hers was just as good a feeling. She immediately came closer and gave me one of the warmest embraces that she had ever given me, then excused herself from the room. She returned quickly with a box in hand, and a huge smile on her face. Wasting no time, she shoved my gift into my hands and stood eagerly awaiting my attempts at opening the package without totally destroying the packaging. She didn't have the patience for that. She needed to know if I would like my gift right then, so she helped me by ripping the packaging. As I opened the box I noticed the Nautica emblem on the red, blue, and green vertically stripped shirt. She couldn't have gone wrong with the brand. It was what most of my wardrobe consisted of. After admiring the shirt for a little while I moved on to the Guess jeans that may have to go back from the size that was listed on the tag. But after trying them on I realized she knew me better than I thought. The box also included a pair of socks, and boxers from Nautica as well. In all this was a perfect gift I couldn't have done better myself, and she could tell from the smile on my face. We spent the rest of the evening laughing and singing Christmas carols with the rest of her family. It turned out to be one of the most enjoyable Christmas experiences that I ever had.

The holidays were finally over and a brand new year was upon us. My decision to attend a different university had finally become a reality. I had already explained my decision to everyone who may have had a concern, which included my parents, Maria, and Cuz. He was the most disappointed about the situation, the way he saw, it we had around three or four years of acting an ass together, but this was the best decision for my future. Luckily I had about two weeks longer than everyone else before school was to start. Maria had already traveled back to school a couple of days prior, after an enjoyable Christmas vacation which included the two of us being together without so much as an argument, or disagreement. This was beautiful, but in the back of my mind the truth had been lurking about, the main reason for our total enjoyment was because it was understood that our time was limited before we would again be separated by distance. So everything was taken with a grain of salt, no need to get angry even though we both knew some of the things that would have ticked the other off, if seeing each other on a regular basis was a possibility. She was even supportive in my decision to transfer, which was unexpected. Her theory was as long as I was in school everything else would work itself out. Being that I did have an extra two weeks with nothing to do, I thought my best move would be to get back up to WMU and pick up the rest of my things, and maybe tell everyone that I was leaving, so I guess a road trip was in order.

After an exhausting two and a half hour drive, I couldn't imagine anything more important than my bed for a quick nap. The skills that I had acquired earlier in the school year of sneaking in and out of the building would've came in handy if I had the opportunity to use them, but as soon as I pulled into the parking lot I was immediately noticed by Phil who was pulling in from work. I made it to my room but that was about as long as I had to be alone on this trip. By the time my head touched my pillow the door was already opening. Thinking to myself I could've sworn I locked that damn door.

"So you were planning on just sneaking in today and not telling anyone you were here?"

Damn Cuz can I get in the door good before you start acting an ass? I was coming down to yo room after I took a nap.

"I'm saying, Phil said he saw you trying to sneak in the building and shit."

Ya'll worse than women, I'll be down there in a little while just let me lay down for a minute or two.

"Yeah what'eva dude, you might as well get some rest now cause we partying from now until it's time for yo ass to go back home. Matter a fact it's a party tonight."

Cool Cuz now can I get some rest, just give me about thirty minutes and I'll be up and bout my businezz.

After not really getting any sleep I ended up in Mal's room with everyone else talking about how everyone's Christmas vacation went and what kind of trouble they got into over the break. Some news was new to me, and at the same time most of the stories I had already received, the Cuz version. It was cool though, most of the guys I hadn't seen for a good month or two anyway so I was just enjoying the company. After about two hours of drinking and talking shit we decided it was around time to get ready for the party. Before heading for my room I decided to stop by Rita's room and see what she was up to. Unfortunately I hadn't seen her since the night she dropped me off at my house, and besides after our two quick conversations on the phone, we barely spoke over the break because I was constantly with Maria. The conclusion was that I would stop by for a second or two, and slide in the fact that I was leaving school, and make sure that we were still cool. As I quietly knocked, she opened the door quicker than I expected. As I took a startled step back, the door swung open and I could immediately see her bright smile and beautiful bronze skin. It felt good to see her, and from the expression upon her face the feeling was mutual. Inviting me in quickly by grabbing my arm and pulling me in, then sitting me down on the couch her smile quickly went away. Instead of the pleasant conversation that I was expecting from her greeting, she began with a playful onslaught of verbal jabs.

"You had me take you home, and then I don't see you the entire break and on top of that I barely spoke to you. What's that about?"

This was the beginning of what ended up being the next half hour of playful verbal sparring between us, in other words we said some things playfully that we actually truly meant but wouldn't dare seriously say to each other. She really just wanted to get the point across that she missed me, and wanted to let me know just how much. After about another hour of sitting and catching up it was time for me to get ready for the party, I really couldn't wait. Especially seeing that most of these people I haven't seen even longer than the fellas. It took me about twenty minutes to get ready, by that time everyone had their drinks and had done everything else they needed to do to get ready for the party. We made it there by midnight, which was usually around the time that we arrived to every party. Probably because we had the notion that the party didn't start until we hit the door anyway. As soon as you hit the party the music was so loud you couldn't hear yourself think. The song was a hit with a base line so hard you couldn't keep the chicks off the dance floor, sexy chicks all over the place, were dancing, shaking everything that mama gave them. It wasn't long before we were all behind some chicks taking in the beautiful views. I took my time and leaned back enjoying my last party as a WMU student, and the fellas did everything in their power to make sure I did too, by sending every available chick in the club my way. That was until they spotted Rita enter the building, with her eyes fixated on my every move, it was almost a surprise that she showed up. When I had last left her presence she had made it clear it wasn't for her tonight. Even still she looked great! Her long hair flowing down her back, and accentuating the sexy black form fitting dress that she was wearing or was it wearing her? As she swayed back and forth gliding across the floor, commanding the attention of both male and female parties, within no time at all she stood before me with the sexiest smile that I had seen all night. She slid her hand around my waist, and whispered in my ear.

"So is this dance for me?"

It seemed as if the music went quiet for just a second and then drowned everything else out soon after she finished talking. The soft ballad of Luther Vandross singing "If this world were Mine" slowly caressing her shoulder, and then allowing my hand to slide down to the small of her back, I pulled her close as I explained that I was happy she made it. She replied that it looked like I was having fun without her. With my usual devilish grin working overtime I responded, "Not as much as I am having now." As Luther sang I put the two-step that I learned as a kid standing on my mother's feet to good use. This may have been her first dance of the night, but it immediately turned into her last, as the DJ stepped the tempo up a notch with R.Kelly reminding us of his damn Jeep! Rita took this opportunity, to violate my ear lobes gently caressing them one at a time with the tip of her tongue. In between licks expressing her desire to escape this party and escort me to her private party. Honestly after the slow grinding, and the job she did on my lobes, I couldn't imagine anything more pleasing. As we exited the party I made eye contact with the fellas, which easily explained my plans for the night. As she led me through the crowd, I gave the I don't know shoulder shrug and the innocent smile as if I didn't have a clue what was about to occur. Seeing that this was another campus party it took us no time at all to reach the elevator of the dorms, and before we knew it we were fiddling with her keys attempting to get her door open as quickly as possible. It probably would've been a lot easier if I would've just let her turn around and put the key in, but that was too much like right. I had to see how talented she was so keeping her pinned up against the door and allowing her to try to open the door by touch was the plan. Finally we stumbled through the door way without breaking our lip lock that had intensified to the point that we were tugging and pulling at each others clothes as if they had to come off for us to live. By the time we made it into her bedroom we were both standing with nothing more on but the suits we were born in. With her standing and me sitting at the edge of the bed I proceeded to slide my hand from her calf up to her inner thigh just to see the expression on her face change. She bent her knees and knelt down in front of me resting her arms on my thighs, and then dropped her head in my lap and began having a deep conversation with her new best friend. This made me feel like I had never felt before, compared to the rookie technique that I received from Maria (maybe she wasn't practicing on someone else, and just wanted to try it on me. Oh well!) She was a bonified veteran at pleasing the member of my body that had complete control at this point. Without slowing down or wavering from her path she continued with her pleasure path until I lost the ability of speech, as well as four of my five senses. I was down to just the sense of touch, because I couldn't hear too much of anything except for the sounds of her lovely mouth at work and since my eyes were closed, sight wasn't being used either. As far as my sense of smell went, I was still hooked on the pear scent that I had rubbed on her months ago, and I had came to the conclusion that since her sense of taste was working over time, mine could be put on the back burner. Before I knew what hit me I felt a twitch in my lower region, and I knew what that was about immediately. I tried to warn her but that was one of the senses that had taken the night off, and by that time it was way too late. I thought for sure that this was going to put an end to this escapade, but the truth was she didn't plan to remove her mouth until she received ever drop of me. She finally removed her head from my lap with a sensual look on her face, and my vision blurred. She explained that she would have to regain his attention because she wasn't done with him yet. Her words alone were enough for me to rebound, and get back in the game, I regained my wits and grabbed her hands pulling her closer to me and exchanging places with each other I slide my finger tips across her pleasure just to check if she was ready for the next part of our adventure. I then pushed her back on the bed, and lowered my body between her towering legs, and placed myself in the perfect position to enter her palace. As I entered I felt nothing, except the moisture that was her, and the only thing I heard were the moans that she allowed to escape her mouth. While I planted myself deep inside her garden I took the time to move her left leg above my shoulder, so that she could feel me in my entirety. After slowly grinding our bodies together for a while, our pace began to increase. To the point that I had to lift my torso up into push-up position to complete each stroke, as her moans quickened and her excitement grew, I took the opportunity to look deep into her eyes, wondering what she could possibly be thinking. With each thrust I buried myself deeper inside her body and would notice a passionate grimace appear on her face each time, so I inquisitively asked if she was okay. Her response introduced me to another sexual plateau, she whispered "Damn baby you're so BIG!" Now I can't speak for every man in the world but this was such a turn on for me, especially since I was just getting over being the BEST, once again even if it wasn't completely true in the right place, and at the right time it sounded great. So for the next couple of hours we experimented with as many possible ways that she could feel just how big I was. It wasn't long before we were both sweaty, then tired, and then passed out from our sexual bonanza. The next three days flew by, and before I knew it I was back on the road heading for the D.

WINTER SEMESTER: Introduction to Trouble

Here I am finally, schools in and I'm ready for action as I strolled campus attempting to find my classes. Giving a half ass smile or nod to each person that I pass by, I'm partly happy to be here and partly a little nervous because of the change. It's all new to me. Never been done to this magnitude before. I'm the new kid, that doesn't know anyone, nor do I know my way around this place. From elementary school all the way up to my first semester in college I was always comfortable with my surroundings because I already knew people when I got to a school mostly because of Cuz, and because most of my friends had attended the same school as me since I was a young child. For the first couple of weeks I pretty much stayed to myself not really talking to anyone. I was straight to class and straight to the car. This way I believed that I would stay out of trouble and not be caught up with a new chick, after all I was in a relationship. This worked for a while, but me being good must come to an end or at least that's how I thought the saying went. I had just about made it out of the month of February when it happened, I arrived to school for my eleven o'clock class right on time just to find out that it had been cancelled due to my professor's family emergency so I was stuck with nothing to due for the next hour. The suggestion I made to myself was to hang out for a little while in the student center and maybe meet a couple new people. When I entered the building, most of the people were sitting around playing cards and just chatting about different topics. I spotted MB in the middle of the room with a group of people surrounding him, most of the chicks were hanging off his every word. The guys in the area were mostly basketball players so I guess most of the chicks could've been considered groupies. Walking over to that area of the room I was immediately greeted and introduced as one of the new players on the team. A couple of eyes turned and gave me a quick look to see what I had to offer. I got one or two smiles from the chicks, but the dudes weren't too impressed. This didn't bother me in the least. I was used to it by now. Most guys aren't friendly right off, especially if you're the new recruit on the team. I was more of a threat than a teammate basically, because I would be challenging one of these guys for their spots next season. After sitting for about ten minutes most of the guys got up and headed out for class. The girls stayed for a little while longer, and held a conversation with me for a while. Most of the questions pertained to my ability, or inability to play basketball. On the court I'm one of the most arrogant and confident people in the world, off the court I was usually more humble so my response was simple "I'm okay, not too good, not too bad." That's when she walked in and sat right next to me. She was a friend of someone at the table and was very quick witted not to mention sexy as hell, she wasn't my usual type. Especially because her first impression was kind of boyish, her hair was covered by a baseball cap and she was rocking some jeans and a pair of Jordan gym shoes, which I had been over since the end of my senior year. I was with out a doubt becoming a stiletto heel man, whether they be boots or shoes if they were cute and made her stand taller on a heel that was barely there I was impressed. She had none of that going for her, but she still had a certain something that kept my attention. Not to mention the smart mouth that had me hanging on her every word. By the time she was done talking I was so intrigued I had to know who she was but refused to let her know I was interested. So she now had my attention whether she knew it or not was another story, not to mention the fact that she might not care if she has my attention or not. Hopefully that question would be answered sometime soon, but until then I did my part and find out who she was.

Hey, how are you doing? My names Chris just thought I'd introduce myself before I get cussed out for sitting at your table.

"Oh I'm sorry, I didn't mean to go off the deep end, but I didn't notice that we had company today. Let me guess you're one of the new basketball players huh?"

Wow, you're good, how'd you know?

"Well it wasn't that hard these two are basketball groupies, and if you weren't a player you probably wouldn't be sitting over here."

Is that right? So if they're groupies what does that make you?

"That makes me the friend of some basketball groupies, nothing more nothing less."

What about the old saying birds of a feather flock together?

"Doesn't apply in this situation, I could care less if a guy plays some dumb ass sport or not. If I'm interested then I am, and if I am interested he'll know immediately."

Well that's good to know, thanks for the information, hopefully I'll get to put it to good use one day.

"Maybe you will, sooner than you think!"

Also good to hear, but I have a class to get to right now hopefully I'll see you soon. I'd love to get to know you better.

"There's no time like the present, how long is your class? I'll be down here for about an hour or two. You should make your way back down this way and maybe we can talk then."

Sounds good!

With that I made my way to class and sat there for half the time thinking about the trouble that I would sooner or later be very deep into if I wasn't careful. After reviving from my daydream I took the time to answer the question that had most of the class stomped for the time that I was under hypnosis. I thought that this simple gesture would make the fact that I was just in a daze a mere formality, which was correct I received high praise for my correct answer, but at the same time I was put in my place because Dr. Peace added to the praise that if I paid attention throughout his entire lecture I might have been able to answer the last five or six questions that he had asked. The smirk of confidence that I had on my face was instantly wiped away and replaced by a look of disbelief, I had usually been able to just get by with doing just enough to show that I had some intellect. By the time the shock was over so was class. I quickly gathered my things and headed back to the student center for my mid-day rendezvous. At that exact moment

I realized that I didn't even know her name. I had sat and talked for about twenty minutes or so without so much as a hint as to what to call my new friend.

Once I finally made it over to the student center I found that she had already left. I was talking to MB and he shared the news with me that a couple of the other guys had been sitting around with him again. They barely said a word but when they did speak, the snide remarks and looks of disbelief had me wondering what was going on. MB explained that I shouldn't worry about them, they just couldn't believe that after all their efforts in trying to bag Shay that they never got any further than hello before being cut into little piece by her quick tongue, and in one meeting I had her investigating as to who I was, and any other information she could find out. So again I found that I wouldn't be one of the more liked guys around campus or at least not by the guys at first. Walking away from the crowd I thought to myself "Hmmm, Shay, so that's her name kinda cute. I wonder where she ran off to?" My thoughts were broken by the beauty of another, it was the sophisticated chick from my first visit to the school and she was looking even better this time. I thought about going over and just introducing myself, but at the same time I decided against it. There was no reason to be greedy, I didn't want every chick at the school, just one maybe two. So I decided to pace myself, sooner or later I would get around to getting to know her better as well or at least I hoped so.

A couple days passed without me hearing so much as a word from Shay. That was until she caught me heading out the door of the student center on my way to my car.

"So is it Chris or Christopher?"

"My name is Christopher, but everyone calls me Chris. I see you've been doing your homework Shay."

"Mmmm hmmm and I see that you've been doing yours as well Mr. Alexander. So why haven't I heard nor seen you in the past couple of days? And don't say it's from a lack of looking either."

"Wow, sexy and you read minds too. What more could a guy ask for? Tell me what I'm thinking right now."

"I don't do x-rated thoughts before the first date. Sorry!"

Extraordinary, you do have psychic abilities! By the way, I like your hair (which she now had braided they were called zillions if I wasn't mistaken.)

"Thanks, glad you like it. So what are your plans for today?"

To be totally honest I don't really have any, just chill'n, what about you?

"My plans include going home and getting in the bed."

Just then I made another observation that caught me off guard just a bit. There was a shade of silver in her mouth and it wasn't on her teeth, no braces of any sort, but I still saw a hint of silver. Hmmm, is it, could it be a tongue ring in my mist? I would've loved to ask her to show me what was in her mouth, but feared that she may have gotten upset. So I politely let it pass, and ignored the fact that the silver tongue ring was sparkling directly in my eyes. I attempted to enjoy the rest of our conversation without bringing up my almost obvious obsession with her mouth. Listening to her every word smiling when appropriate, laughing when necessary, finally it was too much for me to hide. I took what I thought was a quick glance, but turned out to be more of an elongated stare into her mouth. Noticing how her tongue rolled across her ring every time she pronounced any word with the letter R in it, this was a turn-on in itself. My stare was interrupted by her clearing her throat and then saying "Yes, it's a tongue ring! Any other questions?" I couldn't help but laugh, and then I quickly apologized for staring. Then explained that this was my first time noticing that she had one, and it was my first time seeing one in person. The next couple of statements were not expected, but great to hear and opened a whole other conversation that I would enjoy more than anything we had discussed earlier in our meeting.

"No just because I have a tongue ring doesn't mean that I will be sucking your dick. (I was thinking to myself that's not what Chris Rock said) Nor does it mean that I am some kinda freak or anything of the sort. Even though I am it's not because I have a ring in my tongue."

Sweetie slow down I never said any of those things, even though the last bit of information is great to hear.

"Is it really, who's to say you'll ever get a chance to see that side of me?"

Once again you're jumping to conclusions, who said that I wanted to see that side of you? All that I said was it was great to hear.

"What'eva nigga you'd love to see how freaky I can get."

Well I tell you this much I wouldn't mind finding out one day, but I can wait. It's no rush, I have plenty of time to see just how freaky you can get if it comes to that.

"Well I'll have to make sure it comes to that, then won't I?"

Be careful, you're walking on thin ice, I may just take you up on your offer and then show you just how wild I can be.

"Mmmm, I think I might like that! Maybe we can work something out, what are you doing tonight maybe we can watch a movie or something."

Sounds like fun, I don't have any plans as of right now. So around what time would you like me to be there, or are you coming to me.

"Depends on if you make me cum or not! Just kidding you can come by my house around nine, nine thirty which ever is good for you Mr."

Well then it seems as if it's settled I'll give you a call a little later for directions, and I'll see you tonight.

"Yes you will, bye for now."

On my way to the car I couldn't help but think of the trouble I was setting myself up for. I knew exactly what kind of movie watching we were going to be doing. The kind where I'd only see the beginning or the end of the movie because the rest of my time would be spent being entertained by her, and hopefully her tongue ring. By the time I made it home it was already around six thirty, which meant it was only five thirty in Tennessee, and that meant Maria's next class wasn't for another hour or so. I couldn't think of a better time to call than now anyway, I probably wouldn't be home for her call later. So I might as well talk to her now before it's too late. The phone only rang twice before she picked up sounding excited to hear my voice so early in the day. She started the conversation off with "What are you doing calling me so early in the day?" which I quickly responded with "I missed you all day so I thought I would give you a call early. Plus, I wanted to let you know that I would probably be getting home late tonight so I would make sure to call you tonight when I get home from hanging out with the team." We talked for about fifteen minutes, covering all the newest events of our lives and then expressing our love for one another. Our relationship was becoming more of a routine than anything else, the truth was, I didn't know what she was doing at school, except for what she told me, and she had no clue what my days and even worse my nights consisted of here on the home front. I'm sure if she did, this relationship would've been over with by now. I did love her, but this was a long distance relationship, and I did have trust issues. After our enjoyable conversation I got off the phone feeling bad for a second, that was until I comforted myself with the fact she was probably doing the same thing or worse. After all we were in our college years, the time when you're supposed to be wild and crazy. I decided to lay down and wait until later to make my call for directions, I wasn't sure what was in store it would be better for me to be well rested than to get over there tired and ready to fall asleep.

I awoke around ten to nine got up and took a shower. By the time I threw my clothes on and grabbed a bite to eat it was nine thirty. I thought to myself, better call before she thinks she's been stood up. After exchanging pleasantries she informed me that she was about to call me, and see if I had made other plans. I laughed that one off, and told her there was nothing that I would rather do than to watch a movie with her tonight. To which she responded, I'm sure there are a couple of things she could name that I would rather be doing. Once again I laughed this time it was because there was some truth to her statement. From my house it took less than twenty minutes to arrive at hers. As I knocked on the side door you could hear the bark of a huge dog coming from the backyard. Now usually I'm a fan of dogs, but the mammoth creature that appeared behind the rickety gate of the backyard was no ordinary dog. It seemed more like the great two headed fire breathing beast that guarded the gates of hell in Greek mythology. So I had a rush on getting in the house. Once I entered the house she hit me with the same line that every dog owner hits a visitor with, don't worry about Cujoe, he doesn't bite. We headed straight for the basement, which had been finished and turned into an entertainment, slash guestroom. It had all the essentials of both a huge screen television equipped the latest satellite, a full sized bar, and a sectional that folded out into a bed. Not to mention a full-sized bathroom so you wouldn't have to venture upstairs to take care of the Three S's. She sat me down on the couch and asked what movie I would like to watch. I told her it really didn't matter, just happy I had the opportunity to enjoy her company.

With a smile on her face she told me that I was already in the house, so no need to keep trying to run game. I chuckled, and then asked her what my options were. She pulled me off the couch and towards the entertainment center where she had at least two hundred DVDs. I saw a couple of my favorites and then asked her what she was in the mood for comedy or something serious. She responded that I wasn't ready for what she was in the mood for, which left it open for me to take it however I saw fit. So not to be mistaken I made sure that we were still talking movies, the only answer she gave was I could be, or maybe not.

"So what are you ready for?"

"I got a movie we can watch, but I don't know if you ready for this yet, so we can watch a movie of your choice first and then if you still want to watch my movie then I'll put it on. Does that sound good to you?"

"That sounds good. So I'm up first huh, well if that's the case I haven't seen the Devil's Advocate in a while." (Didn't want to seem to anxious to jump to her movie)

"Cool I love Al Pacino, and that's one of my favorite movies."

"Really you're like the first person, especially female that I have ever heard say that, most people didn't care for it because they thought it was too slow. Plus if they watched it, it would be like worshiping the Devil."

"I love the story line, and the fact that it shows the endless possibilities, and the way the devil holds power over human weaknesses."

She put the movie on and then came back and sat next to me on the couch, quickly snuggling up next to me. The warmth of her body next to me was so enticing it took everything in my power not to just lay her down and kiss her entire body. I'm sure she could tell I was fighting with myself to stay off her, because every time she'd look up I would be looking at her, and then quickly turn my attention back to the movie. After about two or three of these incidents she excused herself and traveled upstairs for about ten minutes. When she returned she had on next to nothing, the shorts that were covering her almost perfect ass had turned into a pair of boy shorts that left the bottom of her cheeks exposed. This was arguably the sexiest sight that I had seen thus far (notice how each time it's someone new, they over take the last person as the sexiest person that I have seen thus far.) She sashayed over to the couch, and stopped directly in front my view of the television. She bent over and asked if it was too early to watch her movie choice. I had an idea of what kind of movie she planned on watching, but wasn't completely sure. Even still, I didn't have any complaints, I had seen the Devils Advocate many times before, and I really would like to know what she likes to watch in her spare time. So I agreed that it was time for her movie. This brought a smile to her face. As she walked over to the DVD player and threw her movie in, she rejoined me on the couch this time. She was actually on top of me.

It's going to be kinda hard for you to see the movie in this position, don't you think?

"Truthfully I've seen it many times already, as a matter of fact, I was watching it right before you got here. I really just want to see how you'd react to it."

As soon as the movie started my thoughts were confirmed, it was a porn production. Which normally wouldn't have gotten too much of a response from me, but at this moment I had a beautiful woman in my lap with heat, and moisture seeping from beneath her cotton panties. I watched the first scene, it was one of those cheesy ones with the plot, where the mailman comes to deliver the mail and gets to drop off more than the mail. The lady came to the door in a bra and some panties, and it all started from there. She dropped to her knees and went to work. As I paid attention to the movie, Shay started to imitate the screen play, she slowly slid off my lap and onto her toes squatting down instead of getting on her knees and whispered in a seductive tone " I bet I'm better than she is!" the only thing I could say was "Is that so?" She lowered her head and commenced to showing off her talents, and though I had never been with the chick on the screen if Shay wasn't better with her talent, then I hope I never meet that lady. She worked on me for the complete first scene. Then asked me if I thought I could handle her. For the first time in a long time I wasn't sure, but it didn't stop me from saying that I could handle anything she dished out. By this time I'm at full attention waiting on the next move to be made. As she fondled herself looking directly into my eyes, she took her middle finger and slid it onto her lips, and then into her mouth closing her eyes as if the taste was just that unbelievable. I couldn't help but be turned on by that, not only that, but just her period. I grabbed her hand and pulled her close, and pressed my lips against hers thrusting my tongue into her mouth as if to get the left over residue from her finger. As the intensity of the kiss grew, I laid her back on the couch, and searched for the taste that had her eyes closed and had the look of ecstasy on her face. She threw her head back and let out a soft moan as my tongue probed the lips I had never seen before, she allowed her hands to probe the curves of my head. As I sucked and licked, I could feel the pulsation of her clit. It didn't take long before she couldn't handle the pleasure anymore, and she wanted to feel the pleasure of the rest of me. I lifted my glistening face up to hers and with no hesitation she quickly licked from my chin to my lips, at the same time she took a gentle bite of my bottom lip. That was it, there would be no more playing. She was about to receive everything I had to offer this night every inch of my seriousness. I lowered myself between her waiting thighs as she lifted herself up to meet her knew best friend. As I entered her territory she let out a light scream followed by a low toned moan. From then on every stroke was slow and accurately placed to get her to reach her full excitement. On every deep entry I would receive a deep tissue massage on my back with nothing more than her nails, which didn't bother me in the least. Honestly I liked it, but I didn't need any marks left that may or may not show up on Maria's next visit home. So I stopped that part of our encounter by flipping her over and turning her around, putting her in perfect position to get deep into our escapade. With her ass in the air and her face buried in the pillows of the couch, I began my assault. From the time I entered her walls it was a non-stop moan fest. She couldn't stop calling for people that probably wouldn't be too happy about this situation (Oh god, damn daddy, oh baby). I kept this position going until her body collapsed, and the position was no longer perfect. I wanted to ensure the fact that I would be invited back, and the only way to do so from my understanding, was to either make it one of the best experiences she's ever had or, wear her out to the point were she feels she has something to prove. So instead of being satisfied with her just getting one off, I turned her over and placed her feet on my chest and commenced to giving her all that she could handle. I kept this up until her words turned into syllables, unable to get complete words out, let alone sentences. She took it until her body went limp from exhaustion. I finally thought that she was satisfied, so I excused myself and went to the bathroom while she lay motionless on the couch. As I took a long look at the reflection, I noticed the sweat that I had worked up tumbling down my face from my brow, giving a nonchalant smirk as if to pat myself on the back, and say good job. I returned to my partner who was still resting in the same position that she was left in. I gently stroked her hair and whispered in her ear, I think it's time for me to go. Should I let myself out? She awoke herself from her slumber, and replied, "I'll walk you out." Once she rose the smirk that I thought I had left in the bathroom returned, because her legs wobbled every step of the way to the door. On my way home I couldn't help but think of Maria, and how she would feel if she ever found out about my exploits. I couldn't help the way I was, better yet I didn't want to help it, and I didn't want to change. It seems as if women have a sixth sense, because every time I was about to do something wrong, or as soon as I was done, I would get some kind of sign that my woman at the time was thinking about me or what I was doing. Once I made it home, my theory was more than evident, because I had three voicemails two from Maria, and the third from Rita. The two from Maria had me feeling a little bad about the situation, she sounded so innocent and genuine as if she couldn't possible be doing anything close to what I was doing. However the one from Rita was straight sexual, basically telling me how much she missed me, and how her body ached to feel me inside of her. Kind of amusing, considering that I probably wouldn't be seeing her anytime soon or maybe not ever again.

For the next couple of weeks I spent any free time I had with Shay exploring any and every place, and position possible. We got so wild at one point we found ourselves in the locker room of the gym about twenty minutes before practice was going to start. If we took ten minutes longer we would've had an audience of about ten ball players and three coaches. As sexually gratifying as our arrangement was, it still wasn't enough to stop me from seeking attention from other places, which is where Mizz. Sophistication came into play. I ran into her in the student center's McDonalds line getting ready to order her lunch. I quickly walked in front of her and began to order my meal, and before I knew it her five foot two inch frame was standing next to me explaining that if she wasn't mistaken she was next in line. To which I quickly apologized, and explained that I didn't notice her standing there. I continued my apology by offering to pay for her lunch in order to excuse my rudeness. She politely declined my offer, and said it wasn't necessary the mistake wasn't that big. As we awaited our orders I attempted to keep the conversation going almost to no avail. My guess was, she wasn't having one of her better days. You wouldn't have guessed by the way she looked. As exquisite as I had seen her to this point, in a black business skirt that came just below her knees, with a split in the back that made it up to her mid thigh. Topped off by a black shirt with pin stripes and a black blazer that matched the skirt perfectly. Her short hair curled perfectly in a Halle Berry type cut. I politely asked if she would join me for lunch to which she replied "I'm sorry, but I don't make it a habit of eating lunch with people I just met. I may have made an exception for you, but I have to get back to work, my break is almost over. If this is an open invitation then I will be happy to catch up with you tomorrow. My lunch break starts at eleven so I'll see you then."

If that's the case, I'll happily see you tomorrow.

"Then it's a date, and I'll be looking forward to seeing you then."

That sounds good (I said with a laid back demeanor) by the way, what should I call you?

"My friends usually call me Joi, but since we aren't officially friends it will be Mizz Joi if you don't mind. And you, sir, what should I refer to you as?"

Well everyone calls me Chris, but since we are still unofficial with our friendship you may address me as Mr. Alexander. I hope you enjoy the rest of your day and I'll see you tomorrow.

With everything set up for lunch, I enjoyed the view of her walking away, her miniature body was fully curved and more than enjoyable to watch even if she was walking away from me. Lucky for me she was unavailable for lunch today, because no sooner than I sat down Shay walked in with a look on her face that was hard to explain, it was a mix between being filled with lust, and being distraught. Before she could have a seat I asked what was wrong. In the short time that we had been enjoying each other's company, we had become more than blunt about how we were feeling at any given time. So the next statement out of her mouth didn't surprise me in the least, matter of fact it did more to excite me than the dry ass burger I was attempting to scarf down.

"I woke up horny as hell this morning, and I couldn't find my toy. Then I had to sit through my boring as history class thinking about sex, and after that it took me entirely too long to find you. The point is, I have forty five minutes before my next class is going to start and I want some DICK!"

Well to be honest, I would be happy to help you with any problem you might have, and this problem sounds like its right up my alley. Plus I'm sure you taste better than this dry ass burger I'm eating.

I removed myself from the chair that I was glued to, and began to follow her out towards the parking garage. On the way I tried to explain that we wouldn't make it to either of our houses in enough time to actually enjoy a sexual experience. Her response was quick and to the point, "Who said we were going anywhere?" As we entered the garage she grabbed my hand and led the way to an all black Expedition with tinted windows, as she opened the back door on the passenger side and climbed in I noticed that the back seats were folded down as if she was planning on moving some furniture or something. I stepped in and before I knew it, she had already had her coat off as well as her pants, I didn't have a choice but to follow suit. Before I could get my jogging pants completely, off she had already pushed me down and mounted me as if I was the new ride at her own personal amusement park. She lowered herself on my member hard and then gave an aggressive circular grind. At the same time she pressed her hands against the ceiling of the truck as if to receive some extra leverage. It must have worked to her advantage because I was deeper than I had been before, and it was better than it had ever been before. I wasn't sure if it was the fact that at any minute someone could walk to their car and hear us, or see the movement of the car. Or was it the fact that she had taken the situation in her own hands, in order to get the orgasm that she wanted so very badly. As she continued to press against the ceiling I could feel her walls tightening around my shaft, and with her clit rubbing against my hairs it wouldn't be long before she would be letting herself go. Her grinding slowed immensely, it was almost down to a stop. That's when I figured it was my time to take over. I reached up and grabbed her hands and pulled them down to her side. Holding her arms by her wrist and trapping them between my hands and her wrists, I then planted my feet firmly on the floor of the truck raising my waist, and thighs in the air. All the while pulling her to me, and thrusting upward at the same time. Her moans became more and more intense, as her eyes rolled back as if she was attempting to see what was on her mind. I couldn't help but unleash a devilish smirk, knowing that I was close to solving one of her problems for the day. She begged me to stop, which made me thrust harder. She couldn't have possible thought her next statement was going to get me to stop, especially because she couldn't help but moan it out instead of speaking in a regular tone. "Dammmnnnn babbbeee, I'MMMM ABBBBOOOUUUTT TOOOOO CUUUMMMMMMMM!" I continued an accurate assault on her body, until I could feel streams of her river running down from my head to my shaft, and ending its journey on my sack. When her eyes finally returned to their original place, the only look that was left was that of pure satisfaction, which turned me on even more. Our session was over, I let her know that if we continued she wouldn't be going to class, which I could tell wouldn't have been a problem for her at this point, but I had other things to do today. As we exited the car she again had a slight stagger in her walk as if her legs were weak, once again a smirk came across my face. Since my car was two levels up and she was heading for class, we separated and said our good-byes. As soon as the cold air hit my face I knew it was time to pick up my usually slow paced walk. Before, I could make it in the car good, it happened again my cell rang with a (615) area code. It was Maria again, it was as if she knew what I was doing every time I did something wrong and she would call me just to keep me thinking.

Hello, hey Boo what's up?

"Hello, what are you doing answering your phone? Aren't you supposed to be in class? It sounds like you're in your car, where are you going? Did you go to class today or did you miss it?"

I had to interject: Boo slow down I can only answer one question at a time. First I answered because I'm not in class right now, and no I'm not supposed to be in class it's over already. Yes, I am in my car on my way home, and of course I went to class. Boo, if you thought I was in class what are you doing calling me?

"Well I was just calling to leave a message on your voice mail, but you answered. I was just going to tell you that I miss you, and I can't wait until I come home."

I miss you too Boo, and I can't wait to see you either.

We talked for about ten minutes maybe a little longer, but by the time I pulled up in my driveway. I had already been off the phone for a while. Our conversations did nothing more than increase my thoughts about the obvious, she keeps calling right after I do something, this worried me for a while, but it didn't stop anything at all.

The very next day, I was right back sharing my time with any beautiful woman who wanted my attention. Which according to yesterday's events would be Joi, and I couldn't wait for lunch to get here. As I approached the table that we were to share for our lunch date, she was sitting there looking like she was straight out of a movie. She was almost perfect, from her hair, to her nails, even to the dressed down T-shirt and jean day that she was having. After a quick greeting, that included a beautiful smile, she jumped right into the question portion of our date.

"So what year are you in, and what's your major?"

"Well, this is my freshman year in school and I haven't picked a major just yet. I'm not sure what I want to do with the rest of my life. How about you though?"

"This is my second year and I'm majoring in business administration, I plan on owning my own club once I graduate, and in my spare time, I do a little modeling."

"Wow, is that right? I'm having lunch with a business minded model. How lucky am I? I hope your man doesn't mind us having lunch, I wouldn't want anyone looking for me."

"And what makes you think that I have a man? Even better, what makes you think that I would be here with you if I had a man!"

"My fault, you have a good point! You probably wouldn't be the type to have lunch with someone else if you had a man, but the truth is you are a very attractive young lady, and I have found that when someone looks like you in the "D" they have one of about three things."

"Is that right, and what might those three things be?"

"Well the first is either they have a man which could also include a husband. If that's not the case second would be a CUT BUDDY, and last but not least would be one of these silly ass nigga's who thinks that she is his woman even when she has made it quite apparent that they are just friends."

"Okay, so either a man slash husband for number one, then what did you call number two?"

"CUT BUDDY! You know someone that you just have a sexual relationship with."

"Okay, cut buddy is a sexual partner, then you have number three and that's the silly guy who doesn't know he's just a friend. (The whole time she's speaking she can't help but laugh and giggle.)

"Well am I way off with my conclusion, or do you think there is some truth to it? Oh my fault, some of you are so talented that you have all three at the same time." (Her laughter increased)

"Well if you didn't add the third one in I could've happily told you that you were absolutely wrong, but with that one added I might be in trouble. I try to explain it to him, but he just doesn't get it."

"What did you do to him? You had to do something to him for him to get that way."

"We're not going to go there, but I do have a question. Does that same theory work for men as well? Better yet, let me jump to a conclusion; I hope your woman doesn't mind you having lunch with a business minded model."

"Well I'm sure she wouldn't be comfortable with the idea of me being here right now, but she doesn't know."

"So you do have a woman?"

"Yeah I do, we're in a long distance relationship. She goes to school down south." (I'm not in a habit of lying to women I'm not with, they have the option of either dealing with me knowing that I have a woman, or leaving me alone then and there. Just wanna make sure they know what they are getting themselves into.)

"So what are you looking for from me? Just a friendship, or you think I'm gonna be yo chick on the side? (Now the once sophisticated tone and monologue that she held is slowly but surely slipping away, and you can hear the Detroit chick coming back out that she tried so hard to hide.)"

"Well honestly if ever given the opportunity to see you naked I definitely am not a fool so I would jump at that chance, (by this time in my life I've noticed that I get away with saying certain things that most dudes can't get away with. Things that would usually get a guy cursed out, would get me a giggle and a boy you crazy) but if that's not something you're comfortable with I can always use a new friend to hang out and kick it with."

"Is that right? Well lucky for you I never say never, so who knows where this will lead. I appreciate your honesty, and the fact that you let me make up my mind on whether I was going to continue to talk to you or not.

That statement in itself was enough for me to know that I at the very least would have a new friend and at least one attempt to see that new friend naked. We sat and talked for a couple more minutes before it was time for her to get back to her job on campus, so instead of letting her walk alone I threw my jacket on and took the stroll with her. We walked and talked the entire way. Usually I would have picked up the pace because of the cold air, but I actually walked slower than I usually walk (which everyone who knows me, knows it may very well be the slowest pace on earth), just so I got the full opportunity to enjoy her company. We finally made it to her building, and as I enjoyed watching her walk into the building, I made up in my mind that this would be a friend if nothing more. I can see myself enjoying spending time with her just hanging out. I found myself so deep in thought that I forgot to make sure we exchanged numbers to keep in touch. Luckily this wasn't the last time I would be seeing my new friend.

So far this semester is fantastic. I have my woman and she seems happy we haven't run into any real problems and so far it doesn't seem like she knows about any of my extra curricular activities. Which included an oversexed chick (Shay) who already knew and understood her place, and was happy with it or maybe it was the other way around. Now add in the fact that I had a new friend that I actually enjoyed spending time with, and wouldn't mind laying down. Plus, I still had Rita calling from time to time wondering when I was coming up to visit her at school. I was feeling pretty damn good about myself, and I probably should have stopped there, but that would be too much like right and I'm the furthest thing from right on the planet. My friendship with Joi lasted about two full weeks before it turned into more. She needed a ride home from school, because her car was in the shop luckily for both of us, she got off around the same time that I got out of basketball practice. Instead of being rude and making her wait until I got out of the shower I just went to the locker room and grabbed my clothes so that I could get her home. My plan was to take a shower once I got home, but now that I look back on it maybe it wasn't the plan in the back of my mind. I wasn't too sweaty and wasn't musty at all, after the light workout but I did have that sticky feeling that most people get on those hot summer nights when you don't have the air on. So as we pulled up at her house, I was prepared to watch her walk in the door and then go home and jump directly in the shower. My plan was altered when she insisted that I come in for a little while and chill, and my attempts to explain that I needed to take a shower were ignored. Then a compromise was finally made when she decided that if taking a shower was the only thing that was stopping us from spending time together then my shower would be taken there. It didn't take long for me to agree to the arrangement, but I insisted that she would have to stay away from the bathroom area if I agreed. At first she hit me with a smart comment "Boy, ain't nobody tryna see you naked!" then she got a little more honest with herself, and explained that she couldn't make any promises. As we both tried to laugh the situation off, I noticed that her eyes were fixated on my mid-section and unfortunately the only way that I was able to notice her eyes was because I raised mine up from her cleavage. This may not be one of my best ideas, especially if I want to continue being just friends. I sat in the bathroom pondering whether I should be there or not. Sitting there still fully dressed with the water running I received the answer to my question. There was a light tap on the door and then the knob began to turn. Was she really sneaking in here attempting to get a peek, or did she need something out of the only bathroom in the house? Maybe it was something that just couldn't wait until I was done with my shower considering the fact that I had already been in there for twenty minutes and hadn't even gotten my pants off. Maybe she did need something. I quickly snatched off my shirt and then grabbed the knob, and cracked the door hiding my lower half behind the door. The heat from the hot water in the shower already had me sweating so it looked as if I jumped out of the shower to answer the door.

What up? Did you need to get in here?

"No not at all, I was just checking on you because you had been in here so long."

Oh my fault, I lost track of time. I'm just about done, just need to rinse off and I'll be right out.

"You sure you don't need any help washing your back or anything?"

I thought we decided that you were going to stay out of this area until I was done.

"Actually that was a decision that you came up with. I didn't even agree to it, just listened to you talk."

Is that right? Well I'm just about done. I'll be out in a second or two.

"I'll be waiting."

I quickly stripped down the rest of my clothing and jumped in the now steaming hot shower, and enjoyed the heat that had been trapped for the last twenty five minutes. Standing with my arms and hands against the wall directly beneath the shower head I allowed the beads of hot water to beat against my head and back. With my eyes closed and my body adjusting to the intense heat from the water, I was barely able to hear the door open and her walk in. The only thing that made me open my eyes was the draft of cold air I felt from the door being open. Without opening my eyes I asked the question as if I knew she was there just looking. "So you just couldn't help yourself huh?" Her next move threw me for a loop. Instead of answering she just opened the curtain and allowed the towel that she had rapped around her body fall to the floor. It took a couple of seconds for me to fully focus, but once I did the sight was unbelievable. Everything was a perfect fit for her body type. From her perfectly formed breasts that were just the right size to sit up on her chest without a bra holding them. As I allowed my eyes to admire her body from top to bottom I noticed that she, hands down had the flattest, and most defined stomach I had ever seen on a woman. Attached to that stomach was one of the smallest waists I had seen, followed by beautiful hips and thighs. As she turned to close the curtain, I think it was more so for me to finish my admiration of her body, and that I did. Her ass wasn't big, but it was cuffed so perfectly that it gave the illusion that it was much bigger than it was. She stepped up closer to me blaming the fact that it was a bit chilly when not in the warmth of the water. I wanted to ask what she was doing in here, but it would've been one of the dumbest questions ever asked. She stepped into me, reached her hand out and softly touched from my chest to my stomach. Her hand didn't stop there she continued to my hairs, on down to my awakening member. "Be careful I have one simple rule that must be abided." Her grip tightens as her hand began to move back and forth and she looked up into my eyes and fixed her mouth to ask what that one rule was. I leaned down and whispered in her ear "If you wake him up, you gotta put him to sleep." Her grip tightened again, and with her free hand she grabs my wrist and pulls my hand between her thick thighs, and here I thought the water was wet. She soaked my already wet hands with her juices as my finger tips gently caressed her lips, and clit. With sounds of light moaning and the water beating off our bodies the mood was set, we were both ready for what came next. Exiting the shower I picked her up and placed her on the sink with her legs wrapped around the small of my back, and arms wrapped around my neck. Our lips locked together she then loosened her grip on my neck and reached for the gift between my legs, forcefully pressing me into her wetness and tossing her head back then releasing a deep moan of pleasure. Her movements began before I even had a chance to get my legs in position, first at an alarming rate, and then quickly slowed to a moderate grind. As I widened my stance and gained leverage, her moans became a common sound along with the hot water that was still running, which had the steam so thick it made it hard to breath. It didn't stop our interaction. Our lust had more than taken over and so had our primal selves. Quickly sliding my arms beneath each of her thighs I pulled her off the counter and kept her suspended in the air, and myself deep inside her. Allowing my arms and back to do most of the work lifting her up and down repeatedly, as she pulled herself closer to me she took it upon herself to turn a gentle kiss on my neck into a pit-bull like grip. The initial bite hurt like hell, but after a couple seconds the pain was replaced by what to this day I have no idea, but what I do know is I began to bury myself deeper, and deeper inside her. As I went deeper her grip loosened until once again I could hear her moans over everything else. This motion continued, as I walked her to the bathroom door and pinned her against it so that she could feel all of me. Before long my legs began to buckle knowing what was soon to follow. I quickly exited her pleasure, only to feel her sliding down the door onto the floor mouth ready for what ever I had to offer. After receiving her fill, we stumbled out of the beyond steamed up bathroom, and retreated into her bedroom where we started exactly where we left off. In the next couple of months I learned all sorts of new tricks, not only sexually but I also learned about women. What they like and dislike what they will and won't do. I took the time to learn as much as possible, I even learned how to juggle, women that is, because now not only did I have a woman, and a chick on the side, it turned into a couple chicks on the side. With all that I had learned, I still didn't have it all worked out. Even though that didn't stop me from thinking that I did. It was around this time that I could be found in the student center more and more. Most times I would just sit and play cards during the time I probably could've been studying. My juggling talent working overtime, I would see Joi during her lunch break and any other time would be spent with Shay just having fun giving sneaky sexual advances back and forth. Our friendship was evident, but no one knew to what extent we had taken it. I was always told that if you're going to do some dirt, do it by yourself, because nine times out of ten you won't tell on yourself. Plus I wasn't the bragging type, I didn't need to prove anything to anyone. Most guys that bragged too much either lied about what they were doing, or found themselves in a world of trouble when their stories somehow got back to their woman. Since I didn't need either complication, I kept my doings to myself, and if there was any lying involved it was more than likely me saying that I didn't touch someone that I was being accused of having sex with. Everything was going pretty well, it was going so smoothly, in fact, that I had gotten comfortable being in the same area with both of my CUT BUDDIES at the same time, that is, until someone's feeling once again got too strong.

SPRING SEMESTER: _The Beginning of the End_

It was a beautiful spring day, and I had spent just about the entire night with Shay. Meaning that I hadn't spoken to Joi all night, and I was missing in action according to Maria, seeing as that was the message that she left on my voice mail. First things first, I called and politely explained myself to Maria for she was the only one who I thought deserved an explanation and I didn't mind giving it to her even though it had little to no truth to it. I explained that I had fallen asleep while studying last night, and to an extent it wasn't a lie. Truth was I did fall asleep and in a sense I was studying the only part that was fictional was what I was studying. If I had an anatomy class then my entire statement would have been accurate. After taking care of Maria and also finding out that she would be home for the weekend, I got off the phone and headed for class. Afterwards I went on with my now usual events for the day, I met Joi for lunch. We laughed, talked and she expressed the fact that she missed talking to me last night to which I expressed the same, still offering no explanation. As we talked, I noticed Shay walking into the area. It didn't bother me too much at first, but noticing the look on her face, as she got closer I could see this was going to be a long day. Now seeing that it wasn't a known fact that either of the young ladies were spending time with me outside of school, our interactions were looked upon usually as harmless flirting so it was treated as such. Although there were your unproven rumors going around about me and Shay nothing had surfaced about Joi and me. That all changed after

119

Joi returned from throwing away her garbage and claimed a new seat on my lap laying a small kiss on my lips instead of my cheek like most of my female friends do. I guess Joi felt it necessary to test the rumors she had heard. Shay immediately lost her cool, and stormed out of the eating area. Joi then got up and grabbed her coat on her way back to work, her damage was done. After which I went to find Shay to make sure she was okay, there wasn't anything to explain she knew I had a woman and she also knew the extent of the relationship between she and I. When I finally caught up with her, she was upstairs trying to control her anger. I approached slowly, a little leery of her response.

"What up Shay, you straight?"

"Yeah, why wouldn't I be. It's not like we are together or anything, so I can't get upset."

"Well this is true, but I understand we are only human and if I saw what you just witnessed I would probably be a little upset myself."

"Well I'm not you and I'm not upset! But I will let you know this, I don't appreciate you throwing it up in my face like that. It's already enough that I have to deal with the fact that the man I choose to sleep with on a regular basis has a woman and at any given time she can come home, and I'm forced to share him. If that wasn't enough you think you can parade around with some other chick in my face? Do you think that's really fair? If I was to do that shit, what do you think your reaction would be?"

"Honestly, I can't say. Not sure if we would even be able to have this conversation if it was the other way around. I do apologize for being in your face like that, but it wasn't something that I did. It was her that kissed me not the other way around."

"Yeah I know and you didn't do anything to stop it either. I really hate you sometimes, you make me so sick. You don't have any feelings, you don't have a heart. You just use people for what you want, without any thought of what they might want."

"Maybe your right, maybe I don't care enough. I might even be selfish. This all might be true, and if it is this is all true, it makes it that much more difficult to understand why you deal with me, even better why anyone would deal with me. I can't imagine you have the ability to answer any of these questions, so I'll just leave it at this, I apologize for what happened today and I hope one day you can forgive me."

With that said I began to walk away, feeling a little bad about myself and the way she had been treated on that day, but not as bad as I felt as I hit the top of the stairs and stared down to see Maria with a confused look on her face. It wasn't as if she had seen me with anyone it was more so one of those looks like she was lost, and was looking for someone. Knowing that someone was me, I hit the steps as quickly as possible straight into her arms. Through all my ups and downs throughout the day, I had forgot that it was Friday and we had agreed to meet up after my classes. I was fucking up big time, not only were my buddies on the nut, but now my woman was here and I wasn't aware of how long she had been here. With the way she jumped into my arms as I reached the last stair and showered me with kisses I knew she hadn't been there long and had no idea what had just happened, so I squeezed her tightly and spun her around. While completing the spin I noticed Shay at the top of the stairs looking down with a look of disgust covering her face. She was in perfect position to ruin my entire life, by just coming down a few stairs and speaking her mind. Ending our hug a little sooner than was expected, just so I could look into her eyes or at least that's what I made her believe. We made our way to the door and then to the parking lot and to our separate cars, we decided to go out to lunch, but first we would be going to a private place to spend some alone time even if it was only for a while. It had been about two and a half months of just talking on the phone. This was the first contact that we had in that amount of time. I truly missed her, from the way she smiled at me to the way her lips tasted. Especially the way the smell of her Issey perfume meshed with her personal scent. I hadn't noticed at school, probably because I was so surprised (or scared) to see her, but she had changed her hair color, and the new color looked beautiful on her, it really brought out the color of her eyes. As we pulled up to my house expecting to have it all to ourselves, we were taken back by the rude awakening that was my mother's car in the drive way. There goes that idea, and to make matters worse it wasn't as if we could just pull off and go on about our business because there she sat in all her glory on the front porch. We had no choice, our only option was to park and at least go say hello. Truth was, I saw my mother everyday so I did have a choice, Maria however did not. Twenty or thirty minutes of idol chit chat can seem like a life time, especially when the plan was to be naked by now. At the same time to see my mom take an interest in her meant that she was not only accepted, but she was liked as well. This information was even more important than me seeing her naked, at least at this time. Even though she was only to be here for the weekend, we would still have plenty of time to enjoy each other at another time. Sitting there watching how Maria and my mom bonded had me thinking that all my extra curricular activities had to stop, I had to get rid of the people on the side. Once again my devilish side took over and my thoughts turned dark again "Then again why would I do that? She didn't know anything, and everyone else was okay with the position they played, at least they were at this point. Plus she was only there for the weekend, what would I do when she was gone back to school?" Just as I was coming to my conclusion, I was interrupted by my cell phone ringing on my hip, which also caused the conversation that was going on across the room to grow silent. Sliding the phone from the holster and checking the I.D, I started to act as if I didn't know the number but that would've caused more confusion than answering so I've learned.

"Hello"

"Hey, baby I know I jumped off the deep end earlier today but I just wanted to call and apologize. I didn't have the right to get an attitude I should've just ignored the whole situation, but like you said we are only human and sometimes our emotions take over. Hope you can forgive me one day, I would hate to ruin our arrangement."

"It's cool no big deal, I understand how you felt. I probably would've been upset myself but I'm gonna have to call you back. Maria's in town and we're spending time together right now."

"Oh, my fault I'll let you get back to her, and hopefully I'll talk to you soon."

Even though it wasn't even a two minute conversation the damage was done with her eyebrows squenched together. Maria asked the question that I was hoping didn't come up. "Who was that on the phone?" Here I am again a little less than a year later in the same shit, different toilet. Hopefully this time I'm a little wiser, but who knows. What should I do? "It's MB, we got into it the other day and he was just calling to make sure we still cool." Yeah that sounds good, if only that was the story that came out. What came out next surprised the hell out of me, maybe it was my subconscious telling me that I wasn't handling the entire situation too well, and this was my way out. Maybe it was me telling myself that I should just be honest, with the woman I'm supposed to be in love with, either way the words that escaped my mouth were as follows: "It was just a friend from school asking about a problem that we had in class today." And just like that it was dropped at least for the time being. Mom and Maria went right back along talking and laughing for the next couple of hours, that is until my stomach started grumbling because our lunch date had turned into a dinner date and we still hadn't left yet. On our way to dinner the discussion turned sour. It wasn't as if I didn't expect the line of questioning but I at least thought it might wait until after dinner.

"So how many "friends from school" have your cell phone number? Better yet how many of these so called friends are female?"

"Not too many people have my cell number, and not too many of them are female." (What the hell was I saying?)

"So what do females need to call you for anyway? Do they know about me, do they know you have a woman?"

"I can honestly say yes Boo, everyone knows I have a woman and they know that I love her. I don't pay them little chicks any attention."

"Mmmm hmmm, what ever Christopher. Let me find out otherwise. It'll be hell to pay."

"Boo you won't find out, because there's nothing to find. I'm with you and only you. So calm down!"

"You better be! If you know what's good for you."

"I do know! That's why I'm with you."

(Every man should know that no matter how beautiful your woman is, no matter how intelligent she is, no matter how many compliments she receives daily, she still needs to be reminded that you want her, and only her. So every chance you get she should be reminded of how head over heels you are over her, and complimented to no end. Take it from me it'll pay off in the long run.)

After dinner we decided that it was getting kind of late and we should continue our weekend together tomorrow, so I took her to her car and watched her pull off on her way home. After my call earlier in the day my phone was immediately turned to silent, I didn't need anymore trouble than I was already in. So on the way into the house I took a quick glance at the phone, six missed calls, three from Joi, two from MB, and the last one from Shay. Now Joi was understandable. I hadn't explained that my woman was in town yet, but Shay on the other hand I'd already explained that she's here, so this might mean trouble. I thought I had been clear that I had a woman and she definitely comes first, but eventually it comes down to one of us catching feelings that we shouldn't. I returned the first two calls, and left the Shay situation to handle itself. There was no reason to call and talk about the very things I was trying to avoid, at least not this weekend. Not when I had bigger problem, my woman was uncomfortable, and I was more concerned with that fact than anything else. She may have said she was letting it go, but that was just to get my mind off the problem, thinking I could talk freely again and walk right into her trap. Little did she know, I wasn't your ordinary guy. I spent too much time around my aunt and my mom not to pick up a couple pointers. Over the next couple days Maria was extremely nice, a little too nice for someone whose mate just told them that they get phone calls from the friends of the opposite sex. Being sure not to fall for this I continued to keep my guard up, since I wasn't sure what her intentions were. My plan was to get Maria comfortable, before it was time for her to go back to school and this wouldn't work unless she knew she didn't have anything to worry about. Since I didn't have anything to hide, (considering I had told everyone that my woman was in town, and my phone wasn't ringing of the hook as it usually did) I purposely left my phone lying around so that if she wanted to take a look it was readily available. Theory was this could work one of two ways. Either she would realize that I had nothing to hide, and in turn she had nothing to worry about, or someone would continuously call and ruin the entire ploy. See the goal wasn't to prove that the girls were just friends, the goal was to prove that there wasn't any continuous calling. That way she would be more comfortable believing that it was merely a class relationship instead of anything more. I almost believed it worked until Sunday was here, and I realized that we hadn't been intimate for the entire weekend, I quickly came to the conclusion that I was in much more trouble than I first thought.

Maria was back at school, and I was back to my old tricks. I hadn't missed too much over the weekend. Joi was still interested, and had no problem with the fact that I had to spend the weekend with my woman. Although she did say I would have to make up the fact that I had put her on hold for an entire weekend, like I would mind. I appreciated the fact that she understood what she was into, and didn't attempt to turn it into something it wasn't. We spent just about the rest of the semester together, I had always heard the saying "Sex, Lies, and Videotape" well my version was very similar only instead of the videotape we could probably add more SEX.

THE SUMMER: *A Summer Unfulfilled*

Before I knew it winter and spring semesters had come and gone, and the summer was here. Unlike high school, the days of school being over in the middle of June was over. It was late April, and school was out unless you planned on going to summer school, which was the furthest thing from my mind. I had been through enough this year alone, no need to add more pressure by attending school in the hottest part of the year. On top of everything else I had plans for this summer. It was going to be my time to make up for last summers events. I had to sacrifice one summer already. I'd be damned if it was going to be two back to back. I knew Maria would be here for most of the summer, but I also knew that she had a family reunion to attend in California at the end of the summer, and I had Caribanna to attend. MB had been telling me about this since January, he explained that it was something that I couldn't miss, and it wasn't going to cost me anything, because coach usually took care of everything. All we had to worry about was getting there, which wasn't a problem, because if worst came to worst I would drive my damn self. But I wasn't going to get ahead of myself, I still wasn't in Maria's good graces so the bulk of my summer would be spent getting back where I belonged. The key to our relationship was the fact that she was always number one in my life. When she was here she was the only one in my life. I would go days without answering my phone or returning calls. The problem with this is the chicks on the side would usually get tired of not coming in at all, it was one thing to know you were second, but when you totally get ignored you tend find your attention from other directions. So I eventually lost contact with

Shay, who I believed ended up moving out of state that very summer, and Joi tried to keep in touch, but that only could last so long. As far as Rita went, she wasn't giving up quite that easy, she would constantly leave voice mails, pleading with me to see her sometime this summer. This was anything but possible, it wasn't going to happen. My agenda was filled for the summer it included

1)Maria's good graces
2)Working on my game
3)Last, but not least Caribanna

So unfortunately Rita didn't have a leg to stand on, but as I said before she wasn't a quitter. Maria had been home for more than a month and I still hadn't been with her sexually, I knew I was over due, but I also knew that there was an unresolved issue and rushing her into the sexual part of our relationship wasn't the move. Although waiting patiently wasn't one of my strong suits, I decided that it was my best option. More than half the summer was gone and sex was still never brought up between the two of us. It had almost became a dead issue with me, I still enjoyed her company and we still saw each other daily for hours on end, but the intimate part just wasn't there. Unfortunately, this continued for just about the whole summer all the way up to the time for her family reunion. The day before she leaves, she chooses to bring up the fact that we hadn't had sex the entire time she's been home, as if I didn't know this fact. Then out of the blue she feels it's her duty to blame me for the entire problem saying that I didn't find her attractive anymore, and I must be getting what I wasn't getting from her from someone else. Now this would definitely be another of my pet peeves, I hate getting accused of something that I am not doing. Truth be told a couple months ago she would've had a valid point, and I wouldn't have been justified having an attitude, but this wasn't months ago and an attitude is what I had. So in a very aggressive tone, but as polite as I could possibly be considering my anger I asked,

"What are you talking about? Where in the hell is this coming from?"

"You know what I'm talking about, if you're not getting sex from me then you have to be getting it from some where else."

"Are you serious? What you just felt like arguing today or something? You know damn well I'm with you all day everyday. When do I have time to be knocking somebody else off?"

"You act like it's impossible! You're not with me twenty four seven."

Is that right? So I should make the same assumption about you then huh?

Maria you know this don't make a lick of sense. I can't believe this shit! (I mumbled under my breath)

"What, what did you say? Huh, what did you just say under your breath?"

All I said was I can't believe this shit! So should I assume that you've been getting it from some where else? Since that's the only logical explanation that I can come up with. That's the only reason I could see you coming out of the blue with these accusations, it must be you feeling guilty about your own extracurricular activities.

"Yeah right, you don't believe that yourself Christopher!"

No, I would not like to believe that Maria. But it makes sense, and it's more than possible. As a matter of fact, the more I think about it, the more sense it makes.

"You know what I don't have to deal with this bull shit, I think you should leave."

Considering how angry I was that wasn't her best move, because my next move was to the door. Now this whole argument could've been, should've been avoided especially considering the fact that she had no proof, and according to me she was the one holding out on the sex. What Maria failed to realize is she was leaving in a couple hours, and what was even more serious, I was leaving in less than twenty four hours. On my way to another country to party with women from all over the globe, add that to the fact that I had been exiled to a sexual desert for the past two months and that gives you a recipe for disaster. I really wanted to go back and fix this mess, go back and make her understand that I didn't do anything, make her realize that for the past two months I had been the perfect angel that she would love me to be, but I didn't. Something in me just wouldn't allow me to do so, no matter how badly I wanted to, it wasn't going to happen, not tonight.

Carribanna:

It's a brand new day and the beginning of a long weekend, I don't know what's in store for this weekend, but whatever it is I'm ready. Cuz and the fellas had been to this event last year and I couldn't make it, but no such thing this time. I'm on my way, and a good time I'm going to have. From my understanding, it's guaranteed. It's impossible not to have a good time at Caribanna. After crossing the border we had about a two and a half hour trip until we reached our destination. You could tell as soon as you hit the high-way how lovely the trip was going to be, every car that we passed was filled with women and you could tell exactly what their destination was. MB was driving his car, it supposedly sat four but more realistically, two people would be more comfortable, so that was just enough room for me and him. Just about every car we passed was a double take car, meaning the women in the car were so beautiful that you had to look twice. Now mind you, I did say just about every car, we did pass a couple monsters along the way. For the most part though, every car did pretty damn good. When we finally made it off the freeway, everything was bumper to bumper. It was sick! I hadn't seen traffic like this since Freaknic (Huge gathering that takes place in Atlanta), and the sites that followed made Freaknic look like a snow day in Tennessee, you know when they close the entire city down for a couple flurries. There were people everywhere hanging out of their cars, on top of their cars, some people just jumped out of their cars leaving the driver in traffic while they went to explore the surroundings. MB hit me with it quick "You get out of this car I'm leaving yo ass here!" To which we couldn't help but laugh at. We had every possible taste, if you wanted Vanilla, it was there with two piece bikini's on, or if you were in the mood for a little Caramel, it was oozing out all over the city, beautiful with long dark hair or sexy short cuts. You can't believe how much Dark Chocolate was there and I'm not talking regular old Hershey's I'm talking Godiva top shelf dark chocolate. It didn't get too much better than this, I had died and gone to heaven. As we made our way through the traffic and finally to the hotel, we couldn't wait to get in the room and in and out of the shower so we could get dressed and get back outside. There was really no need to go back outside because we were staying in a hotel filled with beautiful women, women who were in the mood to meet attractive young men and do whatever came to mind. Now considering that we were going to be there for an entire weekend, you really didn't want to chose, or be chosen too early on the trip because you just might miss out on another event. I knew this and had a complete understanding of this fact, but it didn't stop me or MB. The first women that paid too much attention were about to get our full attention at least for a period of time, and before I knew it, it happened and it was more than worth it.

She was as sexy as they come, her dark chocolate skin was perfect. Her hair wasn't quite shoulder length, but it wasn't far from it. She had a sexy slant to her eyes that instantly gave her an exotic look, but if that wasn't enough, her full lips looked a lot more than just kissable. Not to mention once you got past the beauty of her face, you couldn't help but be stunned by her body. Unlike a lot of women, she was blessed in both major departments as far as looks went. Fortunately for me the interest wasn't one sided, she looked at me as if I was her last meal, and she was going to savor every bite. Our first encounter, we both passed each other without so much as a word, just a look that was shared between us. Even though the lobby was packed with people checking into their rooms it was as if we moved in slow motion starring each other down and revealing our excitement. It was all sexual, couldn't be anything else. Before I knew it instinct had taken over, I stopped thinking and began to act. I guess it hit me that even if we were staying in the same hotel there was more chance than not that I would not see her again this weekend. I needed to act fast. That's when it happened. I stepped in front of her on her way to the elevator and asked "So you just gonna look at me like that and not say a word?" She looked amazed at the question

I was asking almost as if she was appalled, and then out of the nowhere she smiled, one the prettiest smiles I had ever seen.

"Excuse me, but if recall you were looking just as hard. Plus I thought it was up to the man to say what he wants from the woman."

"Yes I definitely was looking just as hard, if not harder. So I decided to do something, but as far as men always being the aggressor I totally disagree. We do get tired of getting shot down by beautiful women."

"So you get shot down a lot huh?"

"Nope just don't approach a lot, it's simpler that way."

"Hmmm, so what if I told you that you didn't have to worry about getting shot down. Would you approach me then?"

"Well to be honest I've already done the approach now so there's no need to ask that line of questioning, but it is good to know. So if I'm not going to get shot down can I ask what room you're in, maybe I can stop by after I hop in the shower or something?"

"Well to be honest I'd much rather you let me know where you'll be residing that way I'll feel much more comfortable stopping by your room later."

Understandable, I'm in room 242 you should definitely stop by, whenever you get the chance.

"I'll make sure that I do that, hope it's nothing wild going on when I decide to stop by."

Who me? Do I look like the wild type?

"Hell yeah, why do you think I'm talking to you?" (She laughed)

After my seemingly successful encounter with one of the sexiest women I had seen in my life, we headed up to the room to prepare for the wildest weekend I had ever had. It took less than an hour before we were on the street, better yet on the hunt. There was no need to drive anywhere, we were in walking distance of everything, clubs, bars places to eat, I mean everything. It was so exciting walking up the street on our first night in town, we didn't waste time going in a club, it seemed as if everyone was outside anyway. In any direction that we looked there was nothing but half dressed beautiful women lining the streets. I did a little flirting and a lot of drinking. Between the two, I met a couple new faces, but none that topped my friend that I met earlier. That didn't stop me though, there was no reason to put all my eggs in one basket. I flirted more, and upon request I happily gave my room number out as if it was my phone number. This is when my ego hit an all time high, we were standing on one side of the street with what seemed like about twenty chicks and directly across the street stood a couple of dudes that played football for the Browns looking at us. We were surrounded by women, and they were looking at us as if we were the football stars and they were the ordinary people. I believe they were standing in line for Shaq's party, but they just couldn't stop looking at us, it was a wonderful feeling because no matter the reason they were looking so hard, my theory was they were wondering how we had all these chicks hovering around us like we were somebody, and they didn't. I couldn't help but smile and continue my flirtations. By the end of the night I was beyond drunk, and had given my room number to about twenty different chicks, and through drunken eyes all of them were fine as hell. We didn't make it back to the room until around 6:00am and we both fell out barely making it to the beds that still had our luggage lying on top of them. Our sleep didn't last long at all, around 10:00am one of our other teammates knocked on the door saying they were all going to breakfast. Rolling out of bed was one of the hardest tasks I had endured, my head was banging from all the alcohol I had drank the night before. I made it out of the bathroom just in time to catch the phone ringing, who in the hell could this be I thought to myself.

"Hello!"

"Good morning, how are you this morning?"

"I'm fine. Who is this, and who would you like to speak to?"

"Oh, you don't recognize my voice? That must mean you gave your phone number out a great deal last night."

"Listen my head is killing me, and I'm not a morning person so if getting hung up on is something that you would rather not do please explain who you are calling for."

"Wow, you have an attitude problem in the morning! You met me in the lobby yesterday when you were checking in, but maybe I should try to give you a call back when you're in a better mood."

"Oh no, not at all, I'm good just didn't recognize your voice. No need to call back. I just have a headache, and I'm still tired as hell."

"Well I have a remedy for hangovers that might help. I could bring it around to your room if you not busy, or on your way out."

"I would greatly appreciate that, whenever you're ready I'm just about to jump in the shower."

"Well it seems like this is the best time me to cum then. Oh I meant come by then."

(I snickered) "Yeah this is as good a time as any."

"Well I'm on my way, I'm just around the corner. Be there in a sec."

I hung up the phone and looked at MB, and smiled. He asked who that was, and I quickly explained that it was ol'girl from yesterday. He sat up and asked "The one from the lobby?" Yeah, that's the one she's on her way around here right now. "You want me to get out of here?" I don't think that's necessary, but if it comes down to it you might have to make that move. I wasn't sure that him leaving was a necessity, but I knew he wouldn't have a problem if I did need him to. I ran and took about a twenty second shower, got out and threw my towel around my waist just in time to walk out and catch the knock on the door. I started to tell her to hold on for a second while I threw on some shorts, but instead I just went straight for the door, opening it quickly and apologizing for my attire. To my surprise she didn't have a problem with it at all, I could tell this because after her mouth finally closed, she explained that it was okay. She had thirty-two ounce water in her hand, along with a cup of steaming hot tea. She explained that I had to drink half the water down, and then drink the tea straight, and finish the other half of the water gradually. She also explained that the reason I had a headache was because my body was dehydrated, and the water would replenish my body, and the hot tea was just for the shock factor. She sat on the bed, and I grabbed a chair to sit in not thinking that I was still in just a towel. It wasn't until I caught her starring at the towel that I realized that I might be making her uncomfortable sitting in just a towel, so I excused myself and slid into the bathroom to throw on the basketball shorts that I had got from my bag. When I returned to the room she had a disappointed look on her face as if she didn't want me to change. She had been sitting so long that I hadn't had the chance to notice the Tennis skirt that she was wearing that was clearly made for a young lady who wasn't as blessed as she was in the rear department. I complimented her outfit, and then turned the conversation to whether or not she enjoyed her first night here. All the while MB was still laying in the bed acting as if he was in a deep sleep. She asked once or twice if

I thought we were disturbing him from his sleep, and I explained that he sleeps like a log. After about thirty minutes of small talk she decided that it was time for her to leave, but before she could do so she would at least need a hug as thanks for her remedy that still hadn't kicked in yet. She walked over and grabbed my arms and slid them around her for the embrace. I squeezed tight and she just about melted in my arms. Whispering in her ear, I asked if that was all she wanted for repayment. Her hands rubbing my back in a downward motion reaching my ass, and then coming to a tight grip, she responded, "I'll take whatever you're offering." Instantly my body felt a rush, my head was no longer hurting, possibly because most of my blood was rushing to the lower regions of my body. Before my smaller head took over I realized that not even ten feet away MB was still laying there pretending to be sleep, but she was content with the notion that he was sleeping. I couldn't help but think to myself, was she really that wild, hell was I even that wild? There was only one way to find out, my hand started it's ascension to her hair once making it to the back of her hair I pulled in a downward motion so that it brought her face and more importantly her lips in perfect position for the taking. Applying light pressure to hers at first, and as she became more comfortable adding more. Before long it wasn't just her lips that were there for the taking it was her entire body that yearned for me. As we stood there embracing and patrolling the inner workings of one another's mouths, I could feel her leaning back towards the bed and there was part of my answer. She was that wild! I allowed her to lead me to the bed while continuing the kiss, once we made it there almost tripping and falling over most of the room, she sat down so fast that the skirt that barely covered her assets failed to do it's job. She laid back and I on top of her, her legs wrapped around my calves, I could feel her wanting to feel me. Gently pressing myself against her so that she could feel me through my shorts, she took it upon herself to feel with her hands not her body. Starting at the tip, she stroked my completeness all the way down to my sack, as to judge what she would be working with. MB still hadn't made a move yet, I was starting to think that he was really asleep myself. I slowly reached down to her thigh with my right hand slowly moving it up to explore her wetness, and with my left I reached inside the night stand and grabbed the gold wrapper. This wasn't an intimate moment, I didn't know her, she didn't know me, we were just two people sexually attracted to one another, and that's exactly what it would be sex. I quickly placed the package between my teeth tearing it open to retrieve the prize placed inside, afterwards tossing the package to the floor. This is how I later knew that MB was up for the entire event, because later on this move would be deemed the TEAR & THROW AWAY! She was in such a hurry to feel me that she snatched the condom from my hand and journeyed inside my shorts to roll it down herself, then guided me on the tour of her deepness. Upon entry she let out a muffled sound that was an instant turn on, I didn't know if it was the fact that someone was in the room possibly watching, or was it the fact that I didn't know this chick any better than I knew Halle Berry. Whatever it was I was as hard, and as big as I had ever been ready to put on a show for the ages. Raising her legs above my shoulders, I positioned myself on my toes with my arms fully extended so that only my waist did the work plunging myself deep inside her walls over and over again until I heard the sounds that my ears couldn't wait to hear. From a light moan, to a full blown outburst, that I swear could've been heard down the hall, let alone in the next bed. I continued this movement until I could feel her legs tremble and shake, between the sounds and the movements I couldn't imagine this experience any better. We continued our sexual escapade long through the morning and into the early afternoon, and throughout, MB never moved and kept his sleep act intact. After she finally left the room he jumped up and laughed almost to the point of tears. He finally hit me with the bulk of the jokes all in a row. With the last one being the TEAR & THROW AWAY. (The joke was that I didn't know this chick and instead of strapping up I just tore the condom open and threw it on the floor, just to make it seem like I was using one.) It was funny mostly because it was some truth to the joke. We laughed for the rest of the weekend and continued to have more than a little fun. We finally made it back to the D, Monday afternoon. The craziest part is the fact that I didn't even remember the names of any of the woman that I had just spent the entire weekend flirting with, I couldn't even remember the name of my sexual partner for the weekend.

SOPHOMORE YEAR: *The End is Near*

With about a week before Maria had to go back to school we still weren't on the best of terms. We were talking but not like it used to be, it even got to the point that we discussed whether or not we should continue to be together, it was evident that we were growing apart. At the end of the discussion we decided that we could work through our problem and stay together. By the end of the week we still hadn't made any headway in our relationship woes, the only thing we knew was that we were still going to be together. She went back to school, and I took my time to prepare for my long sophomore year of college. This was a pretty slow year as far as women went, Shay had left after the semester, and Joi had moved to Virginia before the end of the summer so more than most of my time was spent between class, work, or on the court. There were a few women that were more than interested, but it really didn't go anywhere. I was focused on the task at hand, I was on a straight basketball diet. From class to work, back to the gym was my daily routine, and seeing that my job was at a local recreational center it was as if I lived in the gym. For the first three months I talked to Maria every single day, I was doing extremely well, hadn't talked to anyone else for sometime. Besides an every now and then a late night call from Rita, who still hadn't given up, I didn't mind her persistence. Maria and I still weren't at our best, but we were the only ones who could tell. For all that friends and family knew, we were madly in love and nothing could possibly be going wrong, how wrong they were. We were distant it wasn't the same anymore. The love that was once there was gone and had been replaced by comfort. We were so comfortable with each other and the thought of being together, even better everyone else's thought of us being together, that we just did that, stayed together. Now I agree that I wasn't the best man I could be when it came to her being away, but whenever she was there no one else mattered. I had convinced myself that the cheating I had done was just from loneliness, not from the fact that something was missing in the relationship. Maria had her own set of issues, just as I did and they were brought to light after basketball season was over and I took my trip down to TSU. She had already been home twice this year and we decided that I would come down sometime during this school year and visit her. I also wanted to see Kev, at least to see if what I had heard about him was true. According to the rumors, since the break up of him and Sabrine he had become a totally different person. It was late spring and school was about a month from being over when I went down, so the weather was beautiful sunny every day and it was warm. Being at a predominately Black University was totally different from being at a white one. The school was located in the middle of the ghetto, and when I say the middle I mean the middle. If you look out the windows of the dorms you can see boarded up houses, shacks that people shouldn't be allowed to live in with people on the porches sitting as if there was nothing wrong. To be honest it wasn't much different from Detroit's streets, only difference is no one put a school smack dab in the middle of it all. The biggest difference to me was the gigantic hills, and the number of black faces that I saw on campus. As we pulled up in front of the dorms, everyone was outside sitting on the stoops, and just hanging out. Some people were hanging out of the windows talking as if they weren't on the fifth floor. Maria in her second year had long been done with the dorms. From my understanding the rules were worst than if she had stayed home and went to school. So her and Shala, a friend she had met in school last year, who was also from the D, got an apartment off campus. She decided to take me on campus first because she had class, and she wanted me to sit in and see what school was like down there. Over all it seemed more like a family atmosphere. Class sizes were smaller than some high schools in the D. I could appreciate that because it meant you were more than just a social security number. You knew the professor and he or she knew you. The only problem I could see was when you didn't make it to class they would know it. After class we hit the student center, and she introduced me around as her man. I noticed in a couple of introductions she had to hurry up and introduce me before someone said something that I didn't need to hear. I made it easy to introduce me and clear the air because of my slow walking, she had a quicker pace than me so she would get to a person before me and be talking for a couple of seconds before I got there, by the time I would walk up the person was already talking to me like they had known me for half my life. It wasn't long before Kev walked up behind me, and pushed me in the back.

"What up nigga?"

"My right foot took a half step up and I quickly turned around to see his smiling face, this was as fast as I had moved all day."

Kev, what it is? (I said in a laid back tone)

I was happy to see him that is what was left of him. He had lost about thirty pounds, which had him looking pretty good. But this wasn't the Kev that I knew from high school. This was a totally different guy whether it was for the best or not was yet to be seen. His eyes low and lips black gave away the fact that his weed smoking habit had kicked it up a notch or two. So instantly I understood that part of the rumor wasn't exactly a rumor. We stood and kicked it for a while, as Maria made her way around the room mingling, and speaking to just about everyone in the room. While she made her way around Kev introduced me to a couple of his so called friends from that way. Instantly into his introductions, I moved up on his friends list from his boy to his best friend from the D. Out of all the dudes I met the only one that I deemed real was this white dude who couldn't be convinced that he was white. (I mean he knew, but he was so much more comfortable being around black people than he would be around white people.) Now this is how college usually works, especially when you go away to a place where most people don't know you. You get an opportunity to redefine yourself, a chance to be either yourself, or someone you've always wanted to be but never was. From my understanding Kev had taking this opportunity to do just that, he was now an ex-basketball player, and not only that but he was hands down on of the best players in Detroit according to his friends from the south. Now in order for them to believe this Kev obliviously had found a way to stay the hell off the court for an entire year and a half, because it would've only taken one time for them to know better than that, unless they were convinced that the D just wasn't a basketball Mecca. As for the rest of the new Kev, he was a thug with a quick temper and he was one of the biggest weed selling dudes in Detroit. This all had me damn near on the floor dying of laughter, but I tried my best not to ruin his mirage of a life. Every time someone told me more about the new Kev, I just looked at him and held in my laughter. That was my way of truly being a friend, I could've easily put Kev on blast and let everyone know the truth but that wasn't my place. It wasn't for me to do. That was Kevin's job to be true to himself and if he wasn't ready to do so, then who was I to ruin his perfectly unbelievable story? If the new Kev was content with a false existence then I was happy for him.

Finally Maria was ready to go. I don't know if she was just making sure the word was out that she had company for the weekend or what, but she was on a mission. It was evident she might not have had a bonified man here, but she had definitely had someone she was messing around with. It was cool I didn't mind, she was playing the game that many woman had played before. I just hoped she was good at it. She and her roommate lived in a suburban area of Nashville in a two bedroom apartment, it was extremely nice, but I expected nothing less. My Boo did have good taste. We spent the next couple of days either tucked away in her apartment, or at the mall shopping. We were on campus twice for the entire trip, the second time was for some kind of pep rally for a party that was going on later that night. Now as soon as we entered the rally I noticed a couple of people that I probably shouldn't have, but I couldn't help myself. They kept their eyes glued to me the entire time I walked from one side of the gym to the other, and they weren't shy about the fact that they liked what the saw. Maria must have noticed the same thing because her usual rapid pace slowed to match mine. As she grabbed my arm to let everyone know that I was with her, this was the most affection she had shown for just about the entire trip that is besides our trips to the mall. We sat about three rows above the chicks that found me a bit enticing, and every now and then we would catch them glancing up to see how I was enjoying the show. The only reason we were there was because one of Maria's friends was on the cheer team, or so I was told. Afterward instead of going to the party, Maria let me know that she had something else planned for us.

So once again we were off the campus, after driving for about thirty minutes we ended up at the Nashville Atrium. It was connected to one of the most prestigious hotels in Tennessee. It was also one of the most expensive hotels in the south. We walked around and talked for about two hours, enjoying the scenery and the nature. After that we made our way to Downtown Nashville to the Hard Rock Café for dinner. This was the white part of town. Black people were pretty much slim to none, but they were so busy drinking they paid little to no attention to us. Dinner was over and we walked along the pier enjoying the breeze from the water. It was at this time where we seemed to be back having fun like we use to it was just me and her enjoying each other. This too had to come to an end, because the next morning I was on my flight back to Detroit and with exception of a couple hours of being the old us, nothing had changed we still weren't happy. Considering the fact that both of our summers were going to be spent apart, because she would be attending summer school down there and I would be going all over the country for summer leagues, and I would be taking summer classes, this had already been a long school year, and it was going to be an even longer summer.

JUNIOR YEAR: The End and a New Beginning

My junior year was finally here, and after having a very productive season on the court, and a not so productive year off the court I was ready for one to continue, and the other to change. Maria and I were pretty much on the outs. The extended time away over the summer was putting a strain on the relationship that neither of us could handle. It was probably to the point that neither of us wanted to handle it either. I was just about done ignoring advances, especially considering the fact that I still wasn't having a sexual relationship with my woman. Plus the advances were coming from so many angles now it was almost impossible to ignore, I was used to attention but nothing prepared me for the attention I would receive after being one of the best players on a winning team. I could barely walk around the campus without at least five or six references to what women would do to me sexually. The new attention was cool, but it made the whole me and Maria, working-it-out, thing just about impossible. Considering that now when I called her I was regularly forwarded to her voicemail, and every time we did talk it was something negative. If she didn't go with the negativity she was now constantly nagging me about going to church. That was about the final straw for me. She was now somehow holier than thou because she attended a couple services. I can understand someone wanting their mate to have a relationship with God, but to take it to the level she took it wasn't okay with me. This did nothing but drive us further apart. That's when I was most vulnerable, and it's also around the time that I met Andrea. She was standing at the pay phone, which I didn't understand because she had a little red cell phone in her hand. She was gorgeous, once again I met a chick with a high yellow skin but this time it was flawless. She couldn't have been anymore than about 5'1 and had this jet black hair that came down to the top of her back, full lips and a beautiful slant to her eyes that wasn't so deep that she looked Asian, and if not for those lips she could have passed for a Asian American, it was an exotic look. Her small frame is what really took the cake at about one hundred and twenty five pounds, she was thick in all the right places. With a set of full breasts, a small waist and an ass that just would not stop. Her height was about the only thing that was stopping her from being on someone's runway. I wanted her to no end! I passed her the first time on my way to the café. She stood there in her yellow Guess outfit, having a discussion on the phone, and when I returned from grabbing my drink she was still out there. I decided this was my opportunity to say something, so I sat and waited patiently as to not disturb the on going discussion between her and the loser on the other end (he was a loser, because little did he, or she for that matter know, but he had just lost her). As she finished her conversation, she angrily hung up the phone turned and looked at me with disdain. Immediately I responded to her look "Whatever it was, I didn't do it, but if I did I apologize." This in itself brought a slight smile to her face. Although it wasn't enough, I continued by asking if she was alright, to which she responded she would be fine. Her full-lips perfectly glossed had me hanging off her every word. We talked for a couple minutes before we both had to go our separate ways, she had class and I had morning practice. Before leaving, I was granted the pleasure of exchanging numbers with her. As she walked away I was once again blessed with a perfect picture. Lucky for me this wouldn't be the last time that I would see her for the day. After class I was attempting to get to the car before I was caught in the rain. I made it just in time, I was pulling out of the garage and noticed her sitting at the bus stop waiting for one of the slowest routes in Detroit's bus history. I pulled up and asked if I could give her a ride. After convincing her that I wasn't going to kidnap her, or try the old out of gas routine, she finally got in the car. She lived not too far from where I did so it wasn't out of my way at all. On the ride to her house I learned even more about her, she was a freshman, and she was just coming from sitting out of school for a year because she didn't think she was ready for college out of high school. She also let me know that she was having an argument with one of her many male friends, earlier today when at the pay phone and in turn he decided not to pick her up from school as pay back for not seeing things his way. After arriving at her house and dropping her off, I made my way home with on of the biggest smiles that I could muster. I was still worried about my relationship with Maria, so actually calling her was out of the question, at least at first. We would still see each other in school, and speak but that was the extent of our friendship. After about three weeks I finally took out the time to call her and see how she was doing. She was cool, she had the sassy mouth that had always attracted me, and this time it was no doubt she had the attributes to back it up. Not only was she beautiful, but she was also intelligent. After about an hour on the phone she explained that she had to run to the store for her mother and she would call me when she got back. So I told her she should bring me some Oreo's, I said it jokingly thinking she knew that I was just playing. Instead she called while on the road and asked me how to get to my house. Less than five minutes later she pulled up in a white Grand Prix, I walked down the driveway and up to her car to accept my gift. I explained that it was nice to see her, and thanked her for my cookies at the same time explaining that she didn't have to do it. She knew already what she did and didn't have to do, as she politely explained that fact to me, I couldn't help but smile. We sat and talked for about twenty minutes before she announced that she needed to get back home with her mother's car. It was getting late and I had other obligations as well. My Uncle had just recently kicked out tenants at one of his rental properties and asked me to stay there for a couple months until he could get someone else to move in. This worked out perfectly for me because I could have company anytime I wanted to, and even better, they could stay for as long as I wanted to. I had already explained my plans to my mom, and it wasn't a problem for her. She thought it would be a good experience for me to get out on my own and see how it felt. Truth was I would probably be home to eat just about everyday, and I wasn't paying any bills, so it wasn't like I was really going to be out on my own. Andrea called just as she said she would when she got home, we talked for a about an hour then she let me go because she was a little tired. That's when I made my way to the house, it wasn't in one of the better neighborhoods hence the suggestion that I stay there to make sure no one broke in while he found some new tenants. As soon as I got in I called Maria to let her know that I was about ready for bed, and that I would talk to her tomorrow. Our conversations had long since turned from long, to short and far from sweet. Before I knew it I was off the phone, and knocked out.

For the next couple of days I talked to Andrea more than ever, even though we didn't have a lot in common, the things that we did more than made up for the things we didn't. After about another week, she called and invited me over for a little fun. We watched a couple shows on television before our attraction took over, or maybe it was just me (I doubt it). We started out with some playful kissing that quickly turned into much more. It happened so quickly that we weren't sure what was coming over us. We went from a up right position on the couch to her laying back and my lips went from hers, down to her neck gently kissing, licking and sucking. Feeling her hands going wild on my head and back, I proceeded to go lower enjoying the fullness of her breasts equally, as she fought to hold in her moans and sighs, because the house wasn't as empty as we had hoped. With that in mind I really wanted to test her strengths, so I proceeded to go even lower and taste her warmth. Already soaking wet with anticipation I slowly dipped my tongue deep into her sweetness, which sent her over the edge to the point where she had to grab the closest throw pillow and cover her face to hold in her moan. This was unacceptable to me I wanted to see the face that I had twisted in pleasure, I wanted to hear the moans that I had worked so hard to get. I reached up, removed the pillow from her face, and enjoyed the beautiful view in front of me, tasting her fruit until her juices totally covered my lips, and chin. Finally raising my face from the place it was so comfortably nestled, I explained that it was about time for me to go. This really didn't go over to well with her.

"So you think, you're just going to get me hot and bothered and just leave?"

Umm yeah, that's pretty much the plan. I have to get home. You know I'm house sitting.

"Oh hell naw, you won't be going nowhere right now!"

Don't act like that I have to go, plus we can't go any further. Yo mom is in the other room.

"Okay then I'm going with you. Let me grab something to wear tomorrow."

You just gone invite yo'self?

"Nope not at all, so you need to go ahead and ask me to come with you."

Without hesitation I invited her to spend the night with me, it took her about five minutes to grab something to wear and then we were off. I asked if she wanted anything before we made it to the house to which she replied everything I want is already in the car and available. We made it to the house, and I was attempting to play as if I didn't know what we were there for. I asked if she would like to play cards or something, her response was where's the bedroom? Thinking that she might want to change into something a little more comfortable, I told her it was down the hall to the left. She grabbed my wrist and pulled me to the back with her, on the way dropping her bag and purse on the couch. Once in the room she quickly lost her top, and was working on her pants when I tried to slow the tempo again. "You know we really don't have to do anything we can just chill." I guess my statements were starting to irritate her because her response was to ask if I was scared or nervous. Which I can honestly admit now that I was just a bit, why? I have not a clue, but I'd be damned if she would ever know it. So I put a front on and turned the tables back on to her "Scared, scared of what? If anything you better get scared!" This feeling was quickly replaced once she searched my jeans and found what she was looking for, slowly stroking her prize into attention. Any fear or nervousness that I might have had was quickly taken away and replaced with pleasure. Gently pushing her down to the bed, and losing my pants as well as my boxers. I spread her thick, and nicely toned legs apart and buried myself deep inside her. This was definitely the wettest and softest place I had ever visited. She made me feel like I had never felt before, sex hadn't taken me here before and I wasn't sure if I even needed to be here. The deeper I went, the wetter she got until I could feel her wetness on her thighs, as well as mine. She was the best and I hadn't even been inside her for five minutes, and I knew she was the best. It wasn't enough though, I wanted more I had to have more. Exiting, and informing her that

145

she needed to roll over thinking that I would have placed her in my favorite position, she was already moving towards it and by the time I was ready to guide her to perfection she was already there. She had buried her head in the pillow above and placed her ass in the air with the most beautiful arch in her back awaiting my next thrust. I couldn't believe it, she couldn't be serious, I had to be dreaming. This couldn't be happening, I fell in behind her and followed her lead for a couple minutes in awe of how she threw it back. That only lasted briefly before I took over attempting to place every inch of myself inside her, listening to her moans that were being drowned out by her telling me to go deeper. I reached around her side and then under in order to play with her clit, heightening her excitement and bring us both to an unbelievable climax. As we lay breathing hard almost exhausted, we felt each other and came to the conclusion that we had unfinished business. She was even wetter than she was when we started, and she had my complete attention. Wasting no time at all she rolled over, and road me clear into the early morning. Orgasm, after orgasm we enjoyed each other until each of us could barely move.

From then on we were pretty much inseparable, it was to the point where I would miss class, even practice because I was with her. I couldn't imagine what I would do without her. I was replacing Maria, but was still with her. Making the ultimate mistake falling for someone who was just supposed to be a sexual partner. In the beginning we both knew that it was just sex, but before long it grew into something more, something I should've never let it grow into. Being with her made everything else in my life took a back seat, not because that's how she wanted but because that's how I allowed it to be. I wasn't strictly about basketball anymore, and school was slipping. I was beginning to actually need the special treatment that we athletes sometimes received, and Maria, Maria was a distant fourth in the rotation behind the other three. I was so blinded by the incredible sex that we shared, my silly ass attempted to introduce her to the rest of my family like they were going to accept her right off. (It was almost the equivalent of a married man introducing his mistress to the family.) And that's pretty much how it worked out for her in that regard. Never imagined that I would receive that many calls about a decision as small as that one, but I did. It wasn't that they didn't like her, it was that she wasn't Maria and according to them. Maria was perfect. (They didn't know enough to know better.) I still didn't care though, I just wanted Andrea, or so I thought. I had made it, mistake free, until one night I made the mistake of thinking I was the smartest person on earth and disrespecting Andrea's feelings with one of the dumbest and unnecessary lies I had ever told in my life. We were on our way to the house and I politely asked her to remind me to make a phone call when we got to the house, mind you it was about 2:30am, and I hadn't called Maria to say good night yet. I was so young, so disrespectful!

With the exception of that one mistake I was doing pretty well. I had since juggled my way through Thanksgiving by visiting Andrea early that day, because as far as family went, it was just her and her mom. After dinner I immediately left for home to take a shower, and then to Maria's house for her entire family which included her Grandmother who wasn't as quick to fall for my innocent role. By now Christmas was coming fast. We were already out of school and so was Maria, so my juggling relationships was already in full swing. Lucky for me I had a basketball tournament to attend to take some of the pressure off me. About three days of relaxation and away from stressful situations, I was still on edge but I still had an opportunity to just chill. When we returned from the tournament it was two days until Christmas, and I still had shopping to finish. Maria's gift was already taken care of. It had been four years of gift giving that we had shared and I needed to top the past gifts, and top the gift is what I did. Since this was the first year that I was exchanging with Andrea I wasn't sure what the gift was supposed to look like, especially because I wasn't sure where we stood as far as our relationship went. I made it as simple as possible. I just bought an outfit that I knew she would like, not too big not to small. Now came the hard part, spending time with both of them on the most important day of the year. It was Christmas time which meant both of them needed to see me, this wasn't one of those regular days that you could just visit one, and see the other tomorrow. This was the day that people in a relationship are together. It was a little more serious than Thanksgiving, and somehow, some way I was still expected to involved my family in my day. How in the hell was I going to pull this one off? The night started off with a lie, I explained to Maria that I would be helping my parents set up the toys for my siblings for the next day.

When actually all I was doing was spending time with Andrea, because I knew that I would be with Maria most of the next day. Andrea and I opened our presents at midnight and then spent the rest of the time nestled under the tree talking about how much we really liked each other. The next morning I explained to Andrea that I would be with my family for most of the day and I probably wouldn't see her until later on Christmas day. Surprisingly this wasn't a problem for her. She understood, and was happy that I would be seeing her later. It never hit me that she possibly had other places to visit as well. So around 10:30am I was on my way home to celebrate with my family and pick up Maria's gift from the house, and also get dressed for the rest of the day. Once I made it to the house, it was full of life, everyone was up and enjoying Christmas day. My brother, and all my sisters were loud as usual, having more fun than a little bit under the tree. Everyone was having a great Christmas and I was just starting. After sitting with the family for a while I finally decided it was time to jump in the shower and make my way over to Maria's house. By the time I finished it was around 2:30pm. Considering I hadn't talked to her for the entire day I made it a point to call as soon as I jumped out of the shower. She still seemed happy to hear from me so I explained that as soon as I was done getting dressed I would be on my way to see her, and of course I would be bringing her gift with me. Even though I knew this was going to be a one sided gift giving day, I didn't mind. Maria's money wasn't right just yet so my Christmas gift would be coming a couple days late. This didn't bother me in the least, because I was so stuck in the Christmas sprit, and I felt guilty as hell for the way I had been acting towards her for the past couple of months. I finally made it over her house and it was already packed with her family, and her extended family. I understand I was a little late, but damn I wasn't expecting the entire family to beat me there. After being there for about thirty minutes I decided to go out to my car and retrieve her gift. She had been thinking that she would have to wait for about a week for her gift, so again I had surprised her, and once she actually opened the gift she was even more surprised, it shined and glimmered in the light of the family room as everyone took pictures of her face. No it definitely wasn't what you are probably thinking, it was just a watch. Well not just any watch, it was a MOVADO museum watch. I could see the excitement in Maria's face, she loved her gift and

I had surely outdone last year's gift, so as happy as she was I was that much happier. We spent the rest of the night laughing and talking, enjoying each other's company and the company of her family. I still had to visit my Grandmother, so around 10:00pm I said my good-byes and made my way to my car. Little did I know this would be one of the last times I would see Maria, at least see her with the same title that she was holding at that time. Our relationship lasted about another week and I never received my Christmas gift. Her reason, now this was the funny part to me, she said "You don't go to church enough, and I'm trying to build my stance in the church!" Now this would be more than legitimate if we stayed in the same house, or city, shit for that matter she may even have a leg to stand on if we stayed in the same state. Truth was we didn't, so what exactly did her growing religious stance have to do with me? Nothing that I could see, but so be it.

WINTER SEMESTER: *A Familiar Place*

So here it was again. A new year was here and I was in a familiar place. Something drastic was happening in my life that was new to me. I was starting a new relationship in my mind, but in reality this relationship started months ago. It started when I never explained that I had a woman out of town. Who was I kidding? I wanted this relationship to start, at least that's what I thought. I was here now with a beautiful woman, and I was going to make it work as best I could. It all started out fine, we calmed down, I regained my seriousness about basketball, school and all my free time was spent hanging out with her. We even went as far as having study sessions together to replace some of our sexual sessions. She made me feel good about being me, and gave me no reason to want to see other people. It got so serious that I just about completely stopped hanging out with the team, and as far as other women went there were none, with the exception of a call or two to Maria from time to time. Everything was going well until around March, it was a Friday if I remember correctly and I was still at work around 11:15pm and according to Andrea she was getting worried. She had called my cell three or four times with no answer and the line at work was busy (probably because I had been on the phone for the past hour talking to Maria.), so she did the only thing she could think of, she came to the job. As I sat unaware of the problem that was just outside of the front door I was startled by a knock, as I jumped up to see who it was I told Maria that I would call her back. Approaching the door I was relieved to see it was Andrea, at first, at least until I took a closer look at the expression on her face. Upon opening the door my relief was quickly replaced by surprise.

"Who the hell were you on the phone with?"

"Huh, what are you talking about?"

"Do not lie to me, just tell me the truth. I've been calling and the line has been busy for the past hour, not to mention the fact that I have called your cell about four times."

"Andrea I don't know what you're talking about. I just came out of the gym. The phone in the office may be off the hook and that's why the line was busy. Shit I didn't even know it was this late, I lost track of time shooting around. Matter of fact I need to check the doors and get out of here before security comes around." (And then I heard the familiar tone and words.)

"Christopher don't try to play me. You really not that slick! Yo ass was on the phone, and I know it."

Now I'm standing there with one of the most confident look on my face because there was no way to prove that I was on the phone. For as long as I have worked at this Recreation Center and as long as I had been using these phones the biggest complaint has been that the REDIAL button didn't work. So I was as safe as a cow in a room full of vegetarians, or so I thought. I had walked out of the office to check the rest of the doors when I heard her talking.

"Hello, who is this?" (Pause for answer)

"Where you just on the phone with Christopher?" (Pause for answer)

"This is his woman!" (Pause for response)

"For about the last six, or seven months." (Pause for response)

The whole time I went about my business as if nothing was going on, I just knew there was no way she was really on the phone. That was until she called me in the office, and said the phone was for me. I played along with her little charade, by coming in and grabbing the phone. First I looked at her and told her she knew that it wasn't anybody on the phone, then I held the phone to my ear and said hello.

"Hello Christopher thanks for calling back."

(Whatever cockiness I might have had a second ago jumped right out of me.)

"So she's been your woman for six or seven months, huh?"

I was forced to do the only thing that any sane, but dumb ass man would do, I hung up the phone. Then immediately attempted to flip the script, blaming Andrea for being nosey and telling her that I really didn't like her, she should get out and leave me the hell alone. She in turn did as any sensible black woman would do in this situation. She tore the place up and called me every name in the book on her way out. My ignorance didn't stop there. My next move was far dumber than the last, I called Maria back attempting to explain myself which went no where. The names that Andrea left out she finished off, and then hung up on me.

Andrea called throughout the night, trying to get an explanation and I really wish that I had one to give her but I didn't. I had no idea why I acted the way I did, I couldn't explain why I still talked to Maria. I was happy being with Andrea and I really did like her, and was growing to love her. The problem was that I fucked up, and I knew it. I explained it to her as best I could, and hoped she would forgive me. At the same time I understood she needed time to get over my stupid ass decision, and time is what I was going to give her, as much time as she needed. After a couple of weeks she decided to give me another chance, which I was extremely thankful for. I intended to make up for my ignorance, I was going to make it alright. Now even though Andrea chose to forgive me didn't mean that she was planning to forget anything. This was more than understandable considering the previous events that occurred. No matter what happened I was going to try my best to work through our problems, mainly because I felt like I deserved whatever she needed to dish out. For weeks, months I lived life on egg shells apologizing for every little thing that happened between us, agreeing with her on every topic whether I believed her to be right, or wrong. Andrea wasn't going to make it easy to be with her, she had revenge in her eyes and in her heart.

SUMMER BREAK: *The Move*

For months on top of months I worked vigorously on my ability to balance myself on the thin ice of our relationship. Careful with my words, careful with my movements, I was even careful with my decisions. It came to a point where I wasn't happy anymore. I was just in it to make her happy. In the process of trying to make her happy I made one of my more emotional decisions (Emotion: acting without the benefit of intellect). I agreed with the idea of us moving in together, thinking that if we stayed together, and she knew about my daily movements that she would ease up and be a bit more comfortable, and I could take a break from my newfound talent of eggshell walking. I think I've said it before, I've been wrong before, and I was wrong again. This made my day-to-day life that much worse. Now I would hate for anyone to take this the wrong way, there were many good times but they were more than out weighed by the bad. I was no longer around her because I wanted to be around her, it was more so because I knew she didn't trust me to be around anyone else. On one hand I could understand where she was coming from, but on the other hand I couldn't live my life in this manner. My attempts to control myself, and keep her happy were about to be tested to no end, school was just about over and the summer was about to start. I can't speak for any other cold weather cities or states, but I can speak for Detroit Michigan and once the summer hits here there is almost no other place I would rather be. Not because there's so much to do, but because the visions of loveliness, and nakedness dance through my head. The difference between here and the cities that are warm year round is the fact that it gets so cold here that when it does get warm it's a celebration in itself. We have a better appreciation for our summers, because of our winters. The summer was just around the corner, and I promised myself that since I definitely wouldn't be messing with any other chicks, I would at least kick it with MB and Cuz. Considering the fact that my senior year was going to be starting soon and this would be just about my last summer as a student I thought that I might as well make it enjoyable. And enjoyable it was, there was no cheating involved at least not the type of cheating I was use to doing. After about two straight weeks of going out with the fellas, it was explained to me that I was going out too much, and spending too much time with them and not enough with her. This seemed a little hard to fathom considering most of my day was spent with her, and I wouldn't go out until she would decide she was going out with her friends, (which little did I know really meant her girls, and whatever male friends they had in common.) But that's another story. After our little discussion, and my decision to slow down with my going out, I noticed that it was a one-sided decision. Instead of us both being in the house, or being together, I found myself spending more time alone than anything else. So after about a week or two of sitting at home alone with her returning when ever she felt like, I decided it was only one thing for me to do. Enjoy Myself!!! So from then on I was spending all my time with the fellas again, night in and night out we were either at the club, or at the bar. Occasionally we would just chill in the house and play John Madden on Play Station 2, but for the most part it was the club. Unfortunately when I say the club I'm not talking about a regular club. I'm talking about the Gentlemen's club, even though there weren't many gentlemen in the place. Now I wasn't much for paying to watch chicks dance half ass naked, but this is what we did on a regular, and since I was on an honesty kick I didn't mind telling Andrea where I was whenever she called or once I had gotten home each night. My theory was that I wasn't doing anything wrong, unfortunately it wasn't seen that way from both parties. It probably wouldn't have been a problem if it wasn't an every night event. Once again she voiced her opinion about my comings and goings, but this time I also voiced mine and due to the fact that there was no change in her lifestyle there would be none in mine. We continued this charade throughout the summer and into the fall of my senior year.

SENIOR YEAR: *The End is Near*

This was it I had finally made it, I was two semesters away from the biggest achievement of my life, and through it all I couldn't help but think about how miserable I was. I was in a relationship that lacked the communication, and understanding that people in a relationship are supposed to have. Every other day it was a different argument, a different problem. At each turn there was another person in the middle of my relationship, or whatever a person would call what I was in. If it wasn't her being irritating, she would find a way to bring her friends into our problems, or she would get her mother in the middle off things, or worse my mother. As if I didn't have enough problems on my plate, I had a full load of classes, I was still an athlete, and a job that was beginning to work my nerves and for the first time I actually had bills to worry about. Anybody else would've had a nervous break down, but not me. All I could see was the light at the end of the tunnel, and that light was graduation. Now, constant bickering would have any sane person avoiding his or her home life, so it was understood that spending time with each other would be far and in-between. Truth was we did still live together, but our schedules allowed us to not see each other. We had long gotten over the novelty of a sex life. Well, honestly she got over it first and I not so soon after followed suit. I think one of her bright friends convinced her that to get her way she could use sex, or the lack thereof as a tool. More than likely it was one of her friends without a man who did that convincing, because if you ask any man he will tell you that is the quickest way to get yourself cheated on. In the beginning I would ask about it, and here and there even attempt to initiate sex to no avail. After striking out at a couple hundred at bat I finally got the hint, and decided to get on my horse. Now this was wild to me, she attempted to convince me that she was no longer interested in sex. (HAHAHAHAHAHA) She had evolved to a point where if she was going to be having sex, it would be with her husband, and since I wasn't offering a ring of any sort, she wasn't offering anything, but smiles (rarely), and giggles. Now what she honestly wanted me to believe is that in less than a year she had gone from a person who wanted sex every hour on the hour, to someone who can do without it at all. In my mind this was quite impossible, so I formulated a hypothesis of my own. It was simple, if she wasn't getting it from me, she damn sure was getting it from someone else and with that on my brain. Let the games begin.

If there is one thing that I will not be, it's a fool. I refuse to be made a fool of, and I refuse to be a fool for someone. In the instance someone attempts to make a fool of me I will take my time to make a complete fool of them. Andrea's new thing was not coming home until the next morning. Something about she would go over her mother's house to study and would lose track of time then she wouldn't want to be out late by herself. This was funny because the whole point of us moving to Westland (a suburb of Detroit) was so she could feel comfortable with all of her comings and goings. If it were up to me I would've been quite comfortable in the D. At least then I would not be a victim of Driving while Black on my regular drives home. After her second time in the same week trying to pull that one off, I began to thoroughly wash my face, and forehead as to remove the FOOL that had most certainly been written there one night in my sleep. Now I usually go by the three strikes rule, but I saw no reason to wait for a third time for her to attempt to make an ass of me. So I did what most men would do (but not admit to doing), I rode past her mothers house, and during the little drive I made it a point to call. After getting no answer, and not seeing her car in her mother's driveway, I immediately called again this time getting her on the first ring.

Hey Boo, I was just about to run and get myself something to eat. I was just wondering if you were hungry.

"No, not really, my mother cooked, and we are eating now, so I'll pass."

Now the problem with this is she's loud, her mother is loud, and they had a dog that was extremely loud. And all I hear is silence, not a sound except for her voice. Not the sound of a television or the radio and after a quick glance at the clock in the car I noticed that it was ten o'clock. "Law and Order" time. Now come rain, snow, sleet, or hail, her mother does not miss a episode of "Law and Order", and it's never a time the dog isn't barking or tearing something up, unless he was outside lounging but he wasn't I didn't see him on my ride by. She must've really thought I was stupid!

Boo you want me to stop by, so you won't have a problem getting home tonight?

And here was the third mistake, letting me undoubtedly know that she really thought I was a fool. She instantly took something harmless, like me stopping by and turned it into a big deal.

"No I don't need you to stop by, I'll be home in a little while, damn!"

Damn Boo, what's that about? I was just trying to be helpful, but never mind. You enjoy yourself!

"What the hell is that supposed to mean?"

Nothing, nothing at all. Talk to you later.

After hanging up the phone I decided that my plans for pay back should start immediately, but it wouldn't be enough to just go out and have sex with someone, I needed something better. After all, this would be the end of this relationship. I might as well end it with a bang. Now unlike most of my indiscretions in the past, this one would be public. I had a rule, and it was simple, if we were going to kick it on the side, it was going to be pretty much a house thing nothing public, because even though I was disrespecting my relationship I refused to make it undignified. No one would ever be able to come out and say I saw your man with another chick anywhere, at anytime. That was unacceptable to me. But this was going to be totally different, my plan was to be seen by whomever, wherever, however. I wanted it to get back, I wanted her to question me about it, I wanted her to know, not think I had done something. Now the next part of the plan was the who. I needed someone that was better than Andrea, someone she would have to question herself about, and end up at the conclusion that he did this because she had something that I didn't have. This is the most important part, the mistake that most men make in cheating is that they will cheat with a woman that is not better, or at least equal to what they already have. The most important fact is that while you're cheating if you can't see this person as a potential replacement for you woman, don't do it. Cause if caught, you don't need to give your woman any added ammo because the chick ain't as cute as your woman. This was going to be a challenge in itself, because Andrea had it all at least in my eyes and a couple others. What made it even more of a problem is the fact that I wanted to make it personal. On top of everything else it had to be someone she had seen before, or had a problem with. And with that it hit me I had the perfect candidate. She was beautiful, intelligent, had sassiness about her, and to top it all off she was in a Sorority that Andrea wanted to be in. So part two was done, because she had already more than shown interest in me before. She had everything needed to pull this off, unlike most of my previous gal pals, she had a natural beauty no make up, and she wore her hair in its natural curly state. Her skin was the personification of brown, it wasn't light brown, wasn't dark brown it was just brown. She was thin for the most part except in the places it mattered most, she had a huge chest and one of the best asses that a pair of jeans had the pleasure of being worn by. She had the face, and body of Janet Jackson and hadn't even had anything replaced to get it. The best part was the fact that she didn't mind at all being used in my ploy, actually she enjoyed the entire idea. Not to mention we would finally get the opportunity to hang out as we both so badly wanted.

It was a Friday, the day that would undoubtedly have everybody in Detroit out and about, and we were going to Andrea's favorite hang out. Where all the wanna-be ballers, and supposed street pharmacists go for dinner and drinks. We were going to Starters, let me tell it, the place was highly overrated, but let some people tell it if you eat at Starters you were hood elite. It wasn't much to me because we were doing it when it wasn't the hottest spot on Joy Rd, but it would serve as the perfect place to be spotted by all her friends or the niggas who she SUPPOSEDLY ignored because she was with me. We arrived and had a seat in the middle of the room instead of getting a booth that might've hidden us from the on lookers, and ruined the plan. After being seated we took our time to order drinks and appetizers, before the main course. We laughed and joked, while enjoying each other's company and just like I suspected we were noticed by one of her admirers as well as one of her so called friends (I say so called because in the beginning she put her bid in and got shot down, then tried to say I attempted to get with her, excuse my French, but she was a dumb BITCH!) it didn't take long before my phone was ringing off the hook, can't help but love a snitch.

What up Boo?

"Don't fuckin what up me! Where the fuck are you?"

I'm at Starters, why what up? You want me to bring you something back?

"Mother Fucka! I know damn well yo ass ain't out wit a bitch!"

Huh, what are you talking about? I ain't with a bitch, I see one or two, but I'm not with one. Who told you something like that?

"Why you lying about it? Two different people have called me and told me that they are looking at yo ass right now."

That may be, but I'm grown and I don't have to lie about anything. Your name is not Shirley so I can't get in trouble, so there's no reason for me to lie. I'm not with a bitch.

"So you telling me you not at Starters with another woman?"

No, I never said that, and you never asked me that in the first place. I told you that I wasn't at Starters wit a bitch, and that was the truth I'm not.

"Yeah okay, we'll see how smart yo ass gone be when I get there I'm on my way we'll see."

Now the plan was to humiliate Andrea, not put anyone in the middle of a physical altercation. So as to not get the police involved I decided that our job at Starters was done and our dinner should be more along the to-go variety. My date agreed, and we were off to the next stop after collecting our meal. Now if Andrea was truly the genius that she was convincing herself she was, she would've not let me know she was on to me until she was close enough to actually catch me coming out of the bar, but alas she wasn't and in the end she lost her advantage because she allowed her emotions to control her instead of her controlling them. After safely exiting the bar, and being on our way we continued our night not to far away at the house I would be house sitting for the weekend because a family member was out of town. To ensure that there would be no distractions I parked my car in the garage so that it wouldn't be spotted when Andrea was on her city wide search, and I also turned my phone to silent to avoid the irritation of the continuous ringing throughout the night. After enjoying dinner and the amusing conversation that went along with the night, my lady friend and I took our date to the next level. She returned from the bathroom, after freshening up and instead of just sitting on the couch she choose to hike up her skirt a little past her thighs and straddle me. Before I could resist, she forced her tongue into my mouth, recognizing that sexual satisfaction was in order for the role of co-star she had just played in my mini drama. I took it upon myself to make sure that she would be satisfied. I roughly grabbed the back of her head pulling it even further into mine, and at the same time ramming my tongue back into her mouth. I could feel myself awakening as she began to grind in circular motion, as my hand traveled from her head to her shoulders I began a slight raise of my mid-section, and at the same time pulling her in a downward motion by her shoulders enabling her to feel the thickness that was me. There was no more talking, no more laughing, this was no longer just a ploy, this was me back in my essence about to do what I had done so many times before. Cheating on my woman, and this time I was going to enjoy it that much more. As I ripped her top and bra off allowing them to hit the floor, unleashing her beautiful full breasts, taking them one at a time into my mouth teasing each nipple with my lips and tongue until they both stood fully erect, and her intense moisture began to flow down her thighs. Excusing my mouth from her breast, by gently pushing me back just a bit, she reached around to my back grasping the bottom of my shirt and pulling it straight up so that we both sat there topless. She commenced returning the pleasure that I had recently placed on her breast on my chest. Before that night I didn't realize that my chest was as sensitive as it was, but it was great to know. Instead of making her remove herself from the more than comfortable position that she was in, I slid my hands to her back and slid the zipper down giving me the ability to lift her skirt up instead of down. Leaving her in nothing but the sexy black thong that had matched the bra that had been disposed of long ago. As her legs slithered around my waist, I slid even further up to the very edge of the couch and then rose up on my feet. As I started to walk towards one of the bedrooms I slid my tongue across her lips and then into her mouth. With each step our kiss continued until we made it to the bed, as I sat her down she loosened my belt, unbuttoned, and unzipped my pants in what seemed all one motion. As they fell to the floor she wasted no time reaching for the part of me that would satisfy her sexual appetite. By this time he was more than ready to satisfy, and hopefully be satisfied. While lying back on the bed she kept a gentle grip on me pulling, and guiding me at the same time into the place she wanted me most. As I entered, awaiting the usual moan that I had heard so many times before from a woman, I heard something that was a bit different, and without a doubt not as sexy. It wasn't a grunt, but that's about the only way I can describe it. It wasn't a complete turn off, but it wasn't one of the sexier sounds that I had heard. Luckily it wasn't a continuous sound. It only happened now and again when I first entered. After that she was completely normal, the moans of pleasure excited me more and more as she let each one escape. I questioned in a soft voice what she liked, and how she liked it. When she was finally able to get her words together she explained that she couldn't get enough of getting sexed from the back it turned her on to have her ass smacked, adding that just talking about the act makes her cream. I didn't have any other choice. It was my duty to turn her around and please her just as she wanted to be pleased. As I stroked her allowing her to feel all of me, she gathered her words once again. "Smack yo ass!" now this wasn't my first experience smacking an ass, but each woman is different, I wasn't sure how hard or soft she wanted it smacked, so my first attempt was a light tap just to test how she wanted it done. "Harder, smack yo ass harder!" She didn't have to tell me twice, I got just the right angle and just the right distance and smacked her ass as if I was clapping my hands together. The sound echoed throughout the room as her moan turned into a muffled scream since she now had her head buried into the pillow in front of her. With her now totally into our act, I was all into it, I picked up the pace of my stroke along with the depth. As I tried to make her feel me throughout her entire body she began to make a run for it moving up further on the bed with each stroke "Relax baby you can take it." I take it she didn't agree, because she kept moving until she was stuck between the head board and me and from there I pleasured her as she had never been pleasured before. I was so use to being the one with the stamina tiring my partner out, but that wasn't the case this time. She went for hours on end, and every time I thought I couldn't go any longer she got me back in the game, and wore me out again. I kept up until we were out of condoms and, I could no longer move. Unable to move it wasn't long before I was knocked out not waking until morning, and by that time she was gone. And I was left with my phone next to me with twenty five missed calls, with fifteen from Andrea, a couple of the others from numbers I had never seen before and of course both of our mothers numbers were there as well. There was nothing else to do, but to get dressed and go home to face the music. I returned home to a broken game system, torn up pictures and an empty closet. Andrea had moved out, and it looked like it was for good. The thing that bothered me the most is that I would have to find a way to pay the extra bills that I would be receiving, and the fact that she still had a key. Both problems could easily be taken care of, I had already been offered a sales position at one of the local Nextel stores that MB had gotten me an interview with, and I would just get maintenance to change the locks to protect the rest of my things. That was the last time that I heard from Andrea, and I didn't look back one time. Although she did great things to build me up, she did even more to break me down. I didn't enjoy the person I was around her, and for that reason alone I was comfortable moving on.

After the end of the relationship between Andrea and me, I made a promise to myself that I would never be in another relationship. They didn't work and I didn't have any faith in them. It was a waste of time. I was all out of trust and tired of hurting women. From now on, the only thing I would be looking for from women was fun, because anything deep or meaningful would cause trouble for both parties. That way no one will get their feelings hurt, we all know what we are getting into from the beginning.

KARMA: *I Say She's Just a Friend*

Holiday's came and went, I went through Thanksgiving, Christmas, and the New Year relatively alone. I had friends here and there, but nothing serious. I didn't even have a chick that I could take around the family and pretend that I was into. It was getting to the point where they were becoming worrisome. Truth was, I was okay with being alone. It was more of an adjustment for the family than it was for me. I was maturing into the man that I would be for the rest of my life and it was time-out for my wild lifestyle. I was coming into an age that I was serious about my life, and that included my love life. I came to the conclusion that I wasn't going to cheat on whoever I was with in my next relationship, so until I found the one woman who made me not want to be with anyone else I was a student, an athlete, and a young man with two jobs nothing more, nothing less, as if this wasn't enough for the average person on earth. I had been working at Nextel part-time for about seven or eight months, the job was great mostly because it made it possible for me to take care of all my bills, and at the same time allowed me to live an enjoyable life. I found that I was more than good at sales, I was regularly complimented with my direct and honest approach. Which I was told was refreshing in the sales community, where customers are usually bombarded by the used car salesmen types. In other words the type of salesman who's going to sell you what he thinks you want instead of finding out what you need. My secret was that I just talked to people as I would want to be talked to if I was the customer. And on a regular basis I would send a customer out of the store to compare prices, with our rivals, while my counterparts spent their time attempting to down play the other carriers, I spent my time finding out what the customer needed. I continued to work there even after graduation considering I wasn't mentally ready to be a teacher for anyone's children yet. Not to mention the horrible state of affairs that the Detroit Public Schools were in. The summer was upon us and it was almost impossible to get into a school for the summer programs, plus I made very good money as a sales rep. It was May by now and in Detroit that could pretty much be considered the beginning of summer. I was stuck working on one of the most boring days of the week, Sunday. The only good thing about Sunday was we had no manger working with us on the weekends so we made the rules. I was working with MB today and since he wanted to leave early he asked if I wanted to come in a little later. Sundays were the best in that regard, we could come and go as we pleased without the worry of getting in any kind of trouble. It was usually a slow day, so that meant not many customers and if at anytime the manager did call we would just say that the other person was at lunch or with a customer. We handled business like this just about every Sunday and this one was no different. Except for the fact that it was even slower than usual. We had a customer around every forty minutes, and even then that customer basically wanted to pay a bill. Since I had just arrived at 1:00pm and MB had been there since 10:00am and considering the fact we were that slow I told him if he wanted to he could cut out earlier than he requested. I knew the drill. People were waiting until right before we closed to all rush in at once with problems, but it wouldn't be anything I couldn't handle. I was good at my job, and I didn't mind helping any customer, even if they weren't smart enough to get their phone activated by me. And just as I thought the minutes turned to hours and the hours drew me closer to closing the store, but it never fails, store closes at six customers come in at five with a two hour problem and a horrible attitude. Now unfortunately the customer's attitude was much bigger than the problem, and his rudeness didn't make me want to work harder in my efforts to get his problem resolved. Honestly, his rudeness was keeping me entertained for the moment so I made the event a little more drawn out than it had to be, partially to annoy him but more so for my enjoyment. That was all put on hold when I noticed her standing there when I first looked up to let her know that I would be right with her, I couldn't believe my eyes. She was beautiful! She politely smiled and told me to take my time, she could wait. I understood that she could, but I couldn't so I put a rush on the customer that was before me fixing his problem myself instead of waiting for Customer Care to do so. Once he was taken care of, I focused my attention completely on her, she had come in to purchase and activate a Blackberry. Her friend had one and convinced her that she should get one as well. She had just come from on of our other locations and thank goodness they were all out, because that gave me an opportunity to meet her. As I said before she was beautiful and that may have been an understatement, with a smile so bright that it would make the sunlight look like nothing more than candlelight. Standing in a pair of Steve Madden sandals at about five foot eight with the longest sexiest legs I had ever seen, she had a bright yellow tone that had a bronze base. Her jeans fit her perfectly shaped body as well as the Baby T, she probably just threw on but she made it look like she actually took time to match up perfectly with her sandals. The truth was she looked great. There was no denying that, but I was always told everything that glimmers ain't gold. In most cases when you meet a beautiful woman she usually has a less than beautiful attitude to go along with it. Usually great looking people are unapproachable, in most cases they are so stuck on themselves, or hold themselves in such high regard that it takes away from their beauty. In her case I didn't get that sense, she seemed genuine and nice in the beginning of our conversation. I concluded that she was just doing as most women of beauty did, flirt just a little bit to get what they wanted. That theory went down the drain when the flirting and laughing continued after the sale was complete. It took about five minutes to set her up with a line, with a new number and the Internet. She sat around for the next hour, just talking and chit chatting about everything but phones. I enjoyed the conversation so much that I kicked back and relaxed while she talked to me. So relaxed in fact, that I didn't even notice another customer come in. Waiting to be helped after about two or three minutes I finally stopped to help the young lady, with a problem she was having with her phone. It was about six fifteen and my new friend was on her way out of the store when she turned around and told me to enjoy the rest of my night. While I stood in front of my new customer, I watched her walking out of the door (mostly admiring her ass) smiling and then taking a small bite of my bottom lip, I responded in a seductive voice "You enjoy your day." My new customer bust out in laughter, which sparked her to return into the store and ask what was so funny. Immediately saying that it was nothing, so that I wouldn't be put on the spot because of my reckless response. It was too late as soon as the she returned and asked her question, the young lady spilled the beans. Explaining that my response wasn't just a response she told her that I "Checked her out" is how a think she put it, and then bit my lip as well. My new friend laughed and, then winked at me and proceeded to walk back out of the store. I had screwed up, I had let her escape without even attempting to get her number, but at the same time I was sure that someone of her caliber was already taken. Especially considering the fact that she wasn't a stuck up bitch! I closed everything down for the day and counted down the cash. Last but not least, I counted the activations for the day, looking at each name and marking it down until I ran across Ms. Lake. It was laying right here in front of my face, everything I needed to take a chance. A chance at Ms Karma L. Lake, and it was a chance that I couldn't pass up twice. I made a move that I usually would've never made, I called Karma on her new number. Lucky for me, I had put her phone on the charger the entire time she had been in the store so she had more than enough juice to make it home or wherever she was going.

"Hello"

"Hello, uhh yeah umm can I speak to Karma, or Ms. Lake."

"This is she, who is this?"

"Well this is Chris the guy who just sold you your Blackberry."

"Oh hey, I was wondering who it could be cause I haven't even had the chance to give the number out yet."

"Yeah I kinda figured as much, well the reason I was calling is because I didn't get a chance to ask you if it would be okay if I called you sometime or another and maybe we can grab something to eat one day. That is if you wouldn't mind."

"Well I definitely wouldn't mind, but I'm actually with someone right now so I don't think I should."

"Well I understand, I just thought I would ask. If I was out of line in anyway I do apologize and you don't have to worry about me calling anymore unless its business related."

"Well I did enjoy our conversation, and NO you weren't out of line in anyway if I wasn't involved I would've got your number before I left. I think I did a good job of controlling myself."

"I think so too, I hope you enjoy your Blackberry and whenever you get a chance tell you man that he is one of the luckiest men on earth."

"I'll be sure to do that, and tell the same to the woman of your life."

"Don't I wish, bye-bye."

"Bye Mr. Alexander"

Well that was that. I had taken my chance and missed out, just as I had thought. She was taken off the market and I was back to square one. It didn't hurt to try. For the next two weeks I was back to my old self, and more than bored at work. In the middle of another one of our boring ass staff meetings getting ridiculed because I didn't follow protocol when it came to my Follow-Up binder. With the exception of me and MB everyone else did what the company called follow-ups with the customer. After about a week or two you're supposed to call the customer and thank them for their purchase, and make sure they didn't have any problems with their equipment. This had long become something that I dropped from my routine, didn't think it was important, I felt that I had made a impression on my customer during their visit, it was no need to call and pester them for nothing. My customers were comfortable enough with me to call if the ran into any problems, so there was no reason for me to do this part. That was until I ran into a customer that I felt needed to be checked up on. Instead of calling though, I decided to send a text message that way I didn't have to endure getting cursed out if she felt that was necessary. The message was simple and to the point.

"Hey this is your friendly Nextel sales associate Mr. Alexander, just calling to make sure that you are still enjoying your service and make sure that there are no problems with your handset."

About two minutes later I received a lovely surprise, but the surprise was a number that I didn't recognize. Considering I was still at work I had to answer it, but usually this was something that didn't happen, if your number wasn't programmed in my phone there was no reason for us to talk. On the other end of the phone was a lot of noise and a voice that I didn't recognize:

"Hello"

"Hello, Mr. Alexander are you stalking me? No seriously yes I'm enjoying my phone. And coincidentally I was just thinking about you."

Am I stalking you? Well I guess you could say that, or you could just say I'm doing my job. What were your thoughts?

"Well one of my girl friends wanted to get a Blackberry, and I told her she should come and see you."

Well thank you very much, I'll make sure to take good care of her.

"Well don't make it too good, save that for me. But look I'm in Atlanta right now, Is it okay if I call you back?"

(Expecting that this was her nice way of cutting the conversation short I reverted back to the salesman) Thank you for your purchase, and have a great experience.

On my way home that night, I received another call from her that was even more surprising than the first. Considering the fact that I was just about sure she was blowing me off, not to mention that from my understanding she was involved. Nonetheless she was calling, and what was even more amazing to me was that she was making it a point to call back and she wasn't in town. The conversation was short, but enjoyable. Before it was over I thought that I would throw the idea of us being friends out there to see how she would react. She didn't have any objections to the idea, and from then on we became text buddies. Having full text conversations instead of picking up the phone, this was right up my alley because I had long gotten over talking on the phone. Texting was my new manner of communication even though it irritated most of my friends, it was great for her and I. We talked for the rest of the night by text, and for the rest of her trip learning just about everything about each other. I learned that she was usually only in Detroit on the weekends, but Monday through Thursday her job had her positioned in New York and since she really doesn't have anything to do in Detroit she rarely comes and stays most times. She just flies out to different cities to visit her friends. The following Monday she was going directly from Atlanta to New York for work, she began texting the next morning as soon as she woke, letting me know that she was on her way to the airport and even all the way onto the plane until it was time for all devices to be turned off. Before we got off the phone I insisted that she texted me once she arrived safely. Which wasn't a problem, in fact she explained that I was her new friend, and I was stuck with her. We continued our new friendship day and night for the next week, she would text me when she woke up for work in the morning and continue throughout the day. And that was our relationship for the first week that was, until she came back to Detroit the next weekend and made a surprise stop by the store. This was a perfect opportunity to get her back for her little comment last weekend. She came through the door with that smile that lit the room so brightly, and I hit her with it.

Hey Ms. Lake, are you stalking me?

(Laughing harder than I expected)

"Boy if I was, you'd like it. Don't even try to act like you wouldn't!"

She didn't know how right she was. I would've loved it! We sat and talked for about twenty minutes before she left to go shopping, I started to leave work and go with her but I had just got there for the day. So instead we did our usual and texted the entire time I was at work. It wasn't long before the weekend was over again and it was once again a daily long distance text. Now even though we texted on a regular basis, it wasn't anything more than that. We hadn't seen each other outside of the two times she had been to the store. Which wasn't a problem, but in the midst of getting to know each other so well, we did yearn to spend time together. We talked about it through our messages on a regular basis, but I knew that would complicate the situation. I was no fool, I knew myself and I knew damn well that I liked her much more than just a friend. For the next few weeks our conversations continued regularly, but it seemed as if she was making excuses not to come to Detroit almost like she was avoiding it all together. I didn't want to be arrogant and think her entire reason for not coming was me. I couldn't have been that important to deter her from coming home.

KARMA: *The Weekend*

Another week had come and gone, and she still hadn't seen Metro Airport, but there was some good news in store. She explained that she would be in town this Thursday and continued on to express her feelings towards seeing me. I believe her exact words were "I better see you when I get there, and don't make me come find you" or something to that effect. It was pretty damn amusing seeing that I hadn't planned on letting her back out of the city without seeing me. So it was set. We would see each other either Thursday night when her flight got in, if not then definitely Friday. It seemed like Thursday couldn't get here quick enough. I was like a school kid again waiting for that first day of school when you get to wear you new school shoes. I could barely mask my excitement, after I played basketball at one of the local spots. I rushed to the car to check my phone for an "I'm here" text, or directions to wherever she was. Unfortunately, that wasn't what I received. She left a message that let me know she would be getting in later than she first expected. It wasn't a big deal. We were just looking forward to seeing each other as soon as possible. Her plane wouldn't be landing until 11:00 pm, which meant she wouldn't be home for another thirty minutes, and we both agreed that it may be a little too late for us to be visiting especially because she would be tired from her trip. But tomorrow was another day, and we promised each other that we would meet for lunch, we couldn't wait. Friday couldn't come fast enough it was about 9:30am when my phone first started going off:

"Wake up babe, you're losing daylight. And I shouldn't be kept waiting."

Now quite simply I wasn't a morning person. Usually I wouldn't roll over until at least 10:30am (one reason teaching wasn't an option at this time.) But ever since I had been talking to her I was up at the crack of dawn texting back and forth.

(Babe huh this was new) What time are we meeting for lunch?

"Well I usually like to eat around 11:30 or 12:00, you know lunch time. Are we meeting each other at the restaurant or are you coming by to get me babe?"

(Now that's twice) It's up to you, I can meet you there if that makes you more comfortable. Doesn't really matter to me either way.

"Well if that's the case babe you can come and pick me up. Do you want directions now or later?"

(Three strikes and Houston we may have a problem) I'll get them when I'm on my way which looks like it'll be in about an hour.

"Okay, I'll be looking forward to seeing you then."

See you then!

Instead of rolling over and going my ass right back to sleep, I was up and at it, quickly jumping in the shower and out straight to the ironing board. I decided that since it was just lunch I didn't have to over do it, I threw my best dry cleaners crease in a pair of Sean John jeans, and bumped out one of my personalized T-shirts which read "I ALREADY KNOW" in white letters. Not wanting her to think that I was just throwing anything on I decided to dress the outfit up with my Movado watch, and one of my favorite pair of Bacco Bucci shoes in black. I was ready for anything with a style of my very own. After I completed the task of getting dressed, I jumped on the next task at hand. I called and asked for directions she wasn't too far from were we would be going for lunch. My plan before arrival was to pull up and just sit in the car until she was ready to go, but that idea was shot to hell. As soon as I pulled up she wasn't ready just yet so she invited me in. Once again having a great knowledge of self I realized that this was against my better judgment. Still I went in and sat on the couch while she made her finishing touches, actually she was quite quick. Now even though I was only there for a second I had the room down pact, as soon as you walk through the front door there was a mirror connected to a coat rack, below that is were you were supposed to kick your shoes off. Turn right and you have the closet, to the left the living room, which was furnished with a cream leather couch and chair set, a beautiful rug and a big screen television and entertainment center. If it wasn't cream colored it was silver (television, entertainment center, tables) there was no divider between the living room and the dining area although she did have a beautiful round table that matched her decor. The kitchen was boxed in by the counter, which was on the other side of the entertainment center. If you walked past the kitchen and turned left you were headed upstairs, to the right was the downstairs bathroom. It was one of the nicer condos that I had seen in the area. Now when I arrived it was around 11:00am, we left for lunch arriving at the eatery at about 11:35am so everything was on schedule. During our meal we ate and talked about just about every topic under the sun, it was so much fun. Besides being very beautiful, and intelligent she topped it off by being extremely attentive. After we finished lunch I had to sneak over to the waiter and pay him for the meal, because she had been so adamant about going Dutch. After about an hour we finally decided to leave, since lunch was over it was time to take her back home.

Now this is something that I might not have explained about myself. In the past couple of months since I broke up with Andrea, the only thing that women were to me were sexual tools. Meaning if we weren't talking about sex, about to have sex, or just finished I wasn't interested. I wasn't looking for anything serious, just to have fun. I had evolved into a monster, an untrusting, unloving monster. And I didn't want to change.

Once we made it back to the house she invited me in for something to drink, since I had some spare time I decided to go in and have a seat and continue the great time that we were having. Before I knew it an hour had past, and our conversation was as fresh as if we had just started it. I had told my mom that I would take my little brother shopping for an event he had coming up in a couple of days. So before it got too late I made sure to call and check and see if that was still something that needed to be done today. Luckily for me, it wasn't as urgent as mom had previously made it seem. So that gave me a chance to spend more time with Karma and that's exactly what I did. By this time it was already 3:00pm, which was crazy. We had been together for the past four hours and it wasn't on some sexual shit. To be honest, while sitting there with arguably the finest woman I had ever been with sex was the furthest thing from my mind, I was doing beyond well. I was doing extraordinary! We had set out to be friends and I was working over time on keeping it that way. Back to the conversation that just didn't stop, and the voice that I couldn't get tired of hearing, she explained that she had promised to watch her godchildren while their parents went out for dinner. Over thinking things again, I immediately started to think this was her way of letting me know that it was about time for me to leave, but before I could move she asked me if I had any plans for the rest of the day, if not we could watch a movie and if I didn't mind I could help her with the kids. Seeing that I didn't have any plans and I wasn't ready to leave yet, so I gladly accepted her invitation. By the time the kids arrived it was now 7:00pm, and I was still as excited to be there as I was when I first arrived. The only difference was that I had made myself comfortable after our hour and a half nap. Without notice our lunch date had turned into a daylong event. It wasn't long after the kids arrived before they were fast asleep, and we were again alone with our conversation. We took turns explaining how much we were enjoying each other's company. I was having the time of my life, I hadn't had this much fun without sex in so long I had forgotten how good it felt. The conversation took a turn when she asked me why I didn't have a woman in my life. I explained about my last situation, and watched her different expressions as I told the story and at the end of me telling her she didn't judge me for what I had done, but told me that it sounded as if my ex deserved what she got. I explained that I had a couple friends, but that's all they were. I explained that truthfully, they weren't even that. The type of women I had been dealing with at the time had an agenda, they would start off saying that they would just like to be friends some of them even had men of their own, but they just wanted a friend. But when they felt the time was right they didn't hesitate to throw themselves at me, and though most times I took advantage of the opportunity, afterwards they would be upset that they didn't get everything they wanted. Upset that it turned out to be just sex, when some of them really wanted much more. She made sure to interject on that part of the conversation, explaining that this wouldn't be one of those times. She was more than happy just being my friend, plus she was more than happy with her man. A story I had heard before, but for the first time I actually believed it. It was something very genuine about her, she seemed angelic as if she could do no wrong, at least that was the picture I had painted in my mind. It was now 12:15am, and I still hadn't left but I could tell she was getting tired so I faked a yawn and told her that I would be leaving, because I was getting tired. She agreed saying she was a bit tired herself, so I helped her make sure everyone was tucked in and then she showed me out. After a friendly hug I was on my way. Once in the car I was completely taken away. I had just spent thirteen hours straight with her without so much as a kiss and I didn't mind at all. As a matter of fact I was happy about it. It was refreshing to be able to sit and just talk, and not get bored. I was amazed by this, but at the same time I couldn't help but think that maybe I wasn't her type. It didn't even matter. I just enjoyed myself for the better half of an entire day, if I wasn't her type she would've sent me home twelve hours ago.

After attempting to explain what had happen to MB, and him not believing me, I just let it go. I guess if he told me that he just spent an entire day with a chick, I wouldn't believe he didn't do anything either. But it was the truth and I knew it. I just had a hard time convincing others, especially people who really knew me. My friends had become accustomed to me being somewhat whorish, but it was okay I knew the truth. As soon as I was about to get deep into my explanation I received a message to stop my train of thought. "I like spending time with you, so what would you like to do today, Babe?" Instantly a smile came across my face, another day with her how could I pass that up, I didn't waste anytime replying "We can do whatever you like." Playfully responding she told me to be careful what with I say. She might take me up on that, and jump on me. I came up with the idea, of going to play miniature golf, this was the furthest thing I could think of from a date, and considering that we were stressing just being friends it was the best idea I could come up with. So that was it, this time she was nice enough to come and pick me up, just another reason to be turned on simply because I hate driving with a passion. We played on the hardest course. Usually I'm a pretty good player, but today my game was completely off. It could've been the fact that I was so distracted by her in these jeans that fit perfectly. From the way they dipped in at her waist and came out fitting her hips perfectly, she beat me at each and every hole. Usually my competitive nature wouldn't allow me to lose, but I couldn't care less winning or losing because I was with her. On the way out we played a couple video games, and during the game I received the nod and a huge smile from an older gentleman letting me know that I was a lucky man as if I didn't already know this. Truth was we were just friends but he didn't know that. After the bugs got too annoying, we decided that it was time to go. Since it was still pretty early we weren't ready to part company just yet, we decided to go pick my car up from my house, that way I could follow her back to her house to watch a movie. Once we arrived, she popped on Dysfunctional Family (Eddie Griffin's stand up comedy DVD) and for the next hour and fifteen minutes we laughed at his hysterical antics. Afterwards she asked if there was anything else I would like to see, I looked through her collection and saw a couple things that I wouldn't have mind seeing, but decided instead that I would like to talk to her. Just then her phone began to ring, she quickly moved towards the phone, recognizing the number and then answering on her way upstairs. When she returned, her whole demeanor was different, whoever was on the other end of that phone had ruined her night and in turn ruined the rest of mine. Once she returned she was no longer in the mood for company, and soon after I was on my way home. She didn't stay upset too long, because not long after I had left she called and apologized, saying that her boyfriend was acting an ass, and she didn't want to take it out on me. She asked how far away was I, and if I would like to come back. I would've loved to, but declined, convincing myself that in her state she might be easily taken advantage of, and that wasn't something that I wanted to do (yes I did, but I wasn't going to). We decided however that we would see each other early tomorrow, because later on that day she would be getting ready for her flight which she had to catch around 6:00am Monday morning. We texted back and forth until about 1:00am and then said our good nights. By now I had spent the past two days with her, and each time the entire time I wouldn't even answer my phone for other people. I was slowly but surely cutting people off. When I spent time with her nothing else really mattered.

After a couple hours of little sleep, and ignoring calls from individuals who I didn't want to talk to, I finally feel asleep, which didn't last long before my good morning text made me roll over. I was turning into an insomniac. I barely slept at night and I awoke at the crack of dawn texting with her. We discussed what time each of us would be available for our meeting today, and decided that it would have to be around three or four in the afternoon. That gave us time to take care of other things we had to take care of during the day. Who knew the time would fly so fast! Before I knew it she was calling to tell me she was in my area and asked if she could stop by, and pick me up. I told her to give me about twenty minutes and I would be ready. She pulled up with her famous bright smile, hair beautiful and naturally curly, looking beyond great. I hopped in the passenger side and prepared for the ride. As I hopped in I noticed that she leaned over towards me as if she was about to give me a kiss, but before she thought I noticed she caught herself. With no destination in mind after about thirty minutes of just riding around we decided to head for a park located close to her house. She said that she used to jog around a path at this particular park. She asked me if I wanted to get out and walk. I was dressed for the occasion but she wasn't. She had on a pair of light colored heels that weren't made for walking I don't care what she said. Didn't matter she insisted that we got out and walk, and that's exactly what we did. Our conversation started off light, but took one of those turns as it continued. We had just passed a bench when she explained that she might have been mistaken and she needed to rest her feet. "Jump on my back!" I said jokingly, as we turned around and headed back to the bench. We sat down and watched the joggers, and the walkers as they passed by and then disappeared from our sight. After we talked and our conversation got on the topic of attractiveness.

"Well you're really not my type, I mean don't get me wrong you very attractive but I'm attracted to older men."

"Ouch, that hurt! So I'm not your type. Thanks! So I should be happy that most old men that pass by turn you on and I can't. Thanks a bunch!"

"No it's not like that at all, you're just kind of young for me."

"What you got on me about a year, if that? You were the girl in high school that all the guys wanted to holla at, but you had a boyfriend that was like twenty when you were sixteen. Am I right?"

"Yeah you are right, I hate to admit it sometimes but that was me in a nutshell."

She scooted a little closer to me on the bench, I immediately thought back to when I first got in the car and she leaned over. Thinking to myself, was she really about to do what I think she was about to do? I didn't move, then she hesitated on her words.

"I wanna, (she paused for a second and then continued) I wanna do something, but I'm not sure how you're going to respond."

Still not sure if she was thinking of what I thought she might have been thinking of I asked what it was she would like to do. She paused for a couple seconds and then went for it. She leaned in completely, with her lips puckered and glistening and just before she got to my face I jumped back. It wasn't one of those small movements, I literally jumped from my place on the bench to a completely new spot. I was almost ready to laugh when I realized that she was a little hurt by my gesture. I quickly apologized for my actions, but it was too late, she was up off the bench and just about to start walking away when I convinced her to have a seat and talk to me.

What was that all about? I thought you were just kidding. What was I supposed to think? You were just telling me that I wasn't your type.

"I guess I was wrong, I shouldn't have tried to kiss you. But the truth is since the day I met you I have wanted to do it, and I would have but when you told me how all the other girls who claim to want to be your friend end up throwing themselves at you I decided that it wasn't a good idea. And when I finally get my nerve up to go ahead a kiss you, yo ass jumps clear across the park."

I apologize, I didn't know you were serious. I would love to kiss you, but you made me feel like you could never be interested in me. So I thought you were just trying to make me feel better. But if you give me another chance I'll make it up. Kiss me.

She reluctantly leaned in and gave me a peck, it didn't feel right. I couldn't help but think that it would've been different if I went ahead and did it the first time. But no matter, it was over now and I probably wouldn't get another chance at it. I asked afterwards if she was still upset or disappointed with what happened and she quickly told me she would rather not talk about it. As we made our way back to the car, we couldn't help but laugh at a parked car that was moving back and forth with extremely steamy windows. It wouldn't have been funny except for the fact that she walked right up to the window as if she was about to open the door, it was hilarious. I asked her what she was thinking, she just replied they must've wanted someone to look or they wouldn't have been out here, we laughed a little more. We needed something to lighten the somber mood that she had me in since the kissing mishap. After the park, I went home because she had to wake up early the next morning, so we made sure it was an early night. The texting was limited that night mainly because I wasn't sure what to say, and I'm sure she didn't either.

KARMA: More Then Friends

Instead of our usual arrangement where she calls me when she arrives at work, today was different. I couldn't sleep half the night thinking of what might have been if I didn't make the decision that I made. So the questions started early, after asking how she was this morning I immediately asked her about the kiss.

"If I hadn't jumped as I did, would you have just given me a peck or would it have been different?"

"What do you think?"

"I'm not sure that's why I'm asking."

"Well it's over now, we probably won't ever know."

"That's not fair! You're going to hold my mistake against me?"

"You really hurt me when you did that, it wasn't like you just moved back. You jumped back as if the thought of kissing me was disgusting, I took a big chance trying to kiss you and you treated me as if I had some kind of disease of something. You tell me why I wouldn't hold that against you."

"Baby Gurl, (she enjoyed the way I called her that) you know kissing you wouldn't be disgusting. You know that I would love to kiss you anytime, anywhere."

"That's hard to believe! Especially when I tried to kiss you and you responded the way you did."

"I told you the only reason I did that was because I wasn't sure that was what you wanted to do. I didn't want you to regret our friendship in the long run, and if we kissed it was a chance that you would."

"It wasn't like I tried to have sex with you, it was just a kiss, nothing more nothing less. It was a one time thing, it was something that I wanted to do and once I did it that would've been that."

"But what if we liked it?"

"We don't have to worry about that, because it didn't happen."

"But it will, and what if we like it, then what? Can we continue to be just friends is that possible? Because I don't think so, and that's part of my dilemma. I already like you too much."

"I don't know what would be next, all I know is I wanted to kiss your lips. And you can't blame me for it, you make them so enticing, and inviting. They just look so kissable. I try to fight it, but I found myself just staring at them all weekend wondering what it would be like to be kissed by you."

Then it looks like we will have to kiss then, doesn't it?

After that was said and done, our regular daily conversation was back on. From topic to topic we talked day in and day out until once again Thursday was upon us. Every Wednesday and Thursday you can find me at a gym on Ann Arbor Trail and Telegraph playing basketball from 6:00pm to 8:00pm, but tonight her flight was getting in at 7:30 so I had to ponder whether basketball was worth it tonight. I had an agenda, and on the top of it was kissing Baby Gurl, but at the same time her flight wouldn't be here until 7:30 so maybe I should keep myself busy that way I won't over think things. So basketball it was. I played horribly mostly because I wanted to. I didn't want to miss her call so I threw a couple games so I could check my messages in between games, and at exactly 7:32pm, I received a call asking if I was waiting at her house. I called her directly back telling her that I could be there in about thirty minutes, my grandmother lived in the area and I could stop by and take a shower and change my clothes. From there I was on my way, I arrived about twenty minutes after her. Greeting me at the door with a more than friendly embrace. I could tell she was excited to see me, and I was even more excited. We sat and talked for a couple minutes not able to keep our hands to ourselves, constantly, gently touching each other along with many more embraces. Once we calmed down a bit, I decided to have a seat on the floor by the chair in her living room while she laid across the couch telling me about her week at work. Even from her explanations I still wasn't completely sure what it was she did for employment, but I did know it was a corporate job and it paid well, at least it did from my viewpoint. As she told me more, it was pretty much the same as anywhere else, men not being able to accept the fact that just because a beautiful woman holds a certain position she had to sleep her way into the position and she's really not qualified for the position (Some shit men decided to believe to make themselves feel good about their position). Before she finished the story she asked me if I planned to sit that far away from her the entire night. I didn't say a word. I just began to scoot across the floor until I was sitting in front of her as she lay across the couch. She continued her conversation, but now as she talked she rubbed my shoulders, which felt extremely good considering I hadn't had a good massage in months. I couldn't help but think that this was a perfect opportunity for me to lean in and kiss her, but the motions would have been too, much I would've had to turn around, sit up and then lean in and kiss her. The spontaneity would have been ruined. It would've felt planned, but what the hell, I said I would and I've never backed down in my life before, no need to start now. I got up on my knees and turned to look at her face as she spoke I hesitated for a second letting her finish the end of her sentence. And just as she began her last word, I began my descent as the word finished the kiss began. My lips gently pressed against hers, not sure how much of a kiss she was expecting I decided to give her everything she could've possibly wanted from a kiss. Making it rough, but at the same time gentle. Our lips moving in motions neither of us ever imagined. As her lips slowly parted I slid my tongue between her lips and allowed it to explore her mouth. I was assured that she enjoyed the kiss when she raised her arms and placed her hands behind my head holding me there longer than I expected to be there. Eyes closed, hearts pounding we continued to go at each other for seconds that felt like minutes and minutes that felt like hours. The movie that had been put on before the kiss started was now watching us as we continued our kiss. As our facial embrace finally broke, her usually bronzed skin was flush and red. Falling back from my knees back onto the floor, I heard her finally exhale. As I starred at the ceiling, and her at me. We could both feel that this was not over, we could feel that this would continue. She slid from the couch onto the floor next to me asking if I was having regrets about what had just occurred. To which I didn't even waste my time responding I just laid there looking into her eyes, and then without so much as a warning nor hesitation I grabbed the back of her head and pulled her lips to mine. Starting over where we had just left off, as if this was more than enough to answer her question. And it was, because for the rest of the night we continued to kiss and touch until the p.m. became a.m. From that night on this is how we would spend most of our time together. Every weekend we were cuddle up and nestled away in the comfort of her home, a home that I felt more than comfortable in. Even on days when her phone would ring with her man on the other end I would patiently wait while she made short of a conversation, and then placed her attention squarely back on me. In time we became so close and so attached to each other that it was if she was splitting relationship time. I was her weekend man, and was more than comfortable being as such. It had gotten so bad that one weekend she gave me warning in advance that for the next couple of weekends we wouldn't be seeing each other. Supposedly she was going shopping with her girls in Indiana and then they were supposed to check out a basketball game while they were there. She would be flying in on Thursday as usual, but her girls wouldn't be getting in until Friday night and she just knew she needed to rest up for their weekend. So seeing each other would be out of the question, but that didn't last long because as soon as she arrived on Thursday night she called, letting me know that she had caught an earlier flight, and that if I was available she would be home in about twenty minutes. Now this wasn't really fair. Here it was 6:15pm and I was pulling up in the driveway of the gym, and here she was telling me that if I was to see her this weekend this was the way I would be seeing her. So I made the only decision that my heart and lips could go for I threw my bag back in the trunk and headed for her house. On my way to her house I couldn't help but accept how bad I really had it. The best way for me to judge how much I was really into people was to consider what I would be comfortable missing out on for them, to date there we only two people I missed basketball for and each of them I was in a relationship with. Then to take in consideration I had never for either of them actually been at the gym and left early because I wanted to see them, as was the case on this occasion. Upon approaching her house I received a call from her asking how close I was, continuing on saying that she wish I had a key so if I beat her home I could've ventured upstairs and ran her some bath water. This statement caught me so off guard I couldn't even imagine how to begin to respond. We pulled up right behind each other and as she began walking away from her trunk lugging a huge roll away bag, I quickly grabbed the handle for her. Letting go and thanking me at the same time she kissed my cheek.

"Hey babe, I missed you this week. You know I've come accustomed to seeing you on the weekend, so I had a hard time imagining not seeing you. I'm glad you could make it."

"I missed you too baby gurl, and you know I wouldn't miss out on a chance to see you."

"Whatever boy, you know you would rather be somewhere wit you boys, or one of yo chicks."

"Don't play wit me, I was at the gym when you called, and I just picked up and left. And you know how I feel about working out and playing basketball."

"I didn't know you were at the gym babe, you could've talked to me later or seen me next time."

"Next time was supposed to be almost two months away, and I can hoop everyday. I'm sure one day won't kill me, and them nigga's ain't missing me too much anyway."

"Well you know I came home early because I wanted to see you that bad. I know I said it would be about two months but I wasn't waiting that long."

We sat and talked halfway through the night before we fell asleep in one of the most awkward positions I had ever been in. It was so unnatural that around 2:30am I caught one of the worst cramps in my leg that I jumped up off the couch to walk around. Unfortunately, waking her up as well. We hadn't been asleep too long so she probably wasn't deep into her slumber, and she was probably as uncomfortable as I was. She got up off the couch and walked over to me trying to make sure I was alright. The way she strolled over made me forget all about my leg, I hadn't paid enough attention to her when I first arrived because if I had I would've noticed that her shirt came just low enough to expose her stomach that was giving Angela Bassett a run for her money, perfectly toned and cut. She got too close, I didn't have a choice I grabbed her waist and pulled her close, gently biting her bottom lip and then kissing her just the way she liked it. Leaning back against the kitchen counter, which was the only thing that separated the kitchen from the living room in her condo I could feel her melt in my arms from the kiss that we shared. She broke free after she regained control of herself, and explained that if I continued we were going to end up doing something that she didn't think she was ready for. I backed up, and allowed her to have her space. There would be no rushing anything, I didn't want her to feel like she had to do something that she wasn't ready for. I surely didn't want to do anything that I wasn't ready for. We sat back down on the couch and started talking, somehow getting on the topic of her shoe collection. The conversation turned into an impromptu fashion show, she invited me upstairs. Hesitantly I walked to the stairs, heavily debating whether this was a good idea or not. Once upstairs I took a seat in the guest room, and watched as she walked in her closet. During the conversation we came to the conclusion that boots were my absolute weakness, and with that fact in mind she decided that the beginning of our show would be entirely of her boot collection, which started with Steve Madden, and ended with a pair of the sexiest fur boots that I had ever seen. Trying each boot on and strutting her stuff around the room as sexy as she wanted to be. We went from boots to her trying on different swim suits, after she attempted to convince me she couldn't wear a two piece set anymore because she was getting chunky. Couldn't help but laugh at her, after all, I lived in Detroit, home of the two sandwich chick. (Meaning some of women who claimed to be thick were about two sandwiches from being considered fat) She made the swimsuit speak to me, it didn't get any better than the sight that I had the pleasure of viewing, before we knew it is was eight o'clock in the morning. It was time for me to be heading home, I let her know how much I enjoyed the show and that I would miss her until I saw her again, then I made my way to my car. Later on during the day she called and let me know that while rushing to get to her flight she had forgotten to pack the charger for her Blackberry, and wondered if I had one she could use until she made it back home. I said sure I had one that I wasn't using anymore, but I wasn't sure how she would be able to get it. She explained that she wouldn't be leaving for Indiana until Saturday morning and if I didn't mind I could stop by tonight, but to give fair warning her girls would be there if I was going to stop by. I told her that it wasn't a problem for me I could come by before I went out tonight. She instantly jokingly asked where I thought I was going the weekend was her time. We both laughed, and then I told her I would be by around 9:00pm. I knew most of my day would be spent running around the city so I made sure to take the charger with me just in case I didn't make it back home. Just as I thought, by the time I would've run home to get it I would've been running late for the club. After calling and letting her know that I was on my way, I stopped by and dropped the charger off. She invited me in for a second and introduced me to her two friends, and just as I thought both of them were beautiful, both were just about as light as Karma with one being of oriental decent, and the other appearing to just be fair skinned. They were both very nice as well as polite, inviting me in for an interrogation of when, how, and where. Luckily I was in somewhat of a rush so they couldn't finish their full interrogation. Before leaving I gave Karma a hug and once at the door she stopped me and gave me a kiss. On my way out to meet the fellas I texted Karma to make sure that leaving so abruptly wasn't rude in anyway and if it was let the ladies know that I apologized. Just so happened she was texting me at the same time making sure she wasn't rude, because her friends made it seem like she rushed me out. We both answered that there was no problem and neither of us felt the other was being rude. After an enjoyable night with the fellas I ended my night texting her and saying good night. The following morning on her way to Indiana she texted me for the first four hours of the day then she pretty much disappeared. Besides her "I miss you" text, our communication was cut off for much of Saturday. It wasn't the biggest deal considering the fact that I knew she was with her girls shopping and having fun. Saturday came and went without much conversation, then Sunday was pretty much the same, at least until I took it upon myself to call her and left her a voicemail letting her know that I missed her. She immediately called back with an upset tone. I could tell that she was in a crowded area, and then it hit me she was at the basketball game. This was wild because I was quite sure that the game didn't start until later on that night, but whatever, I was much more concerned with the fact that she sounded upset.

"What's wrong Baby Gurl?"

"Christopher you know I have somebody, you can't be calling me anytime you feel like it, I told you I was going to see him, and I would be with my girls this weekend."

(Now I knew this to be fact but this wasn't how we acted everyday, the mere words alone crushed my heart. Felt like a building had just collapsed on it. So I did what I usually did when I was hurt, let the frustration take over.)

"Hold up shawty, you never told me anything about seeing your man this weekend and if you did I wouldn't have called. All you said was you and ya girls were going shopping, and to a basketball game."

"That's whose game I'm going too, but we're not going to go back and forth you just need to be careful when you want to talk to me."

"You know what I'll be more than careful, you don't even have to worry about it. Good-bye Karma!"

"What's that supposed to mean?"

"I'm hanging up now, good-bye!"

After we got off the phone things were cloudy, my mind was going in to many different directions. Too many different thoughts in my mind I couldn't think straight. So that was. She was dating one of the Pacers, a basketball player huh? That's why she had so much spare time on her hands, and traveled so much. I couldn't possibly compete with this, he was an NBA player. Even if it was a dude at the end of the bench he still had six figures at his disposal. He could do things for her that I could only dream of doing. Shit he was in the position that I once aspired to be in. He had things that I wished I had, and one of them was Karma.

Thinking to myself

"So this it huh? This was what SECOND FIDDLE felt like. This is what I made most of the women that I have messed around with feel? Eventually the second place person has to be reminded what their position is and it seems that even I have fallen victim to the SECOND FIDDLE syndrome!

That's when my arrogance took over, and I stopped second guessing myself. She was spending time with me knowing that I didn't have what her man had. She was spending time with me and she knew what he had, and what he could do for her. Yet every weekend she was finding a reason to come home to see me, it was obvious he wasn't doing something right and I was. So I wasn't about to even think about backing down instead I was going to go harder. But not until Karma and I had a better understanding. The way she came off on me was unacceptable and it wasn't something that I had to deal with. The weekend passed and as soon as Monday morning was here my phone was going off as usual, the only difference was I wasn't answering back anytime soon. She would have to wait, it didn't take too many messages before she was asking if I was mad at her because of yesterday. Followed up with the fact that she felt bad for the rest of her trip. She felt like she was cheating on me with her man. This in itself prompted me to respond, but I held out it wasn't going to be that easy. She was going to have to work for my forgiveness, or was she? Her next message was enough to get a response from me.

"I was upset, with myself, not with you because I was supposed to be there to be with him but the whole time I couldn't think of anything but you. So when you called I was happy but I knew I shouldn't have been. So I took it out on you."

Baby Gurl its okay I understand you don't have to apologize, for anything, I'm falling for you too.

I looked at the message again, I couldn't believe that I had just sent that message and couldn't believe that I had made the mistake of verbalizing that I was falling for her. I wasn't even able to ignore her for an hour. She had me gone, I was in bad shape. Between thinking of her, talking to her, and being with her I didn't do too much more. I wasn't sure where this relationship was going but I was sure of one thing I was along for this ride. Once again we had a full day of talking, but most of our conversation was about how we shouldn't actually still be talking. We both agreed that our feelings weren't going to do anything but get deeper, and we should definitely stop but we knew we weren't going to. We were extremely attached to each other, we didn't want to let each other go, and from that day forward even though she said we weren't supposed to see each other for a couple weeks, she made her way to Detroit each weekend for at least a day if not the entire weekend. A month had passed and our mere kissing had turned into much more. We expanded into the exploration of our bodies not just our lips. Our attire had totally changed, instead of seeing each other totally dressed our visits now took on a more comfortable setting. Shorts, and cut off T- shirts had replaced, my usual jeans and button-up shirts knowing that we would be spending our time indoors. With her comfortable cloths took on a whole new meaning, her definition was more, so less is better. Her clothes became closer to under garments than clothing, to which I didn't have a problem at all. Let me tell it, she did it to make my life that much harder, but when she explained that she's most comfortable naked, and if I wasn't there she would be right now. So I happily took the half naked look over the completely naked look. We did the usual talking, kissing, touching for the duration of the night, before we decided it was time for me to make my way home. There had been a couple of times that I had spent the night on the couch, because we had fallen asleep and she didn't want me to take a chance driving home with heavy eyes. Those nights weren't great but weren't too well thought out. We didn't need to get too comfortable with me staying there and waking up together, but it was too late. We were already too comfortable with the idea even though it didn't happen regularly it did happen on enough occasions to become a problem. The truth was each time I spent the night I made sure to stay downstairs on the couch. I was pretty sure that if I made my way upstairs it wouldn't have been a problem, but I refused to do so. There was one particular night when we had an intense wrestling match that ended with us in nothing but the blanket that we used as a wrestling mat. She finally got up and started for the stairs, stopping at the bottom and giving me the nod as if it was okay for me to join her upstairs, my legs froze and I stood in that same spot with nothing but the blanket wrapped around my waist watching her perfectly shaped body ascend the stairs. This would be one of my last opportunities to see her body in all its beauty.

KARMA: _All Good Things Must Come to an End_

The Fourth of July was coming up the following Monday, and I was looking forward to possibility of spending time with her, or if not, at least with my friends, and family. We talked for the entire week, and everything seemed to be going well although she did seem like she was hiding something, but it wasn't a problem. Finally Thursday was here, and she was on her way back home letting me know hours ahead of time. Not only for my information, but also to make sure that I could make my way to her. She had something she wanted to talk to me about, and it had to be in person, texting wasn't an option. I spent the next few hours wondering what could be so important that it had to be told face to face. Deciding not to stress myself out, I let it go. I was too young to worry myself to death. On my way over I had Jill Scott's new CD on repeat listening to one song over and over again. One song and one song only played from the time I pulled out of my parking lot all the way to hers. The chorus spoke volumes of people in love and the things they do to keep that feeling of love.

"What'chu do is crazy babe, guy like belong in an asylum crazy babe. Like the sun in the morning and the moon at night, like the rain falling from the sky, like the trees growing from the ground it's astounding babe. How you loving me, and you touching me, and you kissing me."

I removed myself from the car grabbing the stuffed puppy with the sad eyes and hid it behind my back as I approached the door. She had been asking me for weeks to get her a stuffed animal that would remind her of me when I wasn't around. As I knocked on the door I saw out of the corner of my eye that the blinds were moving, and no sooner than I looked completely to the window the door opened and I was greeted half heartedly. She welcomed me in, and then placed her arms around my neck and hugged me tightly. As I pulled her closer to me, than her embrace had her already, I could feel that her heart was beating at a rapid pace. Once the embrace ended, I pulled the puppy out and let her take a look she instantly noticed the one thing that was going to be the reason that it would remind her of me.

"He has your eyes! They look just like yours, this is so sweet."

"I know you told me to get something that reminded you of me, so when I saw him I saw me and knew that this was it."

Before I could finish my sentence the tears started rolling, I stood in shock for a couple minutes before it really hit me that she was crying. I couldn't imagine what the tears were for, I was lost not only did I not respond well to tears, I definitely wasn't going to respond well to somebody I truly cared about.

"What's wrong Baby Gurl?"

"Nothing, I'm just trippin! I'll be fine, I'm just really messing up and I shouldn't be. I'm supposed to be in love with someone, and here I am falling in love with you. The same shit that those other chicks did, actually I'm worst than them because I have someone who's good to me and that I'm happy with. At least they had men that they weren't happy with. Here I am happy in my relationship and still falling for you. I ain't right!"

Karma it's not your fault alone, we both got into this and just as bad as you're falling for me I've fallen for you! And I knew from the beginning that I wasn't supposed to, but I couldn't help myself.

"Babe this is going to be hard for me, but I'm going to have to let you go. I can't go on being with both of you, it's stressing me out. When I'm there I can't help but think of you, and after I've been with you I think of how wrong I am to be with you. I am in love with who I am with, but I'm falling in love with you. I can't keep this up especially if I want to be married one day."

"Baby Gurl I understand all that, but are you sure that this is what you want to do?"

"I can't go on living for the moment, I must live my life for the future, and my future is to be someone's wife. A good wholesome loving wife, devoted to only my spouse. I can't do that loving two people, and I already know what I have. I'm trying to see if the grass is greener on the other side.

I jus want to make sure that you're making the right decision, and this is what in your heart you truly want to do.

"I don't have a choice and God knows it will hurt, but whatever I need to do to be seen as good in God's eyes is what I have to do, and right now that seems like ending all communication with you."

So how am I supposed to feel in this situation? Am I supposed to just sit back and let the woman I love walk out of my life? Should I just get up and go right now and act as if I've never known you? I should just forget about the way that you changed my life and made me feel a way I thought I would never feel? How can I do that, why would I do that?

"Christopher the bottom line is this is WRONG! I am not happy, and I'm uncomfortable looking my mate in the face because I can't stop thinking about you. If this is not allowing me to sleep at night I have to do something. This has been a continuous battle and we both know how guilty I feel after you leave. No matter how good you make me feel it's only temporary. We both knew that sooner or later one of us would have to wake up and face the facts, and now we're at that point."

We sat for the next couple of hours holding each other as tears rolled down her face and formed in my eyes. Knowing that this was our last night together, we kissed gently and held each other tight. No matter how upset I was, no matter how disappointed our conversation had made me I was still more concerned with her feelings than mine. She was hurting bad, and I hated to see her this way. And if the only way that she would stop feeling this way was for me to leave her alone, then so be it! No matter how much it would tear me apart I had to let her go! We fell asleep holding each other on that night and as the sun began to rise and the rays hit my eyes I awoke to her beautiful glow. All in one motion I got up from the couch picked her up and carried her up the stairs, being careful not to wake her. After tucking her into bed, I gently kissed her forehead and then her lips and left the room. On my way out I stopped by the couch and wrote the last message that I would ever write Karma:

"I find myself sitting here in the wee hours of the morning, still fighting back tears. Having one of the biggest debates of my life with myself. This debate however takes place in many different facets, the first and most important, how to let a friendship that I hold so dear go without so much as a PLEASE DON'T DO THIS! The answer is simple I can't, an even better answer would be that I won't! My emotions won't let me. But to think that this is the bulk of my issues you would be sadly mistaken. My next problem is the fact that I'm not just letting a friend go I'm letting go of a friend that I truly love. A love that is not tainted by lust, or sought after because of sex, but a love that has been discovered by getting to know someone for who they truly are, and not only liking that person but loving that person as well. Accepting the good and the bad. This is a person that in less than four months has gone from not even being considered a friend to one of my best, and from there I took it further, I no longer viewed her as a friend it was more like a companion. I found myself through no fault of hers I must add, ignoring others simply because I wanted to spend my time with her. Whether it be seeing each other, talking on the phone, texting, or merely thinking about her. I saw absolutely nothing wrong with this, and I still don't. Until now! Now when I find myself in tears, not because I'm about to lose a friend, not even because I'm about to lose a great friend. It's not even because I have to now act as if I don't know a person who has had such an impact on my life. It's not because I'm spoiled rotten and she helped me get this way. Unfortunately, it's not even because I love her. IT IS HOWEVER, BECAUSE MY BRIGHT ASS DECIDED TO FALL IN LOVE WITH HER. I won't kid myself, and say I can control it. I won't even say that it's something I choose to do but, I will say I have fallen. And I'll follow it up with the fact that up until the point of this message I loved every second of it. I find myself at my happiest point of my day whenever I'm talking to her, and when I'm not talking to her I find myself thinking about her constantly, anticipating our next meeting. Once I get to see her I find myself wishing time would stop so we could stay together forever. I wanna know everything there possibly is to know about her, and would wait to the end of time for her to tell me. I wanna know about her day at work, and what she is thinking about, I want to know when she's happy, and I want to be the one who makes her feel better when she's sad. I want to

192

be there when she thinks that she is all alone, when she needs an ear to vent and a shoulder to cry on. If she needs a person to depend on I want it to be me she turns to. I really don't want to be selfish, and I would hate making her life anymore difficult than it already is, but I thought she might want to know how I felt before I disappeared forever. I'll end this message like this. He has got to be an incredible person for her to want me out of her life. They must truly be happy together and in love, and truthfully I'm happy for them. I'm sure he already knows this, but I'll say it anyway, he is one of the luckiest men on earth. Yet and still I have to say this Karma (Baby Gurl) please make sure that you are truly happy with him and not just settling for being comfortable."

With the message done I got up from the couch and grabbed what I thought was yesterdays Detroit News and walked to the door. Taking one last look around the house that I would never again enter. I sent the message and closed the door behind me walking slowly to my car, getting in and slamming the car door behind me. I sat there for a couple of minutes sulking, and thumbing through the CD collection finally running into the only music that would help sooth me in this state. Something compelled me to unroll the paper, to my surprise it wasn't a Detroit paper at all, it was the Indiana News and right there on the front page stood Karma and a woman kissing after the Indiana Fever just won the championship. After reading the article, I found out that they had been together for the past seven years. As I pulled off listening to the melodious sounds of Harlem Blues, I couldn't shake the look of shock that was plastered across my face, and just then tears that I had been working so hard to hold back were finally running down my cheeks.

Printed in the United States
59605LVS00003B/133-141